BATTLESHIP OF WAR

DESCENDANTS OF WAR: BOOK TWO

G J OGDEN

Cover design by Laercio Messias
Editing by S L Ogden
www.ogdenmedia.net

CHAPTER 1
VOICES OF DISSENT

COMMANDER DALTON REEVES ducked instinctively as a crude Molotov cocktail sailed over his head and smashed into the security fence surrounding the Sa'Nerran embassy. The liquid inside the bottle caught alight, and an intense orange fireball billowed upward. Soon the flames had spilled over the top of the eight-foot wall and began to lick at a Sa'Nerran warrior standing guard. However, the warrior simply endured the pain, its leathery face and egg-shaped, yellow eyes showing not even a flicker of discomfort.

"I bet you ten credits that was a bottle of Quarr whiskey," said Major Kane. She was standing beside Reeves, and unlike him had not ducked. "That stuff could probably fuel a Jinx-class fighter."

"We might need to fly a Jinx in here to disperse the crowd if this protest carries on much longer," Reeves answered. He noticed that the left shoulder pauldron of the Sa'Nerran guard on the embassy wall was now on fire. He continued to watch the burning warrior, waiting for it to extinguish the flames, but the alien remained statuesque as the flames spread wider. "Either that, or the Sa'Nerra will march out here and do it for us," he added, only half-joking.

"Why the hell are we stopping this protest, anyway?" Kane asked, as another Molotov sailed over the shield wall that an army of Concord Station Security Enforcers had established to hold the demonstrators back. "We could just move out and let them tear these Sa'Nerran assholes to shreds," Kane shrugged. "Problem solved, so far as I'm concerned."

Reeves admitted that the thought had crossed his mind. Unfortunately, in the four weeks since the Sa'Nerra had emerged from Shadow Space and annexed six colony worlds, the ambassadors of all the realms had pressed upon him the importance of keeping the peace. This had not only included Ambassador One, the sentient android which represented the Bastion Federation, but Reeves' old commanding officer, Commodore Jana, too. The Sa'Nerra had to be kept 'happy and compliant' as Commodore Jana had put it to Reeves during a holo-call a week earlier, so that forces could be fully mobilized and the new frontiers established.

"The Bastion Navy isn't ready for an all-out war with the Sa'Nerra yet," Reeves replied to his XO. "And neither are the other five races, for that matter. As much as I'd gladly let this mob loose on these leather-faced bastards, the ceasefire must hold. And that isn't going to happen unless we get this protest under control."

Reeves then saw Sergeant Axia Calera running over to

him from the blockade. She too was dressed in full riot-gear and was armed with a shock baton.

"Commander, my enforcers at the transit stations in Mid-Town are reporting more activists breaking through into zone four on foot," the Quarr security chief said. As usual, Calera was straight to business. "We could have another hundred protestors to deal with in the next thirty standard minutes, unless we disperse this crowd now."

"Then go ahead, Sergeant," Reeves said. He'd already had enough of dodging Molotov cocktails, as well as the insults that were being hurled at him in a dozen different languages. "Deploy the riot-control gas then drive them back using batons. Make any arrests that you see fit, especially if you can find the ringleaders."

"I'm afraid Commander Vito sold most of our riot-control equipment four years ago, sir," Calera replied. The former Quarr-infantry soldier appeared more than a little embarrassed to admit this. "We are lucky to still have this basic riot gear."

Reeves cursed then watched as another firebomb smashed into the embassy wall. A second followed moments later, crashing into the main gate and engulfing one of the Sa'Nerran guards in flame. A haunting, waspish cry filled the air, like a hundred furious Caracals hissing in chorus, and the warrior was dragged from the gate. Two solid thumps permeated the air and Reeves cursed again, as the gate unlocked and began to slide open.

"Sergeant, push this crowd back now," Reeves said, sensing that matters were about to take a turn for the worse.

"Use baton charges or whatever other means are necessary short of killing these folks, but get them out of here now."

"Yes, sir," Calera replied. Her eyes also briefly flicked over toward the gate, before she turned and ran back to the line of enforcers forming the blockade.

"I've got a bad feeling about this," said Kane. She had turned away from the protestors and was now staring at the embassy gate. Her expression was grave, as if she was standing on a beach and had just seen a tsunami approaching.

Reeves glanced behind and saw the reason for his XO's uneasiness. Several squads of armed Sa'Nerran warriors were marching out of the gates, stepping through the flames as if they were mere illusions. The front ranks carried the traditional, serrated half-moon blades that the alien race favored, but to the rear, Reeves could see that others were carrying plasma rifles. Then through the center of the troop of warriors, another figure approached. This one Reeves recognized at once as the imposing, seven-foot frame of the Sa'Nerran military leader, the Grand Imperator.

"I think you're right," Reeves said, pulling his plasma pistol from its holster. "Check your energy absorption shield is fully charged. This could get ugly, fast."

Suddenly, a roar went up from the enforcers in the shield wall, and slowly they began to march forward and drive the crowd away from the embassy. The front row of protestors fought back; some broke through the wall, only to be pummeled into submission then arrested by the waiting security forces to the rear of the line. The roar of the crowd was then matched by a thump of heavy boots coming from behind Reeves. The Sa'Nerran warriors were advancing fast, and the Imperator was leading them.

"I don't suppose he wants to talk?" quipped Kane as the massive warrior marched closer.

"I doubt it," sighed Reeves, reluctantly moving out to head off the alien leader.

The last time they had met, the Imperator – aided by Serena Shepard, the leader of the separatist New Earth Movement – had ambushed him and tried to kill him. Since then, Reeves had mercifully seen very little of the Imperator's wrinkled, leathery face. However, he knew they had unfinished business, and that the alien would not wait forever to claim its second chance at revenge.

"Get back inside the embassy," Reeves called out to the alien leader, who was power-walking straight at him. "We've got the situation under control, so send your warriors back inside those walls."

"You have already lost control, descendant," the Imperator hissed. "Now, we will deal with these vermin ourselves."

The Imperator had chosen to use its favored nickname for Reeves, instead of his actual name. The term, 'descendant' referred to Dalton Reeves' notorious lineage as the only living progeny of fabled Omega officers, Lucas Sterling and Mercedes Banks. A thousand years ago, Lucas Sterling had killed the Imperator of the Sa'Nerra, and now its successor was keen to settle the score.

"Get your wrinkled ass inside that compound now, or I'll treat your warriors no differently to the protesters," Reeves hit back, stabbing a finger toward the alien.

"Remember that the little slice of your empire ends at those gates. Out here, I'm in charge."

The Imperator took another long step toward Reeves, its yellow eyes burning with a hatred that had not diminished in the four weeks since their brawl in the Oasis Gardens. Kane moved just as quickly, thrusting the barrel of her plasma pistol at the warrior.

"Back off, asshole," Kane said, placing herself between Reeves and the alien. The Imperator turned its attention to the station's XO, fixing her with a look that was no less hateful. "Give me an excuse to blow a hole in your gut," Kane added, taunting the warrior. "Please, do it. Just take another step forward."

"Like your ancestor, I see you like to hide behind the strength of others," the Imperator said to Reeves, though it was still watching Kane closely. "Your bloodline was always weak, human," the alien leader went on, now turning its attention back to him. "I have studied your history. Lucas Sterling was a feeble-minded charlatan, who was always afraid. If it was not for his so-called Omega officers, he would have died long before committing the atrocity on my world."

"You mean, when he nuked the entire planet from orbit, and practically wiped-out your entire rotten species?" Reeves replied, ensuring he spoke the words with a venom equal to that of the Imperator. "That doesn't sound like the actions of a feeble man to me."

"Sterling was nothing," the Imperator hissed, ignoring Reeves' retort. "And like your ancestor, you too are riddled with fear and doubt. If you were strong, you would have killed me the moment I stepped beyond the boundary of my embassy."

"You don't know a damned thing about me," Reeves hit back, stepping up to the Imperator so that they were mere inches apart. "But if you keep pissing me off, I promise that you'll find out exactly what I'm capable of."

The Sa'Nerran leader bared its jagged teeth and reached for the serrated blade attached to its armor. Reeves clenched his fists, ready to strike first, when a firebomb erupted to their side. The burning liquid coated Reeves' leg and splashed across the Imperator's back, setting both of them on fire. The alien leader hissed and drew back, as two warriors ran to its aid, trying to put out the flames with their bare hands. Reeves darted away from the inferno, dragging Kane out of danger as he did so. Suddenly, a roar went up from the shield wall behind him. This time it was not the roar of his security enforcers, but a rallying cry from the protestors.

With his flame-retardant riot gear still smoldering, Reeves watched as a section of the shield wall was driven open. A group of protestors charged through, armed with improvised weapons, ranging from crude clubs to jagged, broken bottles. Seconds later, the angry mob collided with the front row of §. Three warriors went down, but the fearless alien soldiers held their ground and fought back with brutal efficiency. Serrated-blades flashed through the air, slicing through flesh with chilling ease. Cries of pain and terror were quickly added to the melee of sounds, and soon dozens of protestors lay dead or dying on the ground.

"Sergeant, seal that breach!" Reeves called over to his

security chief, though Calera was already in the middle of the affray, fighting hard to re-establish control.

Suddenly, Reeves caught sight of a human male running toward him, holding a modified Bukkan plasma pistol in his hand. His eyes grew wide as the weapon was raised and aimed, then he realized the man wasn't aiming at it him, but at the Imperator. A blast fizzed through the air, striking one of the two warriors still working to douse the flames covering its leader's body. The alien's head exploded like an overripe fruit, showering the Imperator in blood and bone.

Cursing, Reeves charged at the man, knowing that if the protestor succeeded in killing the leader of the Sa'N-erra, war would immediately break out across the galaxy. Ducking low, he drove his shoulder into the attacker's gut and pushed the man back. Another blast rang out, but flew high and wide. Slamming the man to the deck, Reeves snapped the protestor's wrist then stripped the weapon from its grasp, before pummeling a fist into the man's face and knocking him out cold.

Glancing behind, Reeves saw the Imperator shrug off the second warrior. Its armor was still burning from the impact of the firebomb, but the alien appeared uncon-cerned by the flames. Instead, its eyes were fixed on his own, though the Imperator's expression was now more angry than hateful. Dragging the decapitated warrior off the deck, Reeves watched in astonishment as the Imperator dug its hand into the exposed neck cavity and tore open the body, exposing new flesh. Fresh blood gushed from the wound, and the Imperator doused himself in it, extinguishing the flames and painting his armor red.

Another flash of plasma raced through the air, and in his peripheral vision, Reeves saw Major Kane open fire toward the crowd. Forcing himself to tear his eyes away from the gory spectacle of the Imperator and its innovative method of extinguishing flames, he climbed to his feet and recovered his weapon before joining his XO in the defense of the embassy. Three more armed protestors that were also racing toward the Imperator with pistols raised quickly went down, toppling like dominoes and causing the demonstrators to their rear to hesitate. Reeves locked eyes with one of them – another human male – and he could see the doubt in the man's eyes.

"Turn back now, or I will kill you!" he yelled at the man.

The protestor glanced toward the Imperator then back to Reeves, before spitting onto the road.

"How can you defend that thing, after what they did?" the man roared at Reeves. "They're murderers. Savages!"

Reeves felt bile swell up from his gut and he tasted the bitterness in his mouth. By rights, he should have turned around then and there and shot the Imperator in the head, but by some perversion of justice, he was the one saving the alien warlord's life.

"Leave now. You won't get another warning," Reeves snarled, remaining resolute, despite feeling like a traitor to his own people.

The protestor shook his head then spat again and turned, calling to the others to withdraw along with him.

Moments later, the shield wall was reestablished, and Sergeant Calera urged her enforcers on. Behind the line, the Sa'Nerra had quelled the unrest with frightening brutality. Dozens of severed limbs lay scattered amongst an even greater number of whimpering, mutilated bodies. Reeves could see at least thirty dead just within a short radius of where he stood. In contrast, only four warriors had fallen. Incredibly, the Sa'Nerra had won the day, without even firing a shot.

Reeves' buzz – his personal communication device – vibrated, and he double-tapped it to answer the call.

"The crowd is dispersing, sir," said Sergeant Calera. Her voice was breathless and Reeves could hear the fight continuing in the background. "I have established a perimeter and have begun making arrests."

"Very good, Sergeant, keep me appraised," Reeves replied before tapping his left palm to close the link.

"Dalton…"

Reeves spun around to see Major Katee Kane, aiming her pistol toward the Sa'Nerran Imperator. The alien leader, splattered a dark crimson red as if it had just undergone a satanic blood ritual, was glowering at him. A dozen warriors stood to the Imperator's rear, many injured and bleeding, though none showed signs of pain. Then the troop of warriors armed with plasma rifles formed up in front of the embassy gates, like a firing squad.

"So, that's how it's going to be, is it?" Reeves said. Only a handful of his own enforcers remained nearby, but even if the tired and injured squad were fully fit, they'd still not stand a chance against the Imperator's forces. "I save your worthless ass, and you just turn around and stab me in the back?"

"You acted only to save your own pitiful existence," the Imperator hit back, its wrinkled brow furrowed in disgust at the suggestion Reeves had saved its life.

"Believe whatever you like, we're done here," Reeves hit back, shaking his head at the alien leader.

Reeves was about to turn away when the hulking warrior advanced toward him, leaving a trail of crimson footprints on the road behind it. As it got closer, Reeves could see that some of the skin on its neck and face had been burned.

"You are going nowhere, descendant," the Imperator hissed, pulling the serrated blade from its blood-stained armor.

Suddenly, the thump of more footsteps filled the air, but this time Reeves recognized the sound as that of regulation-issue combat boots. Moments later, he and Kane were surrounded by twenty station enforcers, led by Sergeant Axia Calera.

"I'm afraid I'm not available right now," Reeves said, while giving a nod of thanks to his security chief, who had arrived literally in the nick of time. "But if you leave a message with my office, I'll get back to you presently."

"Do not take too long," the Imperator hissed. Blood was dripping from its chin and streaking down its golden armor, creating a slowly expanding pool at the alien's feet. "Your time, and the time of the other races born of the Progenitors, is coming to an end." The warrior reached out and wiped its blood-soaked hand on Reeves' chest, smearing a dark-red line across his stealth armor. "But before then, I will kill you."

The Imperator turned and headed back toward the embassy building. The other warriors followed suit, forming up behind their leader and marching toward the gates, seemingly unimpaired by the vicious injuries that many had suffered. Reeves waited, not taking his eyes off the troop of warriors for a moment, until the gates had finally thudded shut, and the warmongering aliens were once again holed up inside their walled compound.

CHAPTER 2
THE ART OF DIPLOMACY

REEVES LOOSENED the collar of his tunic then wiped a bead of sweat off his forehead with the back of his hand. He'd been in the Council Chamber for just over an hour, and the heated exchanges between the ambassadors and himself seemed to have somehow increased the temperature in the room. He observed as Ambassador Gruba launched into another tirade – mercifully, this time directed at the Quarr Ambassador, Titus Vedrix, rather than himself – grateful for a moment of respite. However, the relief was short-lived, as Gruba inevitably returned his attention to Reeves.

"Commander, this situation is intolerable!" Gruba barked, waving his huge, hairy fist at Reeves from behind his podium. "These protestors almost cost us the peace, yet you have not increased security around the ambassadorial district!"

"For the fifteenth time, Ambassador, I do not have enough enforcers," Reeves said. He already had a pounding headache, and Gruba's exasperating persistence was only making it worse. "Now, if the Bukkan Kingdom would like to increase its funding, or transfer some enforcers to Concord Station, I might be able to change that."

The Bukkan ambassador scoffed. "The Kingdom already contributes more than any other realm, yet we do not see a proportionally higher benefit for our generosity. Besides, who would pay for them? We all know you do not have two credits to rub together."

"Unlike you, Ambassador, who has seemed to find the funding to double the private security guard at your Paradise Mansion," Reeves hit back.

The massive Bukkan diplomat bristled at the accusation. "My own affairs are my own business, Commander," Gruba snapped. "In any case, the solution is simple. You should just allow the Sa'Nerra to guard their own embassy," the ambassador went on, swiftly changing the subject.

Reeves laughed out loud, causing Gruba to scowl at him and close his hands into fists. "Just to make sure I'm hearing this correctly, Ambassador; your suggestion is to allow armed Sa'Nerran warriors loose on the station?"

"It would solve the problem in an instant," Gruba barked. "No-one would dare attempt another demonstration with Sa'Nerran soldiers on the street."

Reeves snorted and shook his head. "I'll take your suggestion under advisement," he replied, making a concerted effort to come across as insincere as possible.

"You do that, Commander," Gruba said, appearing to have missed the blatant sarcasm in Reeves' voice. "As for extra funding and enforcers, I propose the other realms pay their fair share, and stop taking advantage of the Bukkan's famous generosity!"

Reeves was itching to slap down Gruba's patronizing and flagrantly disingenuous statement, when Ambassador One spoke up.

"I have conferred with the Bastion Government and the Bastion Navy has agreed to transfer an extra one hundred commandoes to Concord Station to serve as enforcers," the sentient android began. "Commodore Jana says they will arrive within three days."

Reeves nodded respectfully to the ambassador. "Thank you, Ambassador One, at least someone here is willing to step-up, rather than complain." He looked directly at Gruba as he spoke these words, and this time the subtle act of scorn was not lost on the Bukkan ambassador.

"The Quarr Empire will match the Bastion Federation's offer," said Titus Vedrix. "The Sa'Nerra must be kept on a tight leash, and since the Bukkan only care about themselves, we will contribute more, as the commander has requested."

Gruba looked ready to explode at the Quarr Ambassador, but Reeves was quick to head him off.

"And what about the Skemm Confederacy?" Reeves asked the diplomat from the secretive little world. "Will you also help Concord in its time of need?"

Ambassador Thessala Topal looked at Reeves from beneath her hooded cloak, though he could only make out a shadow where her marble-sized eyes should have been.

"This is a fast-moving situation, Commander Reeves,"

the Skemm ambassador replied, speaking in little more than a whisper. "Many matters require our attention, some more pressing than others, but I will take your request to my government."

"In other words, no!" laughed Fang Gruba.

Ambassador Topal slowly turned her head toward the Bukkan diplomat and peered at him from her beneath her cloak of shadow, but said nothing in reply.

"The Eyrhu Geniocracy are scholars, not fighters," Ambassador Hostillian Zeno said, adding his genteel voice to the mix. "We will continue to assist by lending our considerable expertise to the study of Shadow Space, in order that we can penetrate this mysterious barrier, from which the Sa'Nerra have emerged."

"Rubbish, we all know that you are mobilizing your fleet along the tendrils of Shadow Space, just like the rest of us," Gruba barked. "Not that your pathetic vessels and spineless military will be any use against the Sa'Nerra. You may as well send them here to use as cannon fodder!"

Zeno turned to the Bukkan ambassador, but maintained his composure and dignified countenance. "You will find the Eyrhu Soldiery extremely effective, especially against a crude and vulgar enemy. In that regard, you and the Sa'Nerra are alike."

Gruba laughed heartily. "The Bukkan Royal Guard would tear your scrawny soldiers limb from limb." He then pointed to Cana the Wise. "Besides, you couldn't even beat the pacifist De'Vaught in combat, so how do you expect to face a real enemy like the Sa'Nerra?"

Ambassador Zeno now looked on the verge of losing his

trademark Zen-like calm, though Ambassador Cana the Wise was not phased in the slightest by Gruba's tactless comment. However, neither got the opportunity to respond before the doors to the council chamber swung open. All eyes immediately turned to the new arrival, but Reeves had guessed who it was before the seven-foot, armor-clad warrior had been revealed.

"Why was I not notified of this assembly?" the Imperator hissed, addressing Reeves directly.

"I left a message with your secretary," Reeves hit back. "I guess he didn't pass it along, or perhaps he just couldn't read it." Sarcasm was usually Major Katee Kane's domain, but with his XO holding the fort in the CIC, he'd taken it upon himself to be one who delivered the snarky remarks.

The Imperator continued to hold Reeves' gaze for a few moments longer, but chose not to dignify his snippy comment with a response. The physically-imposing warrior then stepped inside the council chamber, followed by two of its honor guard, denoted by their dark crimson armor.

"Those red-breasted assholes can wait outside," Reeves said, pointing toward the honor guard. "You know the rules, Imperator."

The alien leader stopped in the center of the chamber, between Reeves and the semi-circular arrangement of ambassadorial podiums, and turned to face him.

"Rules such as 'all ambassadors must be notified in advance of a council meeting'?" the Imperator asked.

Now that the Imperator was closer, Reeves could see that its face and neck were still burned. It looked like the injuries had not been treated, despite the fact the warrior had clearly changed its clothes and replaced its blood-covered armor with a suit that shone with a golden, untarnished finish.

"Like I said, your invite must have been lost in the mail," Reeves replied. He was in no mood to fence with the alien leader, and he certainly wasn't cutting it any slack. "Now tell your cronies to get the hell out of here, before I throw them out personally."

The Imperator's bulbous eyes seemed to grow larger for a moment, and Reeves felt sure it was about to reach inside its armor for a weapon. However, instead the alien leader turned to the two warriors and hissed a command at them. The honor guard immediately spun on their heels and marched out of the chamber.

"Take your podium, Imperator," said Reeves, gesturing to the empty position in the middle of the semi-circular row.

"I will remain here. What I have to say will not take long," the Imperator replied.

"You have the floor." Reeves didn't care if the Imperator took up its podium or not, so long as it was out of his hair as quickly as possible.

"If my embassy is threatened again, I will crush those responsible myself," the Imperator began, addressing Reeves with his back turned to the other ambassadors. "But know this; an attack against my embassy is an attack against the Sa'Nerra itself." The Imperator slowly turned and scanned its egg-shaped eyes across the faces of the ambassadors. "There will be consequences, for all the realms.

Consequences that reach far beyond the bulkheads of this space station."

For once, it was not the hot-headed Bukkan ambassador that retorted, but the diplomat from the proud Quarr Empire.

"The Quarr do not take such threats lightly," Ambassador Vedrix spoke up. "I remind the Imperator that we have only agreed a temporary ceasefire. The world you seized, and the Quarr lives you have already taken, are matters we have not forgotten."

"Please, this is a forum for diplomacy, not threats," Cana the Wise cut in.

Gruba scoffed loudly. "Diplomacy is just a way of making threats while appearing to make peace," he barked. "Only you have yet to realize that, Cana."

The Imperator turned to Gruba then slowly paced toward the huge Bukkan diplomat. For once, Gruba's bravado failed him and the ambassador looked deeply uncomfortable.

"Threats such as amassing a war fleet along the edges of Shadow Space?" the Imperator said. The alien warrior towered over the Bukkan, managing to make even the hulking frame of Ambassador Gruba look small.

"We are doing no such thing," Gruba hit back, though without his usual gusto. "Besides, that area of Shadow Space is inside Bukkan Kingdom territory. Our ships are merely making routine maneuvers inside our own dominion."

The Imperator held Gruba's eyes for a moment before

stepping back into the center of the room, again between Reeves and the row of podia.

"I know what diplomacy is; it is dishonesty," the alien leader hissed, again scanning the faces of each ambassador in turn "All you do in this room is deceive one another, as you try to deceive me now. I know that you are all amassing forces in the regions where Shadow Space intersects your territories. This is an act of aggression."

"Your Shadow Space continues to encroach deeper into our territory," the Quarr ambassador hit back. Unlike Gruba, the Imperator appeared not to have intimidated him. "You make claims of having no intention to annex more worlds, yet at the same time you extend your reach closer and closer to more of our colonies."

"As I have already told you, the Sa'Nerra do not control Shadow Space," the Imperator replied, sounding irritated that it had to restate this fact. "It flows and expands of its own volition. We simply exist inside it."

"And how exactly do you 'exist' inside it?" Vedrix replied. "No ship or probe has ever penetrated Shadow Space and returned intact, yet if we are to believe your words, the Sa'Nerra have 'existed' inside it for centuries."

The Imperator stepped up to Ambassador Vedrix, though again unlike Gruba, the Quarr diplomat showed no signs of fear.

"The Shadow Space accepted us after the barbarism of the humans left my people scattered and homeless," the Imperator began. Reeves almost laughed, but he didn't want to interrupt the alien leader while it was in the process of revealing new information.

"Are you saying it is alive?" Vedrix said.

"I am saying it is our territory," the Imperator replied, though the evasiveness of its answer was not lost on Reeves.

"So explain why we cannot enter," Vedrix hit back, growing emboldened by his success. "What are you hiding in there?"

"Enough of your questions," the Imperator hissed. "You have been warned. I suggest you heed this warning and stay clear of Shadow Space."

"I suggest you do not make any more threats, Imperator," Vedrix said. The man was small for a Quarr, standing more than a foot shorter than the Imperator, yet he more than matched the alien leader in intensity.

"Your government was supposed to send a more compliant representative," the warrior hissed back at Vedrix. "Yet you seem determined to follow in the footsteps of your predecessor."

"We have not forgotten how you murdered the former ambassador," Titus Vedrix hit back. The diplomat remained unaffected by the clear threat that had been made against him. Instead, hostility and resentment flowed through Vedrix's words. "The Quarr do not forget or forgive those who wrong them."

"I do not seek your forgiveness, now or ever," the Imperator replied. It then stepped away from Titus Vedrix so that it could again address all of the assembled ambassadors. "Heed my warning. Stay away from Shadow Space."

The Imperator turned and marched toward the door, which opened as it approached. The two crimson-armored warriors were stood to attention outside. Both waited for the Imperator to pass between them, then turned and filed in behind their leader.

Reeves let out a heavy sigh and allowed his muscles to relax. He'd already felt on edge before the Imperator had arrived, and the alien warrior's looming presence had only served to create a deeper sense of unease.

"I think we can call it a day for today's session," Reeves said, eager to get out of the council chambers and return to more pressing matters.

Mercifully, none of the ambassadors disagreed, including Gruba who still appeared shaken by his confrontation with the Imperator, and the meeting quickly dispersed. Reeves saw Ambassador One approach his podium and waited for the thousand-year-old android to arrive.

"You were quiet today," said Reeves, as Ambassador One joined him on the podium.

"Diplomacy is the art of knowing when to say nothing at all," the android replied, shooting Reeves a warm and familiar smile.

Reeves huffed a laugh. "I'm afraid that's a skill I'm unlikely to ever master." He then sighed and lowered his voice so that the remaining gaggle of diplomats couldn't overhear. "So, what did you make of what our Sa'Nerran friend had to say?"

"Only that the Sa'Nerra have become more devious during their absence," the android replied. "The Imperator has learned how to lie, a skill that its race lacked, until they encountered humanity."

Reeves huffed another laugh, though this time because he felt affronted. "So, you're saying all this is humanity's fault?"

"Yes, it is," the ambassador replied, cheerfully. Reeves' eyes grew wide, but he was too stunned to comment. "However, you and I must look forward, Dalton Reeves. And to that end, we must accelerate our plans to enter Shadow Space, and to learn more about the Progenitors."

"Surely, it would be easier to take what we know to the Bastion government?" Reeves had been wondering why the Ambassador appeared so eager to keep their underground mission under wraps. "The Sa'Nerra are a threat to everyone; I'm sure they'd devote the resources to help us."

"The more people that know of our plans, the greater the chances that the Imperator will learn of them," Ambassador One replied. "Should a significant force begin to scour the galaxy looking for the Progenitors, not only would the Sa'Nerra reinforce these worlds, but the Progenitors would be alerted and accelerate their plans." The ambassador then smiled. "One ship, especially a ship like the Invictus, can easily go unnoticed, and even if detected would not be considered a threat."

Reeves huffed a laugh. "So, we're too insignificant for the Sa'Nerra or these Progenitors to pay any attention to, is that it?"

"That is my belief, for now, at least," One replied, still smiling. "Though there will come a time when discretion is no longer an option, for any of us."

The android then removed a small disc from the pocket of her pristine white suit. "This contains the details of someone who can help to arrange transportation," the ambassador continued, offering the disc to Reeves. "He can secure you a ship capable of reaching the planet where I placed the Invictus into storage."

"Wait, you're not coming with us?" Reeves replied. He had assumed, perhaps presumptuously, that the ambassador would be accompanying them.

"It would draw too much suspicion if I am seen leaving the station with you at this delicate juncture," Ambassador One replied. "Once you have the Invictus, however, I have a plan that will ensure I am able to join you on future excursions."

"Sounds mysterious," said Reeves. He could have pushed the android for more information, but he knew there was no point. The sentient AI would tell him when she was ready.

"More challenging than mysterious, but I believe I will be ready by the time you have returned," the android replied.

"And where exactly am I returning from?" Reeves added, remembering that the ambassador had yet to explain where the Invictus was hidden.

"It is in an underground bunker on Thrace Colony," Ambassador One replied, still with a cheerful timbre to her voice. "I can give you a map to its location."

"Thrace Colony?" Reeves said. He almost blurted the words out loud enough for remaining ambassadors to overhear, but just managed to moderate the volume so that it was more of muted yell. "That's a damned Separatist world."

"Yes, I agree it is unfortunate," the android replied. "Thrace used to be a planet no-one wished to visit, and was therefore a useful place to hide things one did not want to be found."

"Ambassador, Thrace is a colony full of New Earthers who would love nothing more than to string me up by my intestines and beat me like a piñata," Reeves said. The prospect of traveling to a Separatist world without the formidable combat capabilities of the android felt like a suicide mission. "Surely, there's another ship we can use to find this Progenitor planet?"

"You will be fine, Commander," the android replied, confidently. "So long as you employ stealth, and avoid the native predators on the planet, which are particularly unpleasant."

Reeves huffed a laugh. "It sounds like a fun place all round," he quipped, resigning himself to the facts. He then took the disc and slid it inside his breast pocket. "I'll get onto it as soon as my duties permit," he added, buttoning up the pocket for extra safety.

With all the unrest on the station, Reeves had almost forgotten about their planned clandestine mission to find and recover the old Omega Taskforce warship. After the Sa'Nerran war, the android had taken the Invictus on a centuries-long interstellar joyride, during which time it had uncovered evidence concerning the entities the Imperator had called the Progenitors. The alien leader had revealed little about these beings, other than that it believed them to be the creators of all the seven species, including the Sa'Nerra itself. The Imperator had also ominously proclaimed that, "All the races born of the Progenitors will die," a statement that had compelled Reeves and his android ally to seek out more information. Ambassador One had come to understand that the Shadow Space was the creation of the Progenitors and that somehow the Sa'Nerra was working for these ancient beings, though in what capacity, neither of them knew. However, with the Invictus as part of the arsenal, the ambassador believed they would be able to travel to one of the Progenitor's worlds in an attempt to learn what the Imperator was not telling them. Reeves hoped that it would even allow them to penetrate the veil of Shadow Space itself, and discover just how big a threat the Sa'Nerra truly posed.

"Do not take long," Ambassador One said, tapping the disc in Reeves' pocket. "This contact is, shall we say, a little eccentric, and more than a little untrustworthy. The vessel it has procured may not be available for long."

"I understand, ambassador, I'll get right on it, and let you know when I've secured the ship," said Reeves.

Reeves was used to people making urgent demands on him, and in ninety per cent of the cases, the urgency was not warranted. However, he doubted that the android was one to exaggerate and so took seriously her gentle encouragement to get his ass in gear.

Ambassador One nodded then stepped off the central podium and disappeared into the shadows at the rear of the council chamber. Reeves was about to leave too, when he noticed that Cana the Wise had approached. She stood patiently, hands in front of her waist. The jewels and adornments of her ornate shoulder cape glistened under the lights.

"Anything I can do for you, Ambassador Cana?" asked Reeves.

"I sincerely hope so, Commander," the De'Vaught diplomat replied. "Because without your assistance, I fear that thousands of people are going to die in pain and misery."

CHAPTER 3
A THORNY ENCOUNTER

Reeves walked into the Oasis Gardens and waited for Ambassador Cana to finish talking to the guards, who appeared to know her well, and join him. Her claim that thousands were about to die 'in pain and misery' had certainly got his attention. Frustratingly, however, the De'Vaught ambassador had been unwilling to discuss the matter further within earshot of the other diplomats. The gardens were chosen so they could talk privately and in safety, though considering what happened the last time he'd visited the so-called safe space, Reeves was more than a little reticent to tag along.

"Not wishing to sound uncaring, Ambassador, but I do have other matters to attend to," said Reeves. He was now following Cana the Wise up one of the floating staircases to a vantage point overlooking the De'Vaught section of the gardens. While it was an undeniably spectacular sight, he did feel like he was 'bunking off' from his regular duties.

"You told me you thought a lot of people were going to die?"

"What do you know about the Slum, Commander Reeves?" Cana said, without taking her eyes off the steps ahead of her.

"Only that it's where people land when they're hard up on their luck," Reeves answered. He had kept his eyes focused on the De'Vaught Ambassador's back; looking down was starting to make him feel queasy.

"Hard-up on their luck is something of an understatement," the ambassador replied, stepping on the anti-grav platform, which had been designed to look like a golden halo, floating above the gardens. "Most people who end up in the Slum do so because they have nowhere else to go. They are penniless, often too sick or crippled to work, and have no prospect of leaving the station. The entire section of zone two where the Slum is located has not been maintained properly or patrolled by security enforcers for decades. It is, quite literally, a deathtrap."

"I understand that much already, Ambassador," Reeves said, moving up beside Cana and resting on the handrail. Now that he had something solid under his feet, the dizzying height of the platform seemed less overwhelming.

"Do you also know that people are dying of illness and starvation?" Cana hit back, taking on a harder-edge. Reeves' aloof response to her statement appeared to have angered her. "Children also?" the ambassador added, leaving that part till last for extra impact.

"I didn't know that, no," Reeves admitted, turning to face

the De'Vaught diplomat. "But if you're here to ask for my help, I don't know what I can offer you, Ambassador." He was pre-empting the reason he guessed Cana had accosted him. "We've lost over twenty-five thousand residents since the Sa'Nerra showed up, plus more than two hundred businesses. I can barely keep the lights on right now, especially given the extensive repairs that are needed to our defense platform, not to mention the extra security around the embassy district."

"I appreciate the challenges you are facing, Commander, but the deteriorating circumstances in the Slum will have knock-on effects to your operations," Cana replied. Reeves' quick rebuttal had not deterred the woman, who maintained her calm, determined presence. "Spiraling crime spills over into Mid Town, The Long Market and especially Night Sector, putting extra strain on your enforcers. Not to mention the costs associated with detaining and potentially deporting the offenders, compensation payments to victims and business owners, additional costs of dealing with an increased number of medical emergencies and disease outbreaks..."

"I get the picture, Ambassador," said Reeves, holding up a hand to stop Cana the Wise mid-flow. "If you can't get anywhere by twanging my heartstrings, then pull on my purse strings instead, is that what this is?"

The De'Vaught Ambassador frowned, while chewing over the meaning of Reeves' admittedly very human metaphor.

"I believe the humans have a phrase, 'money talks', do they not?" Cana finally replied.

"They do, or at least they used to," said Reeves, offering

the De'Vaught diplomat a smile. "But contrary to what you may have heard about me, Ambassador, I'm not a heartless wretch. And you're right to point out that problems in the Slum lead to problems elsewhere on the station."

"Then you will help?" Cana asked, raising an eyebrow.

"I'll see what I can do, but I can't make any promises, not while the Sa'Nerra pose an ever-present threat to this station," Reeves said. Then he remembered why most of the eleven thousand De'Vaught were on Concord Station in the first place. "Though, forgive my bluntness, but I thought philanthropic matters were your specialty? Can't your government stump up some extra cash to help deal with the problem?"

"I am afraid that the Sa'Nerran issue has impacted my work here too, Commander," Cana said, beginning a leisurely circuit around the halo-shaped viewing platform. "My government has withdrawn significant funding from our missions here, in order to finance an increased military presence along the veins of Shadow Space. As you know, Shadow Space permeates De'Vaught territory in more locations than any of the other five realms. We deplore violence, but cannot ignore the very grave threat this species poses."

Reeves was surprised to hear a member of the peace-loving species talk about military expansion, but was reminded that the De'Vaught had also fought many wars. Their motto of 'Destiny Guides Us', coupled with the De'Vaught's unusually high physical endurance made them formidable fighters, when called upon to do so.

Reeves then noticed that the circular route Cana the

Wise was following around the viewing platform had brought the upper-class residential district of Paradise into view. Many of the exclusive homes in Paradise were built on a manufactured hillside overlooking the Oasis Gardens. Reeves had only seen a few of the residences from ground level, but from his current floating viewpoint the decadence and extravagance of Paradise was clear to see.

"Maybe you can propose a motion in the council to increase the taxes on those rich assholes," Reeves said, gesturing to the upmarket district.

"A nice thought, Commander, but the majority of those living in Paradise are criminals that use Concord as a sanctuary and tax haven," Cana replied pausing to drink in the view. "You could spend all of your five years in command of Concord trying to squeeze more credits out of them, and still leave a bitter and disappointed man."

Reeves shrugged. "Maybe the other commanders just didn't try hard enough?"

"Perhaps," the ambassador conceded. "Certainly, Commander Vito did not. But others tried, and failed. It even cost one former commander his life."

"I never heard about that." The offhand manner in which the Ambassador had revealed this nugget of information belied the gravity of her claim. "And if someone had assassinated a commander of Concord Station, I think I'd know about it."

"You would be wrong to assume so, Commander Reeves," Cana hit back, again adopting a sterner tone. "His name was Commander Jora, a man from a respected house back on the De'Vaught home world. The official line was that his death was an accident. That report, however, was a lie."

"Why cover it up?" asked Reeves, still doubtful of the ambassador's claim. "What purpose did that serve?"

"The reputation of Jora's house was at stake," Cana replied, again looking deeply sad. "I believe the term humans use is 'blackmail'."

Reeves frowned. "What sort of dirt would anyone have on a De'Vaught? You guys don't even sneeze without trying to pay penance for any offense you may have caused."

Cana's sad eyes took on a suddenly sharper edge. "Humans are famously good at stereotyping others. We are a people of billions, Commander. Not all of us are, as you would say, 'saints'. We have our foibles and vices too, like all the other races. Commander Jora more than most."

Reeves nodded and held up his hands, palms facing out toward the De'Vaught diplomat. "Point taken, Ambassador," he said, respectfully. He admitted he was often guilty of assuming all De'Vaught were the same, when in truth he'd met very few members of the species. "So, who was it that had dirt on this Commander Jora of yours?"

Reeves had asked the question merely to confirm what he suspected he already he knew. There was one person on the station who specialized in extortion.

"His name is Sid Garrett," Cana replied. "I believe you two are acquainted?"

Reeves huffed a laugh. His guess had been spot-on. "Yes, the Lord of Night and I have met," he said, feeling a sudden swell of anger as the man's gaunt face popped into his thoughts. "I already laid down the law with him and, so far, he's been compliant."

"So far..." said Cana, with another subtle raise of her eyebrow. The De'Vaught had a way of looking perpetually sad, but at that moment the ambassador looked practically despairing. "But you should be careful, and not underestimate him. What you did in Night Sector was incredibly brave. Some might say foolish."

"What would *you* say, Ambassador?" Reeves asked, curious to get the wise woman's opinion.

"I would say it was a bit of both," Cana smiled, "but the courage and compassion you displayed then is why I have come to you now."

Ambassador Cana had played her hand well. The erudite diplomat had appealed to Reeves' sense of decency, as well as his pocket, and highlighted dangers that he had, if he was truthful, misjudged. The last thing he needed was for the Slum to descend into chaos, adding another problem to his already very full list.

"I guess I should check out the Slum for myself, and see what I'm dealing with," Reeves said, making his decision. "And I promise that whatever I can do to help Concord Station's own 'unfortunates', I'll do my best to achieve."

Cana the Wise nodded graciously. "I know you will, Commander Reeves." The ambassador's eyes then looked past Reeves and she appeared wary. "Speaking of criminal elements, I believe we may have a problem."

Reeves turned around and saw a human male approaching from the other floating staircase that led up to the viewing platform. The man was dressed in typical Mid

Town clothing that was utilitarian in nature, suggesting he was one of the many employed in zone three's Factory Town. This in itself wasn't unusual – people from Mid Town were allowed to visit the gardens providing they got a temporary pass into zone four. What was unusual was that this particular visitor was holding a tree branch in his hands. Reeves could see from the exposed wood that the naturally thorn-covered lump of timber had been freshly torn from a tree inside Oasis Gardens.

"I think it's time we got you out of here, Ambassador." Reeves ushered Cana the Wise toward the staircase they had originally used to reach the platform. However, he'd only managed to retrace his steps for a couple of seconds before he saw two more humans approaching from that direction too. One was holding the broken-off leg of a metal garden chair, while the other wielded a heavy-looking onyx-black rock. The latter, Reeves assumed, had been taken from one of the many riverside gardens that flowed throughout the walled sanctuary.

"I hope I didn't jinx us by discussing the Lord of Night," said Cana, backing away from the two men.

"No, these aren't Garrett's goons," replied Reeves, while glancing behind to check on the man holding the thorn-covered club. He was at least twice as far away, which meant Reeves would have to deal with the two new arrivals in front of them first. "Unfortunately, the Lord of Night isn't the only one on this station who wants me dead."

"Serena Shepard sends her regards, Devil's Blood," said the man holding the rock. He was patting it against his other hand, like a policeman trying to intimidate a suspect they were attempting to arrest.

"I really don't have time for this," Reeves replied, still ensuring that Cana was behind him. "Just walk away now and we'll forget all about it."

"We're not going anywhere," the other man chipped in. "Not until you're as dead as the millions of people your blood slaughtered."

Reeves sighed then cracked his knuckles. "Stay behind me, Ambassador," he said, addressing Cana without taking his eyes off the two New Earther thugs. "This is probably going to get ugly."

The first man attacked, swinging the metal chair leg at Reeves. However, the man's anger, coupled with a clear lack of skill, meant the attack was clumsy and wild. Reeves dodged the swing and snapped a fast jab into the man's face, stunning him and causing water to stream from his eyes. The second man came at Reeves next, trying to club the rock over his head like a caveman attempting to bash open the skull of a rival tribesman. Reeves avoided the first swing, but the New Earther managed to land a punch before connecting with the rock on his second attempt. The heavy stone thumped into Reeves' shoulder like a hammer and he staggered back, wincing from the pain. Encouraged by his success, the New Earther tried again, but this time Reeves caught his hand and blocked the strike. The pain swelling through his body was now joined by anger and aggression.

Reeves twisted the New Earther's arm then hammered his fist down across the man's elbow, snapping it like old, dead wood. The man howled in pain and the black rock dropped to the ground. The first man attacked again, thumping the metal chair leg into Reeves' side. He cried out then dragged the New Earther with the broken arm in front of his body. The next swing of the chair leg struck the man Reeves was using as a shield cleanly across the side of his head, splitting open the New Earther's skull and showering Reeves with blood. The man dropped and squared off against the remaining attacker.

"Death to the Devil's Blood!" the New Earther roared before charging at Reeves with the improvised weapon.

Keeping his cool, Reeves drove a powerful front kick into the man's gut, propelling him back by almost two meters. The New Earther landed on his face and wheezed blood onto the deck from his mouth, but Reeves hadn't finished. Marching over to the man, he swung a kick at the New Earther's head, striking it so hard that he almost kicked it clean off the man's shoulders.

"Commander!"

The cry had been uttered by Cana the Wise. She was back-peddling toward Reeves, but the club-wielding New Earther was closing on her fast. Reeves rubbed his throbbing muscles where the two thugs had landed blows then paced toward the remaining thug, fists clenched.

"I've had enough of these assholes," Reeves snarled as Cana the Wise quickly slipped behind him.

"When will you get the message, Devil's Blood?" the New Earther said, grabbing the club more tightly in both hands. "So long as you're on this station, we'll keep coming for you until you're dead."

"You can't come for me if there are none of you left," Reeves hit back, circling around the man. "Serena Shepard can send as many of you idiots after me as she likes, and I'll keep knocking you down."

"We'll see about that, Devil's Blood..."

The man stepped toward Reeves and swung the club. He felt a rush of air as the thorn-covered hunk of wood whistled past his face, but unlike the other two thugs, this man had more skill. Feigning an attack, the man came at Reeves again, this time managing to score a glancing blow to his thigh. The thorns tore into his uniform, drawing blood, as if he'd been swiped by a tiger's claws. He cursed and backed away as the New Earther grinned at him, growing in confidence. Spotting the black rock on the ground, Reeves hurried over to it, narrowly avoiding another swing of the club as he did so. Closing his hand around the heavy stone, he was then kicked in the back and sent tumbling across the golden surface of the viewing platform. Aware that his attacker would waste no time in following up, he rolled to one side, hearing the thump of the club as it connected with the metal deck plates. The next swing missed the top of his head by barely an inch, but it gave Reeves the opening he needed. Darting forward, he smashed the rock against the stem of the club, crushing the New Earther's fingers against the dense wood. The man cried out in pain and instinctively dropped the weapon before staggering back, cradling his broken hand. Reeves could see that three of the New Earther's fingers had been crushed so badly that the flesh had split open to reveal the bone beneath.

Rubbing his stinging leg to numb the pain, Reeves picked up the club and rose to his feet. The New Earther's eyes met his own. The man's cocky swagger and confidence had evaporated, like mist off a hot car bonnet, and was now replaced by terror.

"Give Serena Shepard my regards," Reeves said, pulling the club back like a baseball bat, taking a run at the New Earther and swinging with every ounce of his tremendous strength.

The blow connected sweetly with the man's breastbone, launching the New Earther across the viewing platform like a cannonball. The man collided with the handrail and spun over the top of it, out of control. Reeves could hear the man's fading screams as he fell the two hundred meters to the gardens below. Tossing down the club and dusting off his hand, he turned back to Cana the Wise. His heart leapt into his throat as he saw another human male standing behind the ambassador, holding what looked like an improvised blade to her neck.

"Give yourself up, Devil's Blood, or I'll slit her throat," the New Earther yelled.

The man's hands were already trembling. He'd no doubt witnessed what Reeves had done to his cohort. However, far from making the man less of a threat, Reeves knew that he was even more dangerous. This New Earther was desperate, and would do anything to save his own hide.

"Put it down, now," Reeves said, taking a slow, careful step toward the New Earther.

"I meant it!" the man roared, jerking the knife and

causing a thin trickle of blood to roll down Cana's neck. "I'll do it, I swear!"

"Listen to me carefully," Reeves said, holding his position, believing the man would make good on his threat if provoked further. "The only way you get out of here alive is by doing what I say. If you hurt her, I will tear you limb from limb and feed you to the fish."

The man's eyes trembled and he forced down a hard swallow, but Reeves could see that he wasn't about to back down. Like all the New Earthers, he was a fanatic. Heart thumping in his chest, Reeves saw the man's grip tighten around the handle of the polymer blade that the New Earther had somehow managed to smuggle through security. He knew he was about to kill her, and knew he had to act before the De'Vaught ambassador was murdered in his name.

Suddenly, Cana the Wise grabbed the New Earther's wrist and pulled it hard against her chest. The man tried to wrestle the weapon free, but with the knife pinned tightly to the ambassador's body, the New Earther had no room to maneuver. Cana the Wise then struck the man in the groin and twisted her body, stabbing the knife into the man's leg in the process. The New Earther yelped and released his hold on the knife. However, the man's cries were short-lived as the ambassador struck the New Earther again, this time to the throat, crushing his windpipe and sending the man crashing to the ground. It was an impressive display of self-defense; one that reminded Reeves of his highly-proficient XO.

"Are you sure you're not really called, Cana the

Badass?" Reeves quipped, stepping over the incapacitated New Earther to make sure he was really down for good. The man was barely able to breathe, and he felt confident the threat was gone.

"As I said, Commander, the De'Vaught deplore violence," the ambassador said, wiping the blood from her neck with a handkerchief. "However, that does not mean we are incapable of it."

"You should remember that the next time Ambassador Gruba gets all up in your face," Reeves said, smiling. "That guy could do with a good punch on the nose."

Cana laughed. It was a joyous sound that did not appear to match her naturally forlorn-looking facial features. However, it made Reeves realized that he'd misjudged the De'Vaught in more ways than one. They were neither saints nor pacifists, and they certainly weren't joyless, despite their perpetually sour-faced expressions.

"Perhaps you can accompany me to the Slum?" Reeves said, speaking the thought that had just popped into his head out-loud. "You've proven that you can handle yourself, and it would mean you can show me what I need to see."

Cana the Wise nodded. "An excellent suggestion, Commander," she replied, smiling again. Then she looked at her robes, glistening under the artificial sunlight that lavished the Oasis Gardens like golden rain. "Though I should probably change first."

Reeves laughed then realized his own uniform was looking somewhat the worse for wear. However, considering where they were going, he figured that a more tattered look might be appropriate, allowing him to blend in. Reaching down to the still incapacitated New Earther, he stripped the tan leather jacket off the man's back and slung it on.

"How do I look?" Reeves asked, holding his arms out wide.

"Like someone whom I would cross the street to avoid," Cana replied. She then held up a hand. "No offense intended."

"Non taken, Ambassador." Reeves zipped up the jacket to hide his military tunic. "You're right to think it's a good idea to stay out of my way." He glanced at the bodies of the New Earthers and smiled. "If anyone in The Slum believes otherwise, they'll find out to their cost, just like these sorry assholes."

CHAPTER 4
SLUMMING IT

REEVES STEPPED off the transit and onto the dilapidated northbound platform in the Slum. It was one of only two stops in the ramshackle residential district, and was on the border between zones two and three, close to the main hospital. The other platform directly linked the Slum to Factory Town, for those luckier residents who had managed to secure work. Ambassador Cana stepped onto the platform beside him, now disguised in hooded Skemm clothing in order to mask her appearance.

"Would it be insubordinate to say this is a really dumb idea?"

Reeves peered through the throng of other passengers and saw Major Katee Kane resting up against the platform wall, arms tightly folded across her chest.

"Yes, it would be," Reeves replied, heading over to join his XO, whom he'd asked to meet them at the transit station.

"Okay, I won't say it then," Kane replied, smirking.

Unlike Reeves, who had merely slung a jacket over the top of his scuffed and slightly tattered uniform, Kane was dressed in civilian clothing. To his scrutinizing eyes, her clothes and appearance still looked too neat and clean to pass for a resident of the Slum, but to a casual observer he figured she wouldn't look out of place.

"I hope you've come armed," said Kane, tapping a bulge in her jacket pocket, which Reeves guessed was a plasma pistol.

"I have, but we're here to help people, not shoot them, Major." Reeves had collected his pistol from the guard after leaving the Oasis Gardens, exiting just in time to avoid being caught up in the turmoil that followed the discovery of the dead and wounded New Earthers.

"Fine, but we may not get a choice," Kane hit back. "This place is more dangerous than one of Sid Garrett's fight clubs."

"Fight clubs?" Reeves said, recoiling slightly. He then held up his hands. "On seconds thoughts, don't tell me; I've got enough on my mind as it is."

"I suggest we head to the main market," Ambassador Cana cut in. "This will give you a flavor, so to speak, of the Slum's many problems."

Major Kane scowled at Cana, whose face was shrouded by the long Skemm hood. "Do we have a new crew member?" she asked.

"This is Ambassador Cana the Wise," said Reeves, keeping his voice intentionally low. "Though obviously we don't want to draw attention to that fact."

Kane glanced around the station, her eyes flicking

across the sea of faces on the platform, from Bukkan to Skemm to human. While some were trying to hide it, all of them were staring in their direction.

"I think we're already drawing attention to ourselves," Kane said, suddenly becoming more serious. "We should head out before we garner any more interest from the locals."

Ambassador Cana took the lead, guiding Reeves and Kane through the security cage that separated the Slum from the rest of the station, and into the dark, unfinished corridors and spaces of the district. Lights flickered chaotically and liquids seeped from pipes and dripped from the rafters, creating pools on the deck that were sometimes slippery and sometimes sticky. People lay huddled up in corners and alcoves, surrounded by metal crates and trolleys filled with all manner of nick-knacks and trinkets. Rooms without doors were filled with dozens of people, sharing rudimentary cooking spaces and the few comforts they had. Three times in the first ten minutes, Reeves had seen gangs of thugs beating on individuals or smaller groups, sometimes stealing what little they owned, and sometimes just leaving them for dead without even attempting to loot the bodies. He had tried to break away from the group to help these unfortunate souls, but Cana the Wise had cautioned against getting involved, as it would only bring trouble their way.

Turning along another corridor, Reeves passed by an Eyrhu woman, who was lying underneath a torn and soiled blanket by the side of the corridor. Initially, he thought she was simply asleep, but as he drew closer, he realized that she was dead and rigor mortis had already set in. He felt like he should do something or say something, but all he felt was a dull numbness like anesthetic wearing off.

"This place certainly lives up to its reputation," said Kane, as they continued past the corpse and entered a wider space that Cana had said led onto the market street. "I think I'm going to need to burn these boots and clothes when we get out of here."

"Count yourself thankful that you have the option to leave, Major," said Cana the Wise, in what Reeves considered to be a deliberately judgmental tone. "For the thousands who call this place home, they have no such luxury."

"Why don't the governments of each realm do something to get these people out of here?" Kane asked.

Cana's remark appeared to have encouraged his XO to take the situation more seriously, though Reeves knew that her flippancy was just a mask to hide her true feelings of revulsion and sadness. He recognized the tactic; it was a mask he often wore too.

"Money," said Reeves, answering on behalf of the De'Vaught ambassador. "Consider the cost of transportation alone, on top of then having to re-home and rehabilitate these inhabitants, all at the expense of each government."

"So, you're saying it's cheaper to just let them rot here?" asked Kane, sounding suddenly angry.

"Sadly, that is correct, Major," replied Cana. Her face was still shrouded beneath her hood, but Reeves could guess how her already sad features would have sunken further at that moment.

Kane cursed and shook her head. "You'd think that with the brains of six different species, and thousands of years of society to draw on, we'd have figured out something better than money as a way to define our existences."

"Each society has its own social and political hierarchy, Major Kane," said Cana the Wise, "and it serves those who crave power to maintain it. So has it always been."

Kane had progressed from glibness to concerned inquisitiveness to outrage in less than a minute. Reeves had already moved on from outrage and was now simply in despair. He'd shrugged off the Slum as a problem for another time, and while the looming threat of war was undoubtedly a more pressing concern, the fact he was allocating money to plasma turrets and shields when people were literally dying in the corridors seemed abhorrent to him. That he'd arrived in the Slum from the monument to greed and excess that was the Oasis Gardens only made this worse.

"The market is just ahead," said Cana, indicating to the first of a long line of stalls and kiosks that lined each wall of the wider walkway they'd entered onto. "I would suggest you keep your hands pressed to where you have concealed your weapons. The pickpockets in this area are extremely adept."

Reeves did as Cana suggested, slipping his hand inside his jacket pocket and tightly gripping the handle of his pistol. The last thing he needed was for someone to lift his weapon and it end up being used in a robbery or murder. While he was privileged to live far beyond the Slum, his standing on the station was still in the gutter.

"Where do they get all of this stuff from?" asked Kane, passing by a stall that was selling clothes. To Reeves' eyes, the garments looked new.

"A lot of it is stolen from Factory Town and the warehouses, along with residences in Mid Town," Cana replied, moving through the crowds with far greater ease than Reeves, who felt like he stood out more than ever. "Some are offcuts or seconds that are simply discarded. Many of the items are salvaged from the reclamation and recycling center."

Reeves walked over to one of the stalls and found a pair of gloves that appeared to be made from a tanned animal hide or synthetic equivalent. He picked them up and they felt soft and surprisingly well made.

"How much for these?" Reeves asked the human male behind the stall.

"Five Stagni," the man grunted, holding up five fingers, presumably in case Reeves didn't understand the number.

"What's that in credits?" Reeves replied, frowning at the man. He'd never heard of Stagni before – so far as he knew, the only currency on the station was Standard Credits.

"Credits?" the man snorted. "What planet are you from? Now if you're not buying, piss off." He snatched the gloves out of Reeves' hands.

"I'll give you three, not a Stagni more," Cana said, holding out three bronze-colored metal bars the size of chewing-gum sticks. Her face was still hidden beneath the hood.

"Four..." the man answered, resolutely.

"I wish you a good day then," Cana replied, swiftly sliding the metal bars back inside the sleeve of her cloak.

"Okay, dammit, three," the stall owner growled.

Cana returned and slipped the bars into the stall owner's hand. The man thrust the gloves at Reeves, practically punching him in the chest as he did so, and turned away, muttering curses under his breath.

"What the hell are Stagni?" asked Kane, once they'd moved away from the stall and back into the central aisle of the market.

"It is a discontinued form of Quarr currency," Cana replied. "The metal is only found on the Quarr home world and cannot be replicated. However, it has not been in official circulation for decades."

"How did the coins get onto Concord?" asked Reeves. He was as curious to learn about this alternative currency as Kane was.

"Several sacks of used Stagni bars were found in the reclamation center shortly after the station was founded," Cana replied. "Since few in the Slum actually own credits, these pretty little bars became the de-facto currency over time. There is a finite pool of Stagni, however, so many people pay by trading other items."

"Like clothes?" said Reeves pulling on the gloves, which felt great and fit perfectly.

"Very fashionable," quipped Kane, smirking at Reeves and his new purchase.

"You'll be laughing on the other side of your face after you catch some nasty alien virus and I don't," Reeves hit back, flexing his newly-gloved fingers at his XO.

"I guess that depends how many other sticky fingers were shoved inside those gloves before you put them on," Kane replied, still smirking.

Reeves felt suddenly a little queasy, but made a good show of appearing unconcerned, so as not to give his XO any further satisfaction. Or at least that's what he'd hoped, though his XO's near-permanent grin suggested otherwise.

Suddenly, there was a crash of metal and raised voices from a stall to their side. Reeves thrust his hand inside his pocket and was relieved to find his pistol was still there. He closed his hand around the grip, ready to draw the weapon should he need to. The crowd cleared and he saw a group of five Bukkan males, shaking down a stall owner on the opposite wall. The leader of the group, a stocky six-foot brawler, had practically lifted the Skemm stall owner off his feet. Reeves instinctively went to intervene, but Cana raised her arm to bar his progress.

"Again, I would strongly advise not getting involved, Commander," Cana said, as the Bukkan began thumping punches into the Skemm's gut. "It is likely just one of the many gangs that operate here, collecting protection money or some other form of debt."

"This may be the Slum, Ambassador, but the laws of Concord Station still apply here," Reeves countered. "You can't expect me to stand by and let that man get beaten and ripped off."

"Are you going to be here tomorrow, Commander?" Cana asked.

Reeves frowned. The question had caught him off guard. "Well, no, I'm not."

"What about the day after? Or the week after? Or next month?" the De'Vaught diplomat added, with an inquisitive tone.

Reeves realized that he was about to get a lesson from the wise woman, though what it was he didn't know.

"No, I don't imagine I'll be back here all that often, at all," Reeves conceded. "What's your point, Ambassador?"

"If you intervene now, you will not be here to intervene when these thugs return," Cana answered. "You will not help this man by stopping the gang today. You will only help him by stopping the criminality today and the next day and every day thereafter."

Reeves nodded. "So I'll only make it worse by meddling now, is that what you're saying?"

"Correct, Commander," the ambassador answered.

Reeves glanced at Kane, who appeared to be itching to get involved, just as he was, but her resigned expression suggested she'd gotten Cana's point too.

"If you'll follow me, I will take you to the worst parts of the Slum," Cana said, heading away from the scene of the shakedown and through a narrower, darker alley.

"I think I've seen enough already," Reeves said, jogging to catch up with Cana. "You've made your point, Ambassador, and you've made it well. But right now I really must get back to the CIC." It wasn't a lie, but it also wasn't the whole truth. What Reeves had seen of the Slum had already turned his stomach, and he had no desire to see how deep the cesspit ran.

"This will only take a moment, Commander," Cana

replied, unmoved by Reeves' protests. "The location I intend to show you is en route to the exit, anyway."

Reeves reluctantly continued to follow the ambassador, as much out of necessity than anything else. Without Cana as his guide, he'd likely end up lost inside the Slum for hours or even days. At that moment, he didn't want to spend another second longer in the place than he had to.

CHAPTER 5
ALWAYS BET ON BLACK

REEVES AND KANE hurried after Ambassador Cana, who was racing through the rabbit warren of corridors in the lower levels of the Slum, as if she knew them like the back of her hand. The De'Vaught diplomat then swung left, leading them through a walkway containing a dozen or more exits, all heading deeper into the unknown and undocumented parts of the forgotten district. Some of the exits and rooms had doors, but most were covered by dirty curtains or rows of dangling beads that chimed musically as they brushed against each other.

"How much further, Ambassador?" Reeves called out, concerned they were moving further from the exit, rather than nearer to it.

"Not far, Commander, it is just up ahead," Cana replied, in an unconcerned tone.

Shooting Kane an apprehensive glance, Reeves was about to insist that they leave. However, before he could open his mouth, four figures stepped out in front of them and blocked their path. The hairs on the back of his neck stood on end, as if the dank air had become suddenly charged with electricity. It was the sensation of impending violence. Each figure was wearing a full-cover balaclava, so that only a narrow strip around their eyes was visible. Even so, Reeves could see that they were all human; two men and two women.

"Hand over your Stagni and we'll let you on your way," one of the men said. He was perhaps in his late twenties, Reeves guessed, and was well built, though didn't have the thuggish bearing or accent of the Bukkan gang members he'd encountered earlier.

"Let us on our way now, or I'll break your legs," Reeves hit back, figuring that this was not a moment for casual diplomacy, and that a more direct approach was merited.

The shuffle of boots then alerted Reeves to fact another group of masked humans had moved in behind them, cutting off their only means of escape. Again, the group consisted of two men and two women, all of whom appeared serious in their intent to rob Reeves, Kane and the De'Vaught ambassador.

"Maybe you want to rethink that answer?" replied the man, who Reeves assumed was their leader.

"No, I don't." Reeves pulled his pistol from his pocket, but he'd barely raised it to waist height before he was thumped in the back and sent reeling. The weapon fell from his grasp and skidded along the deck as he thrust out his hands to break his fall.

Spinning over, Reeves saw Kane get attacked next and her weapon taken from her. The group of four thugs to their rear had wasted no time in getting the jump on him and the others, and he cursed himself for stalling with tough talk, rather than immediately taking action, as the gang had done.

Suddenly, Ambassador Cana was seized and wrestled to the ground, while Kane continued to fight off the other two. Reeves gritted his teeth and jumped up just as a punch sailed into his jaw, sending him reeling again. All four of the other thugs were on him in an instant. Some were trying to restrain his arms, while other thumped punches into his face and body. Reeves tasted blood; it was hot and metallic, and acted like a shot of adrenalin straight to his heart.

Thrusting his arms out wide, Reeves tossed two of the gang members off him as easily as throwing off a coat. Another punch stung his face, but he was already in the grip of rage. Retaliating with a hard right, he broke his attackers jaw and knocked the man clean out in one. A knife was then thrust into his back, but his military tunic, which was still underneath the jacket he'd taken off the New Earther in the Oasis Gardens, repelled the blade. Spinning around, he swung a backhand at the woman who had stabbed him, but she ducked under it, Reeves' fist missing her head by barely a centimeter. The blade came at him again, tearing through the tan jacket, but again failing to penetrate his tunic. Reeves reached out and grabbed the woman by the neckline of her sweater then launched her into the wall behind him. Turning to check on Kane, he saw her land four rapid knife hand strikes in a row, sending another woman down alongside one that she'd already subdued.

Reassured that his XO was not in immediate danger, Reeves ran over to Cana the Wise, who had successfully held off two attackers, and grabbed the remaining man. Gripping the thug's waistband and the back of his jacket, Reeves launched the man across the corridor and into the wall like a battering ram. The thug dropped to the deck like a sack of flour, blood seeping from the gums around the freshly broken teeth in his mouth.

Blood still pumping in his veins, Reeves turned to the remaining man – the leader of the group – and stormed toward him. However, he'd no sooner taken a step in the man's direction than the leader raised Reeves' own pistol at him.

"That's enough!" the man yelled. "I didn't want any of this. You could have just given me the damned Stagni and been on your way."

Reeves continued toward the man, ignoring the weapon that was pointed at him. "It was your choice to attack us," he hit back, fists still clenched. "Now it's your choice whether you kill me, or just get the hell out of my way."

Cana the Wise suddenly appeared beside Reeves and the thug turned the weapon on her instead. Reeves saw his chance and grabbed the man's wrist to deflect his aim. The pistol fired, thumping a blast of plasma straight through the corridor wall. Screams filled the air and people ran, but Reeves remained calm and stripped the pistol out of the thug's grasp before turning it on the man.

"Commander, there is no need for further violence," Cana said, trying to step between Reeves and the younger man.

"Cana, get out of the way!" Reeves cried, but it was already too late.

The man moved with a speed that Reeves had not anticipated and grabbed the ambassador, pulling her into a restraining hold. Reeves gritted his teeth and aimed the weapon at the man's head, but the thug had carefully positioned himself so that any shot Reeves attempted risked killing the ambassador too.

"Let her go, right now," Reeves snarled, trying to move into a better position, but the thug matched his moves, step for step.

Major Kane appeared at the other side of the corridor, her own pistol back in hand. She too was trying get a shot, but the man had now backed himself toward a doorway, using Cana as a shield.

"Commander, please lower your weapon," said Cana, who had remained impressively composed, despite the mortal danger she was in.

"Commander?" the thug said, scowling at Reeves. "Why did she call you that?"

Reeves didn't answer, but noticed the man's eyes scanning his body. He looked down and saw that the tan jacket he was wearing had been cut open by the knife attacks he'd sustained, and that his military tunic was now clearly visible.

"You're the station commander, Dalton Reeves?" the

man said, piecing together the two chunks of information and coming up with the correct answer.

"Yes, and now you know the shit you're in," Reeves replied. "But I'll make you a deal. Let her go unharmed, and we'll forget this ever happened."

With the thug briefly distracted, Cana elbowed the man in the gut, broke the hold and thumped a palm-strike into the thug's face. As she did so, the hood covering her head fell back. The thug staggered away, holding a hand to his nose; the balaclava was now soaked with blood. Then the thug saw Cana and froze.

"Ambassador Cana?" the man said. Moments later he pulled off his balaclava and the recognition in the ambassador's eyes was instant.

"Mr. Black?" said Cana, lowering her guard.

"Wait, you two know each other?" said Kane, moving beside Reeves, but still keeping her pistol aimed at the man.

"Yes, Mister Chester Black is the leader of a small but fair-minded community down here in the Slum. One that my mission helped to establish," said Ambassador Cana.

"Based on what I've just seen, it would seem that your mission failed, Ambassador," replied Reeves. He realized this may have come across sounding harsher than he'd intended, though he was only speaking the truth.

"Things have gotten a lot worse down here, Ambassador," Black said, helping one of his other masked members back to their feet. "Most of the supplies you provided us with were stolen by one gang or another. The Blood Bear gang have taken over down here, but the fighting with the Skemm gangs is getting worse."

"I take it they're as unpleasant as their name makes them sound?" asked Kane.

"You have no idea," Black replied, answering Kane's trite question with a dark and sober seriousness. "They're Bukkan, but they make their pirate cousins look like do-gooders." Black then turned to Reeves. "You're lucky you ran into us, and not them. They wouldn't have just come at you with crude knifes and fists like we did. And they wouldn't have backed down, even if it cost them their lives."

"You're lucky I didn't just shoot you on sight," Reeves hit back. "A mistake I won't make again, if you or anyone else crosses me."

"I don't enjoy using violence, Commander, but we no longer have a choice," said Black. "In the Slum, mercy and compassion only get you killed."

Chester Black did not appear intimidated by Reeves' warning. If anything, he thought the man appeared dispirited and ashamed.

"I will endeavor to do much more to help your people, Mr. Black," said Ambassador Cana. "It pains me to see you come to this."

Reeves was surprised to see that the ambassador also looked embarrassed, as if the failure of Black's community was her responsibility to bear. On top of this, the news of the worsening troubles in the Slum had hit her hard too.

"Honestly, Ambassador, I'd tell your people to stay well clear of this place," Black replied. "And you should get out now, while you can."

"I promised I'd help the ambassador to clean things up

down here," Reeves cut in, remembering the purpose of their visit. "And I've seen enough to know things need to change."

"No offense, Commander, but I've heard it all before," Black hit back. "Ten or fifteen years ago, maybe there was a chance to turn things around. But not now."

"We'll see about that," Reeves said. He didn't want to come across as cocky or arrogant, nor was he merely offering empty platitudes. What he'd seen in the Slum had made him want to take action, despite knowing that other challenges still had to take precedence.

"The time for words is long past, Commander," Black said, as more of his group recovered and limped to his side, balaclavas still masking their identities. "We have to take care of ourselves now, by whatever means necessary." Black turned to Ambassador Cana and shot her a weak smile. "It's good to see you again, Cana." Then the smile fell off his face and was replaced with a look of such desolate sadness and resignation that Reeves was sure he heard the De'Vaught diplomat's heart break in half. "Don't come back here again."

Black turned and walked away, followed by the battered and bruised members of his once peace-loving community. Reeves had come to Concord Station believing it might afford him the opportunity to play a pivotal role in the war that was surely coming. However, now he realized that the station had already been at war with itself, long before his arrival. And, more surprising than that, he found that he actually gave a damn about the people living there, and especially those condemned to purgatory in the Slum.

CHAPTER 6
MIAOW MIAOW

AFTER THE INCIDENT with Chester Black, Ambassador Cana had no objection to beating a hasty retreat from the Slum. However, despite the dangers they had faced, Reeves did not regret his choice to visit the troubled district in person. Cana the Wise had wanted to show him the suffering in the Slum in an attempt to garner his support, and it had worked. He couldn't deny that the beleaguered district was a swamp that needed to be drained, but it wasn't going to be quick or easy. Even with the best of intentions, Reeves knew it also wasn't going to happen any time soon.

Ambassador Cana had departed the transit in zone four and returned to her own duties, while Reeves and Kane had continued on to zone six. After the fight in the Oasis Gardens and the Slum, Reeves badly needed to shower and change, and catch up on the ever-growing mountain of administrative work that kept piling up on his desk. Major Kane had changed back into her uniform and returned to the CIC, though mercifully, aside from their adventure in the Slum, it was proving to be a slow day. There weren't many of those on Concord Station, Reeves realized, and he was determined to use the lull in activity to his advantage.

While Reeves had been away, the contact Ambassador One had given him had left a message to say he was ready to meet. He'd arranged a meeting with the Bukkan ship dealer in Mid Town later that day, during which time he hoped to secure a vessel that could take them to Thrace Colony, where the android had hidden the Invictus.

"What did I miss, Major?" asked Reeves, stepping inside the CIC while adjusting the cuffs of his new tunic. The uniform he'd worn in the Slum had been removed and thrown in the trash as soon as he'd returned to his quarters.

"Aside from four first interviews with potential new CAGs, not a lot," Kane said, from the main command station.

"Damn, I forgot about those," said Reeves, joining his XO at the console. "How did they go?"

"Let's just say you didn't actually miss anything," Kane replied, raising an eyebrow at Reeves. She tapped a few commands into the console and the holo applications of five candidates appeared above the command station. "This one was a naval academy washout," Kane went on, pointing to the first record; a human female called, 'Donna Day'.

Reeves skim-read the record then snorted. "She didn't even pass basic flight, and she's applying to be our CAG?"

"Oh, it gets better..." said Kane with a whimsical smirk. "Number two is a Bukkan whose claim to fame is that he once sat in the cockpit of a Bukkan Interceptor."

"You're kidding?" Reeves replied, scanning the record of the Bukkan male, named Clothar Beg. "But it says here that he's an experienced and decorated combat pilot?"

"Have you heard of something called, 'Starfighter Prime'?" Kane said, still smirking.

Reeves thought for a moment, his brow scrunching up almost painfully as he did so. "Do you mean the holo video game?" Kane nodded, but Reeves wasn't having any of it. "Come on, Major, now I know you're yanking my chain."

Kane sighed. "He holds the top score on the entire station. Apparently, this makes him qualified to be our Commander Air Group."

"Unbelievable..." Reeves said, shaking his head. "Were any of these candidates suitable, even if we're just talking about potential pilots, rather than CAG material?"

Kane shrugged. "Maybe, but not without some pretty rigorous refresher training, which is going to require an instructor or a CAG to coordinate, and we have neither."

Reeves rubbed his freshly-shaven chin, feeling more than a little despairing, though in truth, he wasn't surprised that the applications had been of such a poor standard. After all, any pilot or potential leader worth their salt wouldn't voluntarily choose a posting on Concord Station, if there were better options available to them. And there were a galaxy of better options than serving on The Abyss. Reeves then remembered that Kane had brought up five records, but had so far only mentioned four interviews.

"Who is this fifth guy?" Reeves asked his XO. He read the name on the application, then scanned the man's record, which seemed surprisingly impressive. "Jesse

Rush... he looks like a pretty solid option." The more he read the more Reeves was convinced the man sounded like a good candidate. "Did he have two heads or really bad breath or something?"

Kane snorted a laugh. "If I was put off by really bad breath then I wouldn't be here, serving with you."

"Very droll, Major," Reeves hit back, scowling at his XO. "So, what's the catch with this Jesse Rush guy? There must have been something wrong with him."

Kane expanded Rush's record then read out the pertinent sections. "Jesse Rush, former first lieutenant in the Bastion Navy, graduated top of his class."

"So far so good," Reeves said, still at a loss to understand why Kane hadn't recommended the man.

"He served for three years then quit about a year ago, after an incident he was involved in resulted in a passenger transport being destroyed," Kane went on. She then paused while she skimmed ahead. "The record says that pirates attacked the transport near the border with Bukkan space. Rush was scrambled to assist and successfully fought off the pirates, but one of the disabled pirate shuttles accidentally collided with the transport, destroying it and killing all on-board."

"How many?" asked Reeves, frowning again.

"Six hundred and thirty-two," replied Kane, meeting Reeves eyes. The playful smirk had been replaced by a much more solemn expression. Like Reeves, Kane knew the cost of war and service, and the scars it left behind, many of which never fully healed. "There was a court-marshal hearing, and he was fully absolved of any responsibility, but he quit anyway and was honorably-discharged."

"The kid had a rough run, but in my mind that doesn't make him unsuitable," Reeves said, still struggling to understand why he hadn't made the cut. "Did he interview badly?"

"I have no idea, he was a no-show," Kane replied, shrugging.

Reeves shook his head again then rested forward on the command console. He had a fairly good idea why the man had chosen not to turn up, and in ordinary circumstances he'd respect that choice. However, he was fresh out of options, and he couldn't afford to let the opportunity to recruit another good officer pass him by.

"Computer, locate station resident Jesse Rush, human male," Reeves said, addressing the computer.

"Jesse Rush is located in zone five, Night Sector," the computer replied.

"Well, that doesn't bode well," quipped Kane.

"Pinpoint his location, computer," Reeves added, ignoring his XO, though he couldn't deny that this wasn't a promising start. "Where exactly is Jesse Rush?"

"Jess Rush is on bar stool six, main bar, Meow Meow, one hundred and one, Red Street, Night Sector," the computer replied, managing to be far more specific than Reeves had expected or required.

"Well, it could be worse," said Kane, folding her arms. The smirk had returned to her lips.

"How could it be worse than our best candidate

blowing off an interview in order to prop up the bar in a club called 'Meow Meow'?" Reeves asked.

"Red Street isn't so bad," Kane replied, shrugging again. "And despite the name, Meow Meow is actually a karaoke bar, not some seedy strip joint."

"How the hell do you know that?" Reeves hit back, scowling at his XO.

"Hey, I like a good karaoke bar as much as the next gal," Kane said, smiling. "Though I haven't had the pleasure of frequenting that particular establishment yet."

Reeves huffed a laugh then rubbed his chin again and considered his options, of which he figured there were only two. He could either leave Jesse Rush to stare into the bottom of a glass, or see if he could change the man's mind.

"Well, I'll let you know what it's like after I get back," Reeves said, making his decision.

"You're going to Meow Meow?" said Kane, as Reeves stepped away from the console.

"This guy is too good an opportunity to pass up," Reeves said, calling back to his XO over his shoulder.

"Hey, bring me along!" Kane called back. "All I've got on here is a couple of basic tanker ops, and Curio can handle those."

The Eyrhu officer's ears pricked up as Kane said this, though the man continued to work at his console, pretending that he wasn't listening.

"I'm going there to conduct an interview, Major, not belt out a few cheesy pop songs," Reeves replied. He stopped then turned back to face his XO. "Besides, we both know that you and karaoke bars don't really mix."

Kane looked deeply offended. "I sing really well, thank you very much," she grumbled.

"It's not your singing that I'm worried about, but you getting mad and punching out anyone that heckles or boos you," Reeves replied, raising an eyebrow.

Kane was about to argue back, but then stopped and thought for a moment. "Good point," she said, backing down. "On second thoughts, you've got this."

"Smart choice, Major," Reeves said, spinning on his heels and marching toward the exit. "I'll let you know how the interview goes," he added, "and whether or not this Rush guy is a decent singer..."

CHAPTER 7
WHAT A RUSH

REEVES COULD HEAR the dubiously-named karaoke bar, 'Meow Meow', long before he'd walked far enough down Red Street to spot the over-sized neon sign above the door. The howl of over-enthusiastic singing and thump of alien synth-pop was so loud that it drowned out the hedonistic beats emanating from all the other clubs nearby. However, upon reaching the venue, Reeves couldn't work out which was worse – the garish red-lit sign accompanied by a holo image of a singing cat, or the caterwauling screech that was assaulting him through the open door.

Venturing inside, matters did not improve. Neon appeared to be de rigueur in Meow Meow, and its use was everywhere, encircling the bar and illuminating the tables, chairs and doorframes. Wherever there wasn't space for a headache-inducing light source, the venue's owner had placed a holo of the cat that could be seen singing and dancing above the sign outside. The holos, which Reeves assumed were representations of the eponymous 'Meow

Meow' herself, were merrily singing along with the current occupant of the stage; a rowdy Bukkan female, who was belting out a song in her native language at phenomenal volume.

The assault to his ears and eyes was almost enough to cause Reeves to turn around and leave, until he saw a human male sat at the bar, nursing a half-empty glass of white liquid. Reeves could tell straight away that it was his guy. The man had a strong jaw and the sort of face that the Navy would have loved to slap on recruiting posters. He was of average build, but from the muscle definition in his forearms Reeves could tell he looked after himself, even though the fact he was nursing a drink in a Night Sector karaoke bar at eleven in the morning suggested otherwise. However, it was the look on the man's face that stuck with Reeves more than anything else. It was an expression that Reeves had seen staring back at him in the mirror only a couple of months previously. Jesse Rush looked totally and utterly lost.

Walking over to the bar, Reeves slipped onto the stool next to Rush. The man didn't look up and simply continued to spin the half-empty glass in circles on the counter top.

"What'll it be, human?" said a Bukkan male behind the bar. Like almost all the Bukkan Reeves had met, this giant was extremely short on charm.

"I'll have whatever he's having," Reeves said, hooking a thumb at the man sat next to him, though Rush didn't bat an eyelid and merely continued to gloomily nurse his drink.

The Bukkan bartender scowled and looked annoyed.

"You want a glass of Yakow milk?" the man said, looking at Reeves liked he'd just asked for a glass of urine to drink. "What is it with you humans and drinking the breast milk of furry mammals?"

"On second thoughts, water is just fine, thanks," Reeves said. He had no idea what a Yakow was, but he knew he didn't want to consume any of its secretions.

"Oh yeah, water, that will help me pay the bills," the Bukkan grumbled. "If you want water, go home and turn on a tap."

"Fine, get me damned coffee then," Reeves hit back. "And none of that expensive Eyrhu stuff. A proper human coffee."

"That's more like it," the barman replied, smiling and shuffling off to a coffee machine on the rear counter.

"And a couple of those nice caramelized biscuits too," Reeves called over, as the man clumsily threw a cup underneath the machine. The Bukkan scowled then grabbed a handful of golden-colored biscuits from a jar, crushing half of them in the process, and tossing them onto the saucer. "And if you have creamer, I'd prefer that to milk, whether it's Yakow milk or any other kind."

"Okay, okay, give me a damned minute already," the barman muttered under his breath.

"And four packets of sugar too, preferably brown sugar," Reeves added.

This time the Bukkan uttered a curse in his native language before finally returning and sliding the coffee onto the counter. Some of the jet-black contents of the mug spilled out and started to soak into the crushed biscuits on the saucer. The barman then reached under the counter, grabbed a sizable handful of sugar packets and creamers, and dumped them next to the cup.

"Will there be anything else, sir?" the Bukkan asked, with a deep insincerity. "Perhaps you'd like me to stir in the sugar, or hold the cup up to your lips so you can drink it more easily?"

"No, you've done more than enough already," Reeves replied, layering on the sarcasm thickly.

The Bukkan slid a credit scanner over to Reeves. "That'll be four credits."

Reeves almost laughed in the hulking alien's face. "Four credits for a damned coffee and a few mangled biscuits?"

"Hey, do you know how much it costs to get Bastion-grown coffee out here?" the Bukkan argued, shrugging at Reeves.

"This had better be the best damned coffee I've ever had," Reeves said, thumbing the scanner to pay for the drink.

"I very much doubt that," the barman replied, before shuffling off to serve another customer.

Reeves emptied four sugars and a couple of creamers into the cup then started to stir it. The liquid certainly had a coffee-like appearance, and it didn't smell too off-putting, though it was hard to smell anything over the scent of perfume and cologne that was wafting across to him from the other patrons at the bar.

"It's better than you'll get in most places," said Rush, still nursing his Yakow milk. The obnoxious Bukkan barman had made Reeves forget why he was in Meow Meow in the first place. "Though if you want really good coffee, you should try out the Bean Bank on Green Street. It's run by an ex-Navy medic called Cathy, and it's as good as anything you'll get on Bastion."

"Thanks, maybe I'll check it out," said Reeves. He took a sip of the hastily-made brew, and found that it was more than tolerable.

Suddenly, Jesse Rush appeared to notice Reeves' uniform and the rank insignia on his collar, and immediately shot to his feet, straightening to attention as he did so.

"Commander, I'm sorry, I didn't realize it was you," the man said, eyes fixed to a spot on the wall somewhere behind Reeves. The man appeared embarrassed and cross with himself.

"Sit down, Rush, I'm not your commander," said Reeves, motioning for the man to return to his stool. "It is Jesse Rush, right?"

"Yes, sir, that's right," the man said, sitting down again, though somewhat reluctantly. "I'm sorry I didn't show for the interview, sir. I'm assuming that's why you're here?"

"Got it in one," replied Reeves. He was aware that the man had continued to call him, 'sir' despite the fact neither of them were currently serving in the Bastion Navy. "So, why did you bail on me, Jesse Rush? From your record, it certainly looks like you have the chops."

Rush looked uncomfortable, and with good reason. The man had clearly escaped to the garish Karaoke bar to avoid having to confront his past again, and have the incident scrutinized by a couple of strangers. The fact that Reeves had cornered Rush and asked him directly was a shitty move, and he knew it.

"I didn't think I was ready, that's all, sir," Rush replied, choosing a vague, but not untruthful response.

"Here's what I think, Jesse, and stop me if I'm wrong," Reeves said, deciding to skip ahead and cut to the chase. "You blame yourself for the deaths of all the passengers on the transport ship, despite knowing that it wasn't your fault. And now, you're bumming around in shitty bars in the ass-end of nowhere, believing it to be some kind of justified penance for what happened."

"Hey, less of the shitty!" the Bukkan barman called over, but Reeves merely waved him off.

"It's not quite that simple, Commander," Rush replied, though importantly he hadn't refuted what Reeves had said.

"So enlighten me," Reeves hit back. "I've read your file. Your commanding officers all spoke highly of you, and had you pegged for a fast track to field officer status and beyond. Why throw that away over something you couldn't have prevented?"

Rush pushed the glass of Yakow milk away from him, and looked away. Reeves could see he was angry for being put on the spot.

"I've accepted that what happened wasn't my fault, but it doesn't change anything," Rush said, staring off into the distance again. "I just couldn't get back into the cockpit again, no matter how hard I tried."

Reeves considered the man's response, using the

moment of pause to drink some more of the coffee, which was tasting a little better with each sip.

"I did some background reading on my way here, and station records say you only came on board two weeks ago, which was after we posted the advert for the CAG position," Reeves went on, trying an alternate line of attack. "Prior to then, from what I can find out, you've flitted from world to world, station to station, never really staying anywhere for more than a couple of months."

"I got nowhere I need to be, and no reason to stay there," Rush hit back, shrugging again. He had returned to twirling the glass of Yakow milk.

"Yet you specifically chose to come here, and file an application to be my CAG," Reeves said. "At least tell me why."

Jesse Rush thought for a moment, finally taking a swig from the half-empty glass of Yakow milk that he'd been toying with. Reeves was careful not to press him for an answer. The man was either ready to tell him or he wasn't.

"I suppose I was soul-searching, as corny as that might sound," Rush finally answered. "Though I guess that's just the same as running away."

"So, what changed?" asked Reeves, trying to keep the man on course, rather than letting Rush's thoughts wander. "What made you file the application?"

"I heard about the Sa'Nerra, and what they did, and I realized I couldn't do a damned thing about it," Rush answered. He sounded angry again, though it was all directed inward, Reeves realized. "Had I stayed in the Navy, I could have been out there, fighting the Sa'Nerra and making a difference, not matter how small." Rush shrugged again. "Now I'm just stuck on the outside looking in, while the galaxy goes to hell."

"I'll tell you what I think, Jesse," Reeves said. He was no psychologist, but he reckoned he already had the measure of Jesse Rush. "I think you're exactly where you need to be, and more than that, you're exactly what I need." Rush straightened up and met Reeves' eye cleanly for the first time since he'd sat down. "Whatever you're trying to work out in your mind, you're not going to get the answer sat at a bar, drinking Yakow milk. You need to do it in a cockpit, fighting for something you believe in."

"So, war is coming then?" Rush asked.

Reeves nodded. "It's coming, of that I have absolutely no doubt. And when it does, we're all going to have to square with our demons and fight. Because if history repeats itself, the Sa'Nerra won't stop until they've killed every man, woman and child in the six realms, or we kill them first."

Rush sighed heavily then nodded. "Can you give you some time to think about it?"

"Okay, but don't take too long," Reeves replied. "Things are moving fast, and I need to get this station ready."

Rush nodded again then stood to attention, his posture confident and assured. "You'll have my answer in the morning, sir," the man said.

"Okay, Jesse," Reeves said, slapping the man on the shoulder. "Enjoy your Yakow milk." Reeves glanced over to the stage; the Bukkan woman was belting out another song, which sounded like a cross between death metal and opera. "Enjoy the entertainment."

Rush huffed a laugh and nodded. "It's usually better than this."

"I'll take your word for it," Reeves replied, smiling.

The two men then parted ways, and Reeves made a bee-line for the exit. His head was starting to hurt and his ears were ringing like the residual chime of a school bell. Stepping out onto Red Street again, he was greeted by the usual sights and sounds of Night Sector. Ordinarily, just walking down one of the many streets in the party district was disquieting enough for Reeves, but compared to the din of Meow Meow, Red Street was positively peaceful.

Reeves turned down an alley in order to take a short-cut to back to the transit station, and tapped his buzz. However, the device merely made a strange spluttering sound, like hot treacle bubbling in a pan.

"Major Kane, come in," Reeves said, double-tapping his left palm again. "Katee, do you read me?" However, the device just made another spluttering sound.

Cursing, Reeves was about to set off again, when he saw someone step out in the alley in front of him. The figure was cloaked in shadow, but from their outline, it was clear the person was large. Reeves' hand immediately went to his pistol and he closed his fingers around the grip.

"Step into the light, nice and slow," Reeves called out, getting reading to draw his pistol if needed.

The figure did as it was ordered and took several paces forward, revealing itself to be a huge Bukkan male, dressed in a sharp suit and silver tie. It was then Reeves realized who it was. The man was Barton, one of Sid Garrett's goons.

"What the hell do you want?" Reeves asked, as the massive Bukkan approached.

"Mr. Garrett would like to renegotiate the terms of your agreement," Barton said, smiling and revealing rows of jagged teeth.

"The Lord of Night won't like how I negotiate," Reeves hit back. "Now tell your boss if he has something to say, he can say it in person. But if he goes back on our agreement, I'll shut him down hard."

"I don't think so," Barton growled.

Suddenly, a cord was slipped around Reeves neck and a knee pressed into his back. The cord tightened like a boa-constrictor, squeezing his throat and cutting into his flesh. Knowing he had just seconds to save his life, Reeves grabbed the cord to release the pressure and backpedaled as fast as he could, eventually toppling the man who was trying to garrote him. However, despite them both falling to the ground, his attacker remained glued to his back like a barnacle on the hull of a ship.

Two more men appeared, both Quarr, and began thumping kicks into Reeves' gut. Powerless to protect against the blows, Reeves continued to fight the man to his rear, finally managing to slip his fingers in between the cord and his skin. He broke the hold, then head-butted the attacker to his rear, before rolling away from the two Quarr and scrambling to his feet.

Struggling to breathe and with blood trickling down his neck, Reeves saw his original attacker plainly for the first time. It was a Skemm male, dressed in the same slick suit as the others. The Skemm threw down the garrote and removed his silver tie, straightening it into a machete with a swift flick of the wrist. Reeves reached for his pistol, but it wasn't there. He cursed and spotted the weapon on the floor behind the three goons, close to where Barton was still quietly observing the fight, grinning and bearing his jagged teeth.

The Skemm darted forward first, lunging at Reeves with the blade. The edge nicked his arm, but Reeves' fighting instincts had kicked in, and he countered with a hard shot to the face, crushing the man's eye socket and popping out his eye. The Skemm was a devious and tricksy species, but they lacked the physical toughness of the Bukkan or Quarr, and were certainly no match for Reeves' strength. The alien dropped to one knee, and Reeves followed up with kick to the Skemm's ribs. Throwing all his weight and aggression into the attack, he crushed the man's ribcage as easily as smashing a nest of spun sugar. Blood poured out of the Skemm's mouth as the man collapsed to the ground, drowning in his own fluids.

The two Quarr moved next, removing their silver ties and transforming them into machetes. Reeves picked up the Skemm's blade and threw it. Adrenalin was coursing through his veins, and combined with his incredible natural strength, the machete flew like a bullet and embedded itself in the Quarr's forehead. For a moment, the thug appeared confused and tried to reach up to remove the weapon, but the blade had sunk so deep into his brain that it would have taken two men to pull it out again. A second later the

Quarr fell, his head splitting open as it cracked onto the ground.

The final thug glanced at its two fallen comrades and hesitated, but the Quarr were not known to back down from a fight. Gritting its teeth, the thug advanced and attacked, but Reeves was now unstoppable. Fighting was in his blood, and once he had given himself over to violence, it would take an army of Quarr thugs to stand in his way. Dodging the first strike of the machete, Reeves blocked the next attack and pounded an overhand right into the Quarr's nose. Blood gushed down the thug's face and the machete fell from his grasp. Following up with an even harder left, Reeves' hit the alien again, crushing the Quarr male's regal, pronounced cheekbones and sending it down for good.

Teeth still gritted, Reeves then turned to face Barton, fully intending to give the goon the beatdown of his life. However, the hulking alien was standing calmly in the alley, holding Reeves' plasma pistol and aiming it at his head.

"Mr. Garrett said you would not want to negotiate, or to come willingly," Barton said, taking a step closer to Reeves. "In which case, he asked me to settle the matter on his behalf."

The massive Bukkan grinned then added pressure to the trigger. Suddenly, another figure flashed into view out of the shadows and slapped the pistol from the alien's grasp. Barton spun around to face the new arrival, swinging a punch at the figure that was powerful enough to knock down a building. The shadow ducked underneath the blow then landed a ferocious combination of blows to the body, striking the Bukkan to the equivalent of its kidneys. The alien roared and staggered away, but the figure did not let up the assault, hammering more kicks and punches to Barton's body and head. Then the mysterious figure grabbed the Bukkan henchman by the back of his neck and pulled down hard, slamming a knee into Barton's face. The Bukkan goon hit the deck so hard Reeves was sure that the ground shook under his feet. The figure paused for a moment in the shadows, waiting to make sure the alien was not about to get up, then stepped toward Reeves. The light from the many neon signs on Red Street caught the man's face, illuminating it in a melee of bright, garish colors. It was Jesse Rush.

"I take it that you've already made your choice then?" Reeves said, massaging his throat where the cord had dug into his flesh.

"I have, sir," Rush replied, standing to attention in front of Reeves. "I'll return for my interview at the earliest opportunity."

Reeves laughed and extended his hand toward the man. "That was your interview," he said, waiting for the man to take his hand, "and I'm pleased to inform you that you passed."

Rush smiled, took Reeves' hand and shook it firmly. "Thank you, Commander."

"Report to Major Kane at oh nine hundred tomorrow, Captain Rush," Reeves said, adopting a more formal tone, now that the nature of their relationship had shifted. "We have a lot of work to do."

CHAPTER 8
DOCKING BAY 99

REEVES HEARD the clack of boots on the deck plates behind him and glanced over his shoulder to see Major Katee Kane approaching. He'd arranged to meet his XO on the viewing gallery in docking garage one, in advance of their appointment with the mysterious contact, who Ambassador One said could procure them a ship. His early arrival was partly so that he could check out the location of the rendezvous in advance. He was tired of getting jumped by New Earther thugs or Sid Garrett's goons, and wanted to make sure he'd scouted the likely locations for an ambush prior to the meeting. He was also early because he happened to be in the area anyway, after visiting the hospital to get his wounds tended to and regenerated.

"Do we know which ship we're getting yet?" wondered Kane, leaning up against a pillar and peering down into the docking garage.

The enormous garage was largely occupied by passenger transports and cargo vessels, ranging from small light freighters to larger haulers. The personal yachts and cruisers belonging to the wealthier visitors and inhabitants were all docked in garages three and four, in the more salubrious zone four of the station.

"It's probably some kind of light freighter or transport shuttle," Reeves replied. He pointed out into the sea of vessels and aimed a finger toward a Skemm shuttle in bay forty-three. "My money is on that Skemm type-sixteen courier shuttle," he added, feeling fairly confident in his guess. "The records show it's been impounded here for the last two months due to non-payment of docking fees."

"I'd say that Amity Class De'Vaught transport is more likely," Kane replied. Reeves followed the line of her finger and saw the vessel docked in bay twenty-one. "If anyone was likely to punt us a ship, it would be the goody-goody De'Vaught. They wouldn't even ask what we wanted it for."

Reeves hadn't considered this and it made him reassess his own prediction. Then his buzz vibrated and he read the message on his palm. It was from their contact, telling Reeves that he was ready to meet.

"Well, it looks like we're both wrong," Reeves said, noting the bay number on the display. "Our ship is in bay ninety-nine. Ambassador One's contact is there with it now."

"Bay ninety-nine?" Kane said, scowling. "Bays ninety to a hundred aren't in use at the moment. Chief Raspe's latest report says they're unsafe."

Reeves huffed a laugh. "Well, that's not a great start." He sighed and shrugged. "I guess we have no choice but to check it out though. If it looks like a deathtrap, we'll just have to go back to the drawing board."

Reeves and Kane took a conveyer to the end of the docking garage then walked past the neat banks of vessels docked in bays eighty to ninety, until they reached a section that was cordoned off with bright yellow hazard tape.

"This really doesn't bode well," muttered Kane, as Reeves ducked under the tape and continued on.

"Let's reserve judgement until we actually see the ship," said Reeves, trying to remain optimistic, though he couldn't deny that the omens were not good.

Bays ninety-one to ninety-eight were either empty or filled with ships that looked like they hadn't flown for a century. With his sense of foreboding peaking, Reeves finally reached bay ninety-nine and stepped inside. A Bukkan male was waiting for them. The man, who was small in stature for a member of the bear-sized race, was smiling at them. Reeves thought the Bukkan had the hungry look of a dodgy car dealer who was about to sell him a lemon. Behind the alien was small transport vessel that appeared Bukkan in design, though it was clear it had been extensively modified, and Reeves didn't recognize its class.

"Welcome, Commander and Major, it is good to see you," said the Bukkan, cheerfully. "I am Boril Ghazi. I was told that you were looking for a ship." The alien then gestured to the vessel behind him, as if he were unveiling a brand-new ship in a showroom. "And here she is. What do you think?"

"It's a Bukkan pirate ship," said Kane, who had begun promenading around the vessel to get a better look at it.

"A Bukkan trading vessel, if you please," the alien dealer said, eager to correct Kane. "I am confident that this ship has not engaged in pirate activities."

"Exactly how confident are you?" Reeves cut in.

Boril Ghazi shrugged. "*Reasonably* confident," the alien replied, smiling broadly while attempting a charm offensive. "I can say for sure that it has not engaged in piracy for at least six months."

"And how can you be sure of that?" Kane said, while running her hand along the hull of the ship.

"Because it was seized and impounded here six standard months ago," beamed Ghazi. Reeves was not impressed with the Bukkan's flippant reply, and the alien appeared to recognize this. "Do not be concerned, Commander, I assure you that the vessel is no longer on any interstellar wanted lists. Its captain and crew are imprisoned on this station, and will not be released for another three standard months. Until then, this ship is available for hire."

"How come you're the one hawking it out for charter?" said Kane. She had crept up behind Ghazi and startled him.

"Its current owners placed it under my care, until their release," Ghazi said, edging away from Kane as surreptitiously as he thought he could get away with, without appearing obvious. "The rental fees will go toward paying off its accrued docking charges." The Bukkan then shrugged. "Minus my cut, of course."

"Of course," said Reeves, raising an eyebrow.

"Who's in 'ere?"

Reeves turned to see another Bukkan male stomp into the docking bay. The alien was dressed in Concord Station work overalls, and Reeves realized it was Chief Raspe.

"Oh, Commander, I didn't know it were you," said Raspe, looking embarrassed. "These bays are off-limits until I can get 'em sorted out."

The station's chief engineer then spotted Boril Ghazi. Reeves noticed that the smaller Bukkan had moved behind the ship's forward landing strut and appeared to be trying to hide from Raspe.

"What are you doing 'ere, Ghazi?" Raspe bellowed. "I've warned you before about sneakin' around in 'ere."

"Mr. Ghazi is procuring us a ship for a little trip the Major and I need to take," Reeves cut in. "An off-the-books trip..."

Raspe's oval eyes widened and the man stroked his pointed chin, which was covered in several days' worth of black stubble.

"Right, I get you, Commander, say no more," Raspe said, shooting a wink at Reeves. "All cloak and dagger stuff, right? Nice, nice, I like it!" The chief then turned his attention to Ghazi once more. "Though I wouldn't trust that crook as far as I could punt him," Raspe went on. "You'd better let me check 'er out first, guv. You know, just to make sure this thing'll get you where you need to go, and back again, of course."

"Sure, go ahead, Chief, thanks," said Reeves, inviting Raspe to take the lead. "Though I'm sure Mr. Ghazi wouldn't hire us a ship that's unsafe to fly, isn't that right, Mr. Ghazi?"

"Of course, of course," the smaller Bukkan said, again adopting the saccharin smile of a dodgy car salesman. "Everything is in order, nothing to worry about."

Reeves glanced at Kane, though she looked equally unconvinced. "I guess we should check out our new ride then," he said, nodding toward the lowered rear hatch.

Reeves went inside the Bukkan pirate ship and found Chief Raspe busily pulling open maintenance panels and plugging wires into half a dozen different diagnostic devices that he'd either removed from his many pockets, or had strapped to his forearms. However, it was the stench of the ship that was the first thing that struck Reeves.

"What the hell is that stink?" said Kane, jogging up the ramp to meet Reeves. "It smells like something died in here."

"Somethin' did, guv," said Raspe. The Bukkan kicked open a cargo panel and three Slum Rats rolled out. The flesh was rotten and filled with maggots, and the sight and intense, pungent smell of them turned Reeves' stomach. "I'll get a cleaner drone to give her a good once over before you head out," Raspe went on, though he was mumbling the words due to having a bunch of wires clamped between his teeth.

"Is there such a thing as a fumigation drone?" asked Kane. "If not, can you stop by the Oasis Gardens and transport a couple of rose bushes inside to take away the smell?"

"You'll get used to it, guv," said Raspe. Reeves had given up on trying to get the chief engineer to call him and Kane, 'sir' rather than 'guv'.

Raspe then found a partially-eaten snack bar on a shelf.

He sniffed it then pulled back the wrapper and took an enormous bite.

"Chief, that bar has probably been festering on the shelf for months," Reeves said, grimacing at Raspe. His engineer's disgusting eating habits turned his stomach even more than the decaying rats.

"Ah, these things last fer years, guv," Raspe hit back, dismissively wafting a hand at Reeves. "They taste better after a bit of a breather. Y'know, like wine?"

"Everything okay in here?"

Reeves glanced behind to see Boril Ghazi on the deck outside.

"Apart from the dead rats and trash, you mean?" Reeves said, pointing to the rotting carcasses.

"Oh, I'll throw them in for free," Ghazi replied, again offering Reeves a double-dealing smile. The alien apparently expected his joke to cause a ripple of laughter to erupt inside the cargo hold of the pirate ship. However, the unimpressed stares from Reeves and Kane soon wiped the smile of the Bukkan's face. "I have another appointment, so I'll leave you to finish the inspection," the man went on. "Assuming everything is in order, just contact me when you're ready to leave and I'll have the ship moved to an operable docking bay, so that you can be on your way." The Bukkan then skulked out of sight without waiting for a reply.

Reeves frowned at his XO. "I wonder why he was in such a hurry to leave?"

"All I know is that I don't trust him," replied Kane. The station's XO turned to Chief Raspe. "How much longer will this inspection take, Chief? I don't want to hang around in this disused section of the docking garage any longer than necessary."

"Won't be a jiffy, guv," mumbled Raspe, still with a bundle of wires between his teeth. "Pass me that K2 wrench will ya?" He pointed to one of the many tools he'd pulled out of his seemingly never-ending range of pockets. "I just need to re-wire the life-support system. Bukkan prefer it cold and dry, and by default you can't whack up the temps to more than about two-eighty-eight Kelvin."

"What's that in figures I can understand?" asked Reeves.

"Oh, about sixty of your foreign-heights," Raspe said, taking the wrench off Kane. The Bukkan then repeatedly hammered at something inside the hatch he was working on, as if he were trying to smash open a safe.

"You're right, that is a bit chilly," Reeves agreed, making an assumption that the chief had meant to say Fahrenheit.

"And I hope yer can read Bukkan'r," Raspe went on, still bashing away at the component with the wrench. "Cos this ship ain't got no Bastion-English translation package installed."

"Major Kane and I will manage," Reeves said, coming across more confidently than he had a right to. His Bukkan'r was terrible, but he recalled that his XO's language skills were more polished.

Suddenly, the sound of metal crashing against metal filtered in from outside. Reeves frowned again. It sounded like someone or something had knocked over a fuel canister in the bay.

"Did you hear that?" Reeves asked his XO.

"It was probably just another Slum Rat, scurrying around outside," Kane said, shrugging.

"Ain't no Slum Rats in my garages, guv," Raspe cut in. He had stopped hammering and was now shoving the bundle of wires back inside the maintenance hatch. "I personally set traps all over the place for the blighters."

"That's decent of you," said Reeves, impressed that the Bukkan would want to make the docking garages a pest-free zone. "Seeing a Slum Rat scurrying around isn't likely to make a very good impression to visitors landing here."

"Oh, it's not fer the arrivals, guv," Raspe replied, slamming shut the hatch with considerably more force than was necessary to close it. "They're actually pretty tasty if you roast 'em for long enough, with a bit of De'Vaught garlic. I can sell 'em to the Bukkan food stalls in the Long Market for four credits per rat. It's a nice little earner."

Reeves shook his head, though he shouldn't have been surprised at his chief engineer's entrepreneurism. Raspe was a Bukkan, after all.

More sounds filtered in from outside, and this time Reeves was sure it sounded like bootsteps. Instinctively, he drew his weapon out of its holster, and noticed that Kane had drawn her pistol at almost exactly the same time.

"That wasn't a rat," said Kane, stalking toward the rear ramp of the vessel.

"No it wasn't."

The deep, booming voice had come from outside the

ship. Moments later, the hulking figure of Barton stepped into view. The goon's suit was scuffed and dirtied from when he'd hit the deck after Jesse Rush had laid him out cold back in Night Sector. Dried blood covered his face like a rash.

"Mr. Garrett is very insistent that he wants to see you," Barton continued, removing his tie and straightening it into a machete. Six more Bukkan thugs then appeared outside, all armed with plasma pistols. "And this time, I'm going to take you to him in pieces if I have to."

CHAPTER 9
THE NUTCRACKER

REEVES HAD ALREADY WARNED Barton to stay away, and he wasn't about to waste his breath warning the man for a second time. His next response was going to come from the barrel of his plasma pistol. Squeezing the trigger, Reeves blasted Barton square in the chest, knocking the massive alien to his back. The Bukkan thug cracked his head on a storage crate on the way down and appeared to be out cold. Kane also opened fire and together they managed to scatter the six other goons and buy themselves some time.

"Chief, are you armed?" Reeves called back to his Bukkan engineer, while moving into a better position.

"This K2 wrench is pretty handy in a fight, guv, but if you mean a plasma weapon, then nah, sorry," Raspe called back. "Give me a sec', though. I've dealt with enough pirate scum in my time to know what sort of tools these gits keep to hand."

The engineer began throwing open storage lockers and chests at the rear of the hold as Reeves and Kane continued to hold off Garrett's goons. Raspe then laughed and shot a toothy grin at Reeves.

"These should come in 'andy," the engineer called out.

Raspe tossed a small metal shield about the size of a ping-pong paddle across the deck to Reeves, before continuing to rifle through a large storage trunk.

"Chief, I don't think this will be much use against six of Garrett's goons," Reeves said, as Raspe tossed a similar device to Kane.

"They're shield bucklers, guv," Raspe answered, while pulling on a bulky, reinforced jacket that looked like a cross between football armor and a medieval scaled cuirass. It was so massive that Reeves thought it could probably stop a missile in its tracks. "Grab the handle and squeeze the knobbly red button on the side."

Reeves picked up the buckler and did as his chief engineer instructed. A force field expanded from the metal plate, first forming a wide circle, before adapting its shape to cover Reeves from head to toe.

"Okay, I take it back, these are pretty useful," Reeves admitted.

"So is this little puppy," said Raspe, hauling a heavy-look metal pole out of the trunk. He held it out, smiling at it like it was his favorite thing in the whole world.

"I'm not sure that whacking them with a big stick is going to cut it, Chief," said Kane, hiding behind her energy buckler and looking at the Bukkan engineer like he'd gone mad.

"Depends on the stick, dunnit, guv?" Raspe hit back, smiling.

The engineer twisted the handle of the metal bar and four prongs sprang out from the top quarter of the pole, arranged in two opposing pairs. A deep bass hum followed and two arcs of dark blue plasma formed between the sets of prongs, making the weapon look like a giant battle-axe. The difference was that instead of sharpened steel, the blade was made of searing hot energy.

"I can't shoot for toffee, guv, but I've plenty of experience stoppin' pirates boardin' me ships." He shrugged. "Well, apart from that last time, anyway."

"So long as you still remember how to do it, that's all that matters," Reeves said, as two of Garrett's goons darted into view and started taking pot shots at them. One blast clipped the top edge of his shield buckler but the forcefield held strong.

"Don't you need a shield too?" asked Kane, hustling across to the opposite side of the cargo hold, ready to move out.

"Nah, I'm a walkin' shield, boss," Raspe replied, confidently.

The Bukkan then slapped a badge in the center of the jacket and additional armor panels slid out and began to encase the chief's arms and legs. Finally, a scaly hood grew over the top of the man's huge triangular head. Reeves had seen a lot of strange things, but right at that moment, Chief Quitto Raspe beat them all. He looked like an iron golem from a dark fantasy story.

"How about I clear a path, and you follow after and mop up the remains?" Raspe said, stomping toward the lowered ramp.

"Sounds like a plan," said Reeves, shrugging at his XO.

"Beats any idea I've got," Kane agreed.

"I'm gonna enjoy this," said Raspe, as a pot-shot from one of the goons bounced off his armor and ricocheted into the roof of the cargo hold. "My De'Vaught therapist said I need to work on me 'anger issues'."

Reeves was fairly sure that the therapist in question wasn't referring to fighting six armed thugs, but he wasn't about to question his chief engineer.

"Right, let's clear this scum off me deck," Raspe continued, stomping down the ramp with the energy axe humming in his hands.

Blasts hammered into the engineer's armored shell, and quickly Raspe was taking all the incoming fire. Seeing his opening, Reeves moved out, returning fire and driving the goons back. Nodding to his XO, Kane raced down the ramp and took cover behind the storage crates that Barton had knocked himself out on earlier. Blasts thumped into the crates, but seconds later Raspe had gotten into the line of fire and was soaking up the incoming blasts again. Reeves moved next, finding similar cover outside the ship. He spotted one of the Bukkan goons advancing and opened fire, blasting the alien square in the center of its wide, triangular head, killing it instantly.

Suddenly, Raspe put on a surprising burst of speed, closing the gap between him and the nearest goon, who was in cover behind a support pillar. The axe hummed through the air as Raspe swung it with all his might, cutting through the pillar like it was made of plywood. The weapon continued on course, slicing off the left arm of the goon just below the shoulder. The Bukkan thug roared and staggered back, staring at the cauterized stump in disbelief, before Raspe ploughed through the goon and steamrollered the man to the deck.

Reeves and Kane both pressed the attack, taking down two more of the thugs with headshots. Still the incoming fire was focused on Chief Raspe and his menacing armored suit. Reeves could see that sections of the armor were glowing hot, while others appeared to be buckling. Yet Raspe staggered on, like a knight in full plate armor that was growing fatigued from the rigors of battle.

Using Raspe for cover, Kane advanced again, blasting the fourth of Garrett's goons in the chest. This time the armored business suit failed to save the goon, and the blast cored a hole through the man's substantial sternum directly to his heart. Raspe pressed on, swinging the plasma axe and slicing through the body of a goon just above the man's waist, splitting the alien in half. It was such a devastating exhibition of ghoulish violence that the sixth and final goon threw down his pistol and thrust his hands up in surrender.

"Shall I dissect him, guv?" Raspe asked, holding the humming blade of the axe next to the goon's neck.

"No, I want this one alive so he can go back to the Lord of Night with a message," Reeves said, moving alongside his engineer and glowering at the surviving member of Barton's brute squad. He then turned to Kane, while holstering his pistol. "Watch him for me. I'll be back in a second."

"Aye sir," Kane replied, raising a curious eyebrow at her commander.

Reeves could tell she was confused by the order, but

she kept her weapon trained on the goon, while also keeping a curious eye on Reeves, as he walked to the foot of the ship's ramp. Grabbing Barton by the collar of his shirt, Reeves hauled the massive man up, making full use of his incredible strength. He then dragged Garrett's senior henchman in front of the remaining goon, who eyed his unconscious boss anxiously.

"Wake up," Reeves said, slapping Barton around the face. "Come on, sleepy time is over," he added, slapping him again, much harder.

Barton roused, mumbling and groaning as if someone had just woken him from a deep sleep in a comfortable bed in the dead of night.

"What? What the hell is this?" Barton growled. The Bukkan tried to wrestle himself free, but Reeves' hold on him was unbreakable.

"Tell your boss that the next moron he sends after me will end up like these sorry assholes," Reeves said. He was addressing the sixth henchman, while specifically pointing to the Bukkan thug Chief Raspe had sliced in half. Reeves then slapped Barton around the face. "As for this piece of shit, he's going to enjoy the hospitality of Concord's jail, where he'll remain until his bushy eyebrows turn a bright, silvery gray."

"No judge will sentence me," Barton sneered, turning his wide triangular head toward Reeves. "You should know by now that they're all in Garrett's employ." The Bukkan smiled, revealing his jagged, gold-capped teeth. "Why do you think I'm still wandering the streets after all this time?"

Reeves nodded. "Thanks for the information," he said

before smashing the Bukkan's head against one the pirate ship's landing struts and knocking him out cold again. "I'll be sure to have all the judges replaced," he added as the hulking alien thumped to the deck. Reeves turned to his XO. "Until then, have Sergeant Calera keep Barton as a guest in the cells in the security wing. I want him under guard, day and night."

"Aye, sir," said, Kane, tapping her buzz and stepping away to make the call to Calera.

Reeves returned his attention to the sixth goon. "Do you understand the message you're to convey to your boss?" he asked, before opening a hand toward Raspe. "Or do we need to give you a reminder?" The Bukkan shook his head vigorously. Despite his tough appearance, the goon was clearly terrified. "Good, then piss off," Reeves added, kicking the thug in the chest. The Bukkan staggered back and tripped over a raised deck plate, before hurriedly scrambling to his feet again and running like the wind for the bay's exit.

"If you don't mind, guv, I'll change out of this getup now," Raspe said. Reeves glanced over to his chief and saw that steam was rising from the many locations where he'd taken plasma blasts. "It's gettin' a bit toasty in 'ere."

"Permission granted Chief," Reeves said. He had no desire to see his engineer roasted alive in front of him. "What is that thing anyway?"

"The pirates call 'em nutcrackers, boss," Raspe said, hitting a panel on the armor and causing the scales to retract again. "They use 'em to board ships once they've grappled on."

"Why do they call them nutcrackers?" Reeves asked.

"Because you'd be nuts to stand in the way of anyone wearing this thing," Reeves said, beaming a smile at Reeves. His face was coated in a thick sheen of sweat. "And if you're nuts enough to get in their way, you end up gettin' your 'ead cracked open."

"Or sliced in half," Kane said, returning to Reeves' side.

"Yeah, maybe that was bit excessive, guv," Raspe admitted, shrugging his massive shoulders. "It was fun, though. Just like old times."

Reeves raised an eyebrow at his chief engineer, but he considered that now was probably not the time to question Raspe's idea of entertainment. This was especially true considering the hefty Bukkan engineer had just saved their skins.

"I'll let you return to your duties then, chief," Reeves said. "The Major and I have places we need to be."

Raspe grinned again. "Oh right, I get it," the chief said, tapping the side of his huge nose and waggling his bushy eyebrows. "Cloak and dagger, cloak and dagger. Say no more..." Kane snorted a laugh, but it was well meaning. "Anyway, she's good to go, bar needing decontamination," Raspe added, pointing to the pirate ship. The station's chief engineer then removed the Nutcracker armor and tossed it to the deck, before flexing his arms and shoulders and tucking in his shirt to cover his substantial belly. "I'll put this through as overtime, shall I?" the man added.

Chief Raspe didn't wait for Reeves to answer, and simply belched loudly before sauntering off toward the exit.

CHAPTER 10
THE WASP

REEVES DROPPED into the pilot's seat of the Bukkan pirate shuttle and found himself lolling around in it like a baby in a car seat two sizes too big. It was easily large enough that he and Kane could have both comfortably fit inside. The control yoke was similarly oversized, at least for human hands, and all of the buttons and secondary controls seemed slightly too far away.

"I feel like someone shot me with a shrink ray," Reeves said, while fiddling with the seat controls in an attempt to get a better flying position. "I can barely reach the pedals."

Kane smiled then assisted Reeves in his adjustments, finally managing to maneuver the enormous bucket seat into a position where he could comfortably reach all the controls.

"Are you sure you don't want me to fly this thing?" Kane said, returning to her own seat and performing a similar set of adjustments. "I don't want you hitting the wrong button and ejecting us into space," she added with a wry smile.

Like Reeves, Major Kane had changed into civilian clothing while the shuttle had been cleaned and fumigated. Their uniforms would not have gone down well on the famously anti-establishment world of Thrace Colony.

"I'm going to need to get used to the controls sooner or later," Reeves replied, "and it's better I do it while we're in moderately-friendly territory, rather than figure it out when we're under attack."

"Who said anything about us coming under attack?" Kane hit back.

"Considering how many fights I've been in already since taking command of Concord, I think our chances of finding the Invictus and getting back here without coming under attack are pretty much nil," Reeves said.

Reeves focused back on the controls and flipped a sequence of switches, which he assumed was the main reactor start-up sequence. Moments later, a bellowing alarm blared out inside the cockpit.

"I'd suggest we don't dump our fuel while still in the launch bay, sir," said Kane, raising an eyebrow at Reeves, while also lifting a lever and flipping two more switches to cancel whatever action he'd performed. The alarm stopped blaring.

"Damn it, sorry," Reeves said, squinting at the Bukkan'r writing next to the dial. "I don't suppose you have a label gun to hand?"

"It'll come back to you," Kane said, though to Reeves' ear she didn't sound particularly genuine. "But until it does, how about you stick to the flight controls and leave the rest to me?"

"Sounds like a plan, Major," Reeves replied, activating the thrusters to lift them off the deck.

"Transport Omega One, this is Lieutenant Curio in the CIC," came the erudite voice of Concord's operations officer over the comm-link. "I have your departure slot approved, Commander Reeves. You are clear to launch."

"Thank you, Lieutenant, but remember not to refer to me by name or rank over the comm," Reeves replied. "We're trying to keep a low profile, remember?"

"Understood, Commander," Curio replied, causing Kane to snort a laugh. "I have updated your ship's registry ID to show you as an independent mercantile vessel, and have uploaded the relevant transit passes that will you allow you to enter Bastion Federation space as a freelancer."

"Very good, Lieutenant, Concord is yours until I return," Reeves replied. "I trust you to hold the fort."

Despite his foibles, Harpax Curio was an extremely efficient officer, and Reeves felt confident that the clever Eyrhu could manage his duties for a few days.

"I do not suppose you are able tell me where you are heading yet, sir?" Curio asked. This was the third time Curio had probed Reeves for an answer; the Eyrhu officer was nothing if not persistent. "Knowing this would help me to monitor your progress through the nav relays, and also contact you should there be a serious issue requiring your attention."

"I'm afraid not, Lieutenant, but we should only be gone

a few days at most," Reeves replied. "In the event of a serious issue, you'll just have to step up, understood?"

"Yes sir. Thank you, sir," Curio replied, sounding delighted to receive a vote of confidence from his commander. Reeves could imagine the Eyrhu officer's chest swelling with pride as he had spoken the words.

"Just play it by the book, and don't start a war while I'm gone, okay?" Reeves added. He wanted to end on a cautionary note, just to make sure Curio's ego didn't inflate to the point of bursting.

"I will endeavor to avert such an eventuality," Curio replied, a little peevishly.

Reeves saw the launch control panel turn green, signifying that their launch tube was cleared and ready. "I've got a green light, Lieutenant. I'll see you in a few days, Reeves out." He hit the button to close the comm-channel, but instead a holo TV screen switched on above the main control yoke. It resumed the playback of what looked to be a Bukkan porno movie that the previous captain must have been watching, prior to his arrest and capture.

"I didn't think that sort of thing was really your bag..." quipped Kane, as the holo image of the four naked Bukkan resumed their orgy, grunting and screaming like tennis players at Wimbledon.

"Commander, is everything okay?" said the voice of Harpax Curio. Reeves cursed realizing that he'd left the comm link open.

"Yes, Lieutenant, everything is fine," Reeves said, growing slightly panicked as he struggled to find a way to turn off the holo and the comm link.

"It sounds like there's a... struggle on board?" Curio went on.

Reeves looked over to Kane, but she was crippled with laughter, to the point where she looked to be physically in pain.

"Katee, don't just sit there, turn this damned thing off!" Reeves growled at his XO, having to raise his voice to a level above that of the ensuing climax on the holo porno.

"But it's just getting to the good bit," Kane hit back, looking at the holo through her fingers, as if it were a slasher horror movie.

"Major!"

Reeves' firmer and more desperate cry finally prompted Kane to take action, and she shot out of her seat and flicked a button to shut off the holo. Her intervention was timely, as Reeves was about to get assaulted by the screams and moans of the production's climactic moments.

"I trust everything is still okay for launch, sir?" said Curio, after a few moments of blissful silence.

"Yes, we're good to go, Lieutenant, Reeves out." He then hastily reached for the switch to turn off the comm link, before hesitating and checking with his XO.

"This time you got it," Kane said, still slightly red-faced from being subjected to one of what was surely the pirate captain's extensive library of adult movies.

Reeves flicked the switch and the comm-link closed. He grabbed the control yoke, somewhat more reluctantly this time, considering that the pirate captain's hands would have also been all over it in the past, and prepared to launch.

"I'll let you run the launch sequence, Major," Reeves said, glancing over at his XO. "Just in case I accidentally blast a hole in the launch tube instead of engaging the launch thrusters."

"You got it, Commander," said Kane, operating the required controls, though she still had to lean forward out of the seat slightly in order to reach some of them. "Launching in five..."

Reeves watched the launch indicator count down in Bukkan'r numbers then the pirate shuttle's engines engaged and the ship was propelled through the launch tube and into space.

"I have control," said Reeves, throwing the shuttle into a few simple maneuvers in order to get a feel for the ship, which was twice the size of the station's Jinx-class Heavy Fighters.

"How does it handle?" asked Kane, who was busy adjusting the scanner readouts and holo controls to place them at a more manageable height.

"It feels a little heavy, but it maneuvers well enough," Reeves replied, genuinely surprised at how well the shuttle responded. "The Bukkan may not know how to put together a pretty ship, but they can sure as hell bolt together something that flies."

"Unfortunately, this little shuttle doesn't have a tunneling aperture field generator, so we're going to have to stick to the established routes," Kane said. She threw up a course projection on the holo overlay that was now hovering at the correct height in front of Reeves. "Thrace Colony is one of the inner Federation worlds. It'll take us five hops to get there; four if I can eke out a little more power from the field generator."

"That's fine, Major, we're not in any rush," Reeves replied, finishing his brief series of shakedown tests and setting the pirate shuttle on course for the first aperture. "At least while I'm on this ship, I know that there's no chance of having my throat slit by either Serena Shepard's thugs or Garrett's goons."

"True, but if you snore there's a still a high chance that you might be murdered by someone much closer to you," Kane said, smirking.

"Duly noted, Major," Reeves replied, shaking his head.

Reeves' primary scanner readout then chimed an alert. He looked at the holo and saw that a ship had launched, but curiously it hadn't left from Concord Station.

"Are you picking that up too?" Reeves asked his XO.

"Affirmative, it's a launch from the Sa'Nerran Battle-cruiser," Kane replied. Her familiarity with the Bukkan language allowed her to assess the readings more swiftly than Reeves could. "It looks like a small, one-man craft."

Reeves felt his throat tighten. "Tell me it's not heading for us," he said, already fearing the worst.

"Actually, it's not," replied Kane, though she sounded as surprised as Reeves was by this fact. "It's heading away from the station, bearing zero three zero, mark zero one zero."

"Where will that take it?" asked Reeves. The Sa'N-erran ship may not have been on an intercept course, but it wasn't exactly heading away from them either.

"Looks like it's on a course to nowhere," Kane

answered, shrugging. "At sub-light speeds it might pass reasonably close to Censoria in Quarr space in a few hundred years."

"I somehow doubt that's where it's headed, Major," Reeves said, shooting his XO a withering look. "Can you put this thing up on the viewer?"

Moments later, an image of the vessel appeared inset on the holo viewer, which was overlaid across the cockpit glass of the shuttle. Reeves studied the ship, which was a design he hadn't seen before. It was half the size of the Jinx-class fighters and shaped like an arrow head.

"It's basically a flying plasma cannon," said Kane, highlighting the new ship's primary systems on the holo read-out. "It's just a gun attached to an engine with a cockpit that's barely large enough to fit one of those leather-faced assholes inside. Bastion Federation archives only has one thing on record that resembles it; a one-man fighter called a Wasp, from back during the Sa'Nerran war."

Reeves studied the ship for a few moments longer, before returning his eyes to the navigation systems and increasing thrust. They were still about three minutes out from their first surge point.

"Try to figure out where our shields are, Katee," said Reeves, while at the same time scanning his console for the weapons controls. "I don't think that arrow-ship launching just after we did is a coincidence."

No sooner had Reeves finished speaking than the Sa'Nerran fighter craft turned sharply and accelerated. Kane cursed then overlaid its trajectory onto the holo.

"It's now on an intercept course," Kane said, switching

up to a heightened level of urgency. "It's charging its primary cannon."

"Raise shields," Reeves said, pushing the engines even harder, but the Sa'Nerran fighter simply increased thrust too, and adjusted course to match.

"Shields online, but from look of that fighter's cannon, we might only be able to withstand two or three blasts at most before they buckle," Kane said.

The comm system chimed an alert and Reeves answered it, remembering which switch to flip that time.

"Commander, this is Lieutenant Curio, we're monitoring a Sa'Nerran vessel on an intercept course with your shuttle," Curio said.

"We see it, Concord Station, and stop calling me Commander over the comm, damn it," Reeves hit back. He was angry that the Sa'Nerra had gotten wind of their departure, and while he didn't think it was Curio's constant gaffs over the comm link that were to blame, he was eager to learn what was. "Are we still inside Concord's perimeter of authority?"

"Barely. You will exit our defense perimeter in sixty seconds at your current velocity," Curio replied. "Lieutenant Rosca has a lock on the Sa'Nerran craft with our beam cannon. He is asking if we should open fire?"

Reeves gritted his teeth and glanced at Kane, inviting her input, and hoping that her thoughts differed to his own.

"If Concord attacks a Sa'Nerran ship without provocation, you can bet your ass the Imperator will retaliate," Kane said, unfortunately confirming Reeves' own opinion.

Cursing again, Reeves returned to the comm-link. "Negative, Concord Station, we do not require assistance."

There was a brief pause before Curio answered. "Message received, but..."

"No buts, just do it," Reeves said, cutting across his operations officer. "We'll deal with this ourselves."

"Understood, Transport Omega One," Lieutenant Curio replied. "Good luck. Concord Station out."

The resonant thrum of the surge field generator began to permeate the ship, and Reeves saw that they were within sixty seconds of aperture threshold.

"Throw as much power into the shields as you can, Major, then prepare to surge," Reeves said, tightening his grip on the control yoke. "I'm going in slightly hot to see if we can lose this thing before it gets a shot off."

"If by 'slightly hot' you mean dangerously fast, then you're right on course," Kane quipped. She then flipped a series of controls and adjusted the shield balance on her holo screens. "I've angled the shields to face that fighter and beefed them up as best I can, but it's already within weapons range," his XO added.

Plasma flashed out from the darkness of space and the pirate shuttle was rocked hard. Alarms blared out inside the cockpit and Reeves saw that their shields had already dropped to fifty-two percent.

"Damn it, that little ship kicks like a mule," Kane said, still working furiously to keep their defensive barrier intact. "Another one of those and the shields will buckle."

The raider was thumped by a second blast from the Sa'Nerran fighter and this time secondary consoles to

Reeves' rear blew out, showering him with white hot sparks. Fires began to crackle inside the cockpit and the automatic suppression systems kicked in.

"Shields have collapsed," Kane announced, though the confirmation was hardly necessary. "Armor is holding. All systems nominal, but if that thing hits us again, all that will be left of us is dust."

"That's not going to happen, Major," said Reeves, standing ready to manually trigger the surge field generator. "Throw everything you have left into the forward weapons array then hold onto your seat. If that bastard follows us through the aperture, we're going to be ready for it."

"Aye, sir," Kane replied, still working frantically.

Reeves executed the surge maneuver, triggering a powerful pulse of surge energy that opened the aperture and propelled them into the surge dimension. The ship dissolved around him, as if it had only ever been a mere apparition, and for a moment there was an absence of everything except pure thought and consciousness. It was peaceful, but empty – like existing somewhere between a dream and death. Then reality exploded into existence again and Reeves found himself back in the pilot's seat of the Bukkan shuttle, tightly gripping the controls. This time, however, he wasn't going to run; he was going to fight back.

CHAPTER 11
GOOD-LOOKING BUKKAN

ALARMS WAILED as the Bukkan pirate shuttle spiraled out of control as a consequence of the hazardous surge maneuver. Reeves wrestled with the control yoke, grateful for his abnormal strength, which allowed him to pilot the heavy-handling ship in a way few other humans could. Finally gaining control, he pulsed the main engines and arrested the ship's forward velocity, aiming the nose of the vessel at the surge aperture.

"Is there any sign that Sa'Nerra fighter is following us?" said Reeves, checking his instruments then activating the targeting systems. A holo reticule appeared on the cockpit glass directly ahead of him.

"The readings are still a jumble from our own surge," Kane replied, scanning her own set of consoles. "It would be hard enough to make sense of them in Bastion English, never mind having to translate on the fly from Bukkan'r."

"Let's assume it's coming," Reeves said, pushing the

throttle forward and positioning the Bukkan raider closer to the mouth of the aperture.

Kane raised an eyebrow. "If it's coming then the first thing that arrow-ship will do is spear us directly through the middle."

"We're going to have to take that chance," Reeves hit back. "That fighter is faster and more maneuverable than we are. This is the only way we'll get on its tail long enough to take a shot."

"So far, all I'm picking up is a dozen rude messages from the ships waiting on this side of the aperture," Kane said.

Insults and complaints flooded onto the console screen from the ships Reeves had just recklessly surged into the path of. Reeves glanced behind and saw the chaos that his dangerous, unscheduled surge had caused to the vessels waiting in the shipping lane.

"But there's still no sign of that Sa'Nerran..." Kane continued, then paused and focused on the aperture readout. When she spoke again, her tone was urgent, but controlled. "Wait, I'm picking up a surge field. There's a ship coming through."

"Hold on..." Reeves called back as a blinding flash of light briefly dazzled them. Suddenly the arrow-like shape of the Sa'Nerran fighter raced overhead. Alarms wailed and the cabin shook as the shuttle was caught in the wake of the alien ship's thrusters.

"Holy crap, that thing missed us by less than a meter," Kane said, her voice breathless. "Any closer and it would have stripped a layer of paint off the hull."

"Hang tight, I'm coming about," said Reeves, struggling to maneuver the pirate shuttle into a pursuit course. The engine wake of the Sa'Nerran fighter was still buffeting them like a dingy in rough seas. "See if you can boost the engines; we need to get close as possible to that fighter and hit it with everything we have."

"You got it," Kane said, throwing off her harness and darting to the rear of the cockpit. "There's a dirty hack that used to work on Bastion Navy Gunboats, but I've no idea if these shuttles are built the same way."

"Hurry, it won't be long before that leather-faced bastard realizes what we've done," said Reeves, racing toward the Sa'Nerran fighter like a heat-seeking missile chasing down a Russian MiG.

"One second, I've almost got it," Kane called back, her voice muffled due to being neck-deep in wires and flashing circuit panels. Then there was a crack of electricity and smoke puffed out from the maintenance hatch she was working inside. "Try it now." Kane coughed and wafted smoke away from her eyes.

Reeves felt the boost kick in and within moments the shuttle was directly on the fighter's tail. Then his console blared out an alert.

"It's detected us," Reeves said, locking onto the fighter with the shuttle's retro-fitted plasma cannon. "Firing..."

A staccato thrum rattled through the deck plates as the pirate shuttle's plasma chain cannon whirred into action, spitting dozens of blazing-hot rivets of energy into space. The Sa'Nerran fighter tried to alter course, but was caught directly on its center of mass. The alien ship's shields collapsed and plasma blasts raked along its hull.

"Direct hit," Kane said, confirming what Reeves had already seen. "Moderate damage to the Sa'Nerran fighter's ventral hull armor and main engines."

"That's it?" said Reeves. He had expected – and hoped – for more.

"That's it, I'm afraid," Kane replied. "It's a tough little ship..."

"Hopefully it's enough to keep it off our ass," Reeves said, turning and burning hard for their next aperture. "It's a short-range fighter, so my guess is it won't have the fuel capacity to chase us half way across the known galaxy."

"I wouldn't put any credits on that bet," Kane hit back.

Reeves locked in the course and kept the engines at maximum thrust, while anxiously watching the Sa'Nerran fighter on the holo scanners. The alien ship had already aimed its arrow-shaped nose toward the shuttle and was accelerating hard.

"Damn it, that thing is still coming," Kane said, shaking her head at the scanner readout. "It'll catch us again before we reach the next aperture."

Reeves gritted its teeth and checked the navigational scanner readouts. Their first jump had put them inside Bastion Federation Space, close to the heavily-patrolled border with the Quarr Empire. He ran a wider scan to pick up all the contacts between the shuttle and their destina-tion aperture and smiled.

"I'm altering course," Reeves said, making the adjust-ments and pushing the engines to one hundred and ten percent. He knew the engines couldn't handle that level of thrust for long, but he only needed a brief burst of extra speed to get him where he needed to be.

"What have you seen?" said Kane, checking her navigational scanner readout.

"This is our old stomping ground, Katee," Reeves replied, glancing back at his XO. "I'm hoping whoever they assigned to replace us on these border patrols is as keen to intercept Bukkan Raiders as we were."

"But hopefully not as keen to blow them up as we were," Kane added, with a cautionary tone.

An alert blared out from Reeves' consoles. "It looks like they've taken the bait," he said, watching the formation of three Bastion Navy Destroyers alter course. The contacts then blinked off the navigation scanner readout and Reeves gripped the control yoke more tightly, preparing to ride through the spatial distortion that was about to hit them.

"Three surge fields forming, dead ahead," said Kane. She was gripping the sides of the Bukkan seat, also in preparation for the arrival of the destroyers.

Three pulses of intense white light burst out in space ahead of them like mini supernovas. Moments later, three Bastion Navy Destroyers exited the aperture dimension directly in the path of the shuttle. Reeves threw the Bukkan vessel into full reverse, causing the entire ship to shake like it was about to fly apart at the seams.

"Weapons lock, detected," Kane called out. "They're not playing around, Dalton..."

"Power down our cannon, Katee," Reeves said, stopping the shuttle and releasing the control yoke. "Let's make sure we don't look like a threat."

"Aye, sir," Kane replied, her fingers flashing across the console screen. "Weapons are offline; we're now a sitting duck."

Reeves watched the Bastion destroyers aim their cannons at their shuttle then flicked his eyes down to the navigation scanner. The arrow-shaped Sa'Nerran ship was still coming at them hard and fast.

"The Sa'Nerran fighter has locked weapons," Kane called out. She was still gripping the side of her seat.

"How are our shields?" said Reeves, glancing over at his XO.

"What shields?" Kane replied, her eyes growing wide.

Suddenly the two destroyers escorting the lead ship peeled off and powered past the shuttle, buffeting it with their engine wakes. Reeves sat up and peered at the holo image of the Sa'Nerran fighter, urging the Bastion Navy ships on.

"Come on, take that bastard out!" Reeves said, shaking his fist at the holo image, like an eager sports fan trying to urge his team on to victory.

"The fighter is firing," Kane said. "It's too late."

The lead destroyer suddenly powered toward them and Reeves instinctively raised his hands to shield his face, as if doing so would stop a million tons of spaceship from smashing into him. The cockpit was cast into darkness as the destroyer loomed over them like a dark, angry raincloud. Reeves saw a blast leave the alien ship's cannon and he braced himself, but the shuttle wasn't hit.

"They extended their shields around us!" said Reeves, finally realizing what had happened.

"The other two destroyers are engaging the Sa'Nerran fighter," Kane added, also gripped to the holo viewer.

Powerful blasts from the destroyers' cannons ripped through the Sa'Nerran ship, reducing it to dust and smoke in an instant.

"Holy shit, that was close," Kane said, flopping back in her seat and blowing out a heavy sigh. Her console then blared an alert and she read it, without sitting up again. "We're being hailed by the lead Bastion ship."

Reeves nodded and straightened up. "Put them through."

The commander of the destroyer appeared on the holo and Reeves couldn't help but allow a smile to curl his lips.

"Well, you're just about the best-looking Bukkans I've ever seen," said the female officer, clearly surprised to see Reeves on the other end of the call.

"Thanks, you're not so bad yourself," Kane replied, still from her slouched position next to Reeves.

Reeves huffed a laugh. Kane knew Commander Isa Gray as well as he did; they'd all gone through the academy together, and he couldn't have hoped for a better person to come to their aid.

"Thanks for the assist, Isa, you sure know how to make an entrance."

"I've got so many questions, Dalton, I don't even know where to start." Commander Gray folded her arms and narrowed her eyes at Reeves. "Aren't you supposed to be on The Abyss?"

"Me and Katee are just taking a little vacation, that's all," Reeves replied, shooting the commander an innocent smile.

"A vacation, huh?" replied Gray, while reading their ship's ID and travel pass on her console screen. "It says here that you're a privateer trading ship," Gray went on, raising her gaze to look at Reeves again. "There's nothing about a vacation."

"We like to trade in rare and exotic items on our holidays," Kane chipped in. She then shrugged. "It's a hobby."

"Uh huh..." said Gray, now raising an eyebrow at Kane. "And you like to pursue this hobby while flying around in a Bukkan pirate raider and being chased by a Sa'Nerran fighter, the likes of which we haven't seen for a millennium?"

"We're a little strange, I admit," quipped Kane.

"Uh huh..." Gray repeated, while again turning her attention to Reeves. "Well, your ID and permits are in order, so I see no reason to detain you further," the commander continued, while swiping away the holo screen that contained the data on the Bukkan shuttle. "Enjoy your vacation, I guess?"

"Thanks, Isa," Reeves said, still smiling at the commander. "I owe you one..."

Reeves knew that Commander Gray could have been much tougher on them, to the point of boarding their ship and even detaining them for questioning over the incident. Instead, she had chosen to mind her own business. Had they run into a Bastion patrol commanded by an officer they didn't know, Reeves knew they wouldn't have been so lucky.

The holo image of Commander Gray fizzled to nothing, and Reeves watched the three Bastion Navy Destroyers form up then surge back to their original patrol route. Once they were gone, Reeves also decided to flop back into his seat, feeling suddenly weary.

"I think you can take the controls for the next leg of our vacation," said Reeves, trying to relax and let the tension ooze out of his muscles.

"To hell with that, I can barely move the control yoke," Kane hit back. She then slid out of the seat and headed aft. "I'll tell you what, I'll see what kind of food this Bukkan tub has and make us a snack."

"Fair enough, I am feeling hungry," Reeves said, sitting up and taking the controls. They still had several more surges to complete before reaching Thrace Colony. "Just steer clear of anything back there that looks like it's still alive."

"What do you mean? That's the best stuff!" Kane replied.

"No, Katee, I mean it, I hate live Bukkan food..." Reeves called out, twisting in his seat in an attempt to get his XO's attention and stall her. However, Kane was already gone, and all Reeves could hear was the quavering chirp of Bukkan crickets.

CHAPTER 12

IT'S GOING TO BE ROUGH

THE BUKKAN SHUTTLE exited the surge dimension and exploded back into reality in front of the remote blue planet known as Thrace Colony. At one time an independent 'Void Planet', Thrace became a member of the Bastion Federation as humanity expanded its borders in the centuries after the Sa'Nerran war. Now, however, Thrace was under the control of the New Earth separatists, led by Serena Shepard, making it a dangerous place for anyone who didn't follow the movement's doctrine.

"Of all the planets that android could have picked to stash the Invictus on, why the hell did she pick Thrace?" said Kane.

Kane was analyzing the planet using the shuttle's sensors, but it didn't take an advanced scanning array to see that Thrace Colony was a wild world. Reeves could see swirling storms over several of the continents and oceans, and lightning frequently crackled across the globe, like synapses firing in a brain.

"I guess if you wanted to hide something then choosing a place that no-one in their right mind would ever choose to visit isn't a bad idea," Reeves suggested. "Did you know that this place was mentioned in the historical archives of the Sa'Nerran war?"

"Did it mention never to come here?" quipped Kane.

Reeves snorted a laugh. "In a manner of speaking, yes. Let's just say that the inhabitants of Thrace a thousand years ago were not fans of Earth's united governments. And a hatred of the establishment is something that successive generations seem to have taken to heart."

"That's putting it mildly," Kane replied, while continuing to scan the world. "Thrace was the first planet to break away from the federation and join Shepard's New Earth Movement, though Bastion still doesn't recognize it as an independent world."

Reeves' navigational scanner blurted an alert and he checked the holo display, noting that an orbital platform had been detected.

"I don't remember Thrace having a space station," Reeves said, frowning at the data, which was still populating his screen. "There are only around a hundred and twenty-five thousand people on the entire planet. A space station seems excessive."

Kane switched to her navigation scanner readout and employed her superior Bukkan language skills to adjust the settings and enhance the signal. The orbital platform then appeared on a holo viewer that was overlaid in front of the cockpit glass.

"What the hell is that thing?" asked Kane, staring at the

odd-looking installation. "It doesn't look like a Bastion design, at least not one I recognize." Kane's eyes narrowed. "Could the New Earthers have engineered their own orbital platform?"

Reeves shrugged. "I guess it's possible, but it would need more resources than this hostile little world could sustain, and what would be the point?"

"A trading post?" suggested Kane. "Maybe they figured more people would do business here, knowing they didn't have to run the gauntlet of storms to land on the surface."

Reeves' navigational scanner sounded another alert, this time notifying him that the location of the Invictus on the surface had been established.

"The computer has identified the rough location of the Invictus from the co-ordinates Ambassador One supplied," Reeves said, turning away from the mystery of the unknown space platform. "It looks like it's inside an old breaker's yard on the outskirts of a lake-town called Lone Water."

"A breaker's yard?" Kane frowned at the readout. "I hope we haven't come all this way just to find a bunch of rusted old scrap metal." She then focused on one scanner readout in particular. "That's interesting. It looks like that space platform is in a stationary orbit directly above where we're headed."

Reeves shrugged. "Lone Water is one of the major settlements on this world, so I don't think that's anything unusual." He then quickly reconsidered his nonchalant response, remembering that very little of their experiences so far had come under the label of 'normal'. "Keep an eye on it, though, just in case."

Reeves navigated the Bukkan pirate shuttle toward an entry-point in the atmosphere that would take them down to the settlement of Lone Water. The course inevitably took them closer to the mysterious orbital platform. Slotting the shuttle into a high orbit, he began plotting a course for atmospheric entry, a task made harder by the violent storms that continued to ravage the planet.

"I'm getting a much clearer reading on this platform now," Kane said, as the space installation grew large enough to be visible outside the cockpit glass. "There's still something about it that doesn't add up. The material composition and power design is nothing like Bastion tech."

"Maybe they paid one of the other races to build it for them?" suggested Reeves, while continuing to steer the raider on course to the planet. "The Bukkan maybe?"

"It's definitely not Bukkan, and Thrace is too far from the Skemm border for it to be worth their while making the long trip out here."

"I can't see the Quarr lowering themselves to do a small job like this, either, especially not working for humans," Reeves added. "You know how those stuck-up bastards feel about us."

Kane snorted, though it was a distracted, half-hearted chuckle, rather than one of her more unrestrained belly laughs. She was still preoccupied by the riddle of the space installation's origins.

"I'm more concerned that we've not heard a thing from Thrace Colony yet." Reeves had been anxiously watching his comms panel for incoming messages, but they had yet to pick up any transmissions from the surface. "Considering we're arriving in a Bukkan pirate shuttle, you'd have thought someone would have challenged us by now, or even sent a ship to intercept us."

"Who would intercept us, though?" said Kane, glancing over at Reeves. "After Thrace declared for the separatists, the Bastion Navy bugged out, and I doubt a colony this small has their own patrol ships."

Suddenly, both of their consoles ejected a far more urgent alarm. Despite their shuttle being Bukkan in origin, Reeves knew a warning tone when he heard one.

"The orbital platform has opened gun ports," Kane said, translating the warning message. "It's locking on!"

"How come we didn't spot this thing was armed?" Reeves said, deactivating the atmospheric entry program and hurriedly raising what was left of their shields.

"It's pumping out some sort of scanner jamming interference, though I haven't seen anything quite like it before," Kane answered.

Suddenly, the shuttle was hit by a bolt of plasma from the orbital platform. The blast was so intense that Reeves felt the physical shock of the impact reverberate through the control yoke.

"Shields have buckled!" Kane called out. "That blast packed one hell of a punch."

"It's a Sa'Nerran weapons platform," Reeves said, diving hard toward the planet in an attempt to evade the installation's guns. "The energy signature of that blast matches the Sa'Nerran fighter."

"How the hell did the Sa'Nerra manage to build a platform inside Bastion Federation space?" Kane said, holding on tightly to her seat as the shuttle accelerated rapidly.

"That's a question for another time," Reeves grunted, desperately trying to steer the pirate shuttle away from the platform's firing arc. "Right now, we need to get down to the surface before that thing turns us to atoms."

"I'm working on getting the shields back up, but that last hit burned out a generator coil," Kane said, risking injury by moving aft and burying herself inside the maintenance panels again.

"Don't worry about that now, just strap yourself back in," Reeves called out to her. "The only way we get out of this is by evading those guns, not relying on our shields to save us."

Two more blasts of plasma streaked past the cockpit and fizzed into the atmosphere, missing the shuttle by only a few meters. Reeves adjusted course, but the orbital platform continued to track his movements.

"Shields are back up at twenty percent," Kane said, bouncing from wall to wall of the cabin before she finally managed to grab hold of the huge Bukkan seat. "That's it though. If we take another hit, our shields are gone for good."

An explosion ripped out from the rear of the cockpit and Reeves was pelted with debris rebounding off the walls and cockpit glass. Flames began to lick around the sides of his seat and smoke quickly filled the cabin.

"Katee, report!" Reeves called out, looking to his left, but his XO's seat was shrouded in inky black fumes.

"Katee, are you okay?" he called out again, but the bitter black smoke was suffocating and his voice was barely more than a hoarse rasp.

Fire suppression systems kicked in and pumps whirred, emptying the cabin of smoke. The flames that had begun to ignite Reeves's chair and the sleeve of his jacket were also extinguished by the focused puff of inert gases or force-field bubbles that surrounded the fires and starved them of oxygen. He desperately wanted to check on Kane, but the yoke had gone slack in his hands, and fire had engulfed the ship from friction with the atmosphere.

"You probably don't need me to tell you that we're hit…"

Reeves glanced left and saw Kane clawing herself back into her seat. Her clothes were scorched and she was bleeding from a cut to her head, but he didn't feel the need to check on her further to know she was fine. Her immediate employment of sarcasm was enough to indicate his XO was not badly injured.

"The controls have gone sloppy," Reeves said, frantically adjusting the flight systems in an attempt to stabilize their descent. "I'd say we've lost an engine and at least a couple of thrusters."

"You're right, engines one and two are completely destroyed and we only have around fifty per cent thrust on three and four," Kane confirmed. She was back in her seat and working on what remained of her consoles. "The reactor housing has also cracked, and about a dozen other systems are failing as we speak."

Two more blasts fizzed past the shuttle then a third

glanced across the nose section, scoring a deep groove into their hull.

"That last hit took out our scanner assembly," Kane called out. She had abandoned any further attempts to revive the dying ship and was adjusting her harness, pulling it as tightly across her body as it would go. "You're going to have to land this the old-fashioned way, Dalton."

"I think 'land' is far too generous a description for what I'm about to do," Reeves warned.

The shuttle had now punched through the upper atmosphere and was speeding like a ballistic missile toward Lone Water on the horizon. Reeves threw as much power as they had left into the anti-gravity stabilizers and maneuvering thrusters, and hoped it would be enough.

"I'm going to set down in the hills above the town," Reeves continued, wrestling with the controls to keep the shuttle on a level descent. "Though I think it's pretty safe to say that we're not welcome here."

"I'll scout some locations for us to hide in," Kane said, resorting to using the limited computing functions of her buzz, given that the orbital platform had obliterated the ship's scanners. "I'm reading the remains of a ruined settlement at the fringe of the forest," Kane went on. Reeves' buzz then vibrated and he chanced a quick look at the screen on his palm, realizing that Kane had sent him an image of her proposed landing site, plus a rough bearing to reach it. "We can use the buildings for refuge, and escape into the forest if needed."

"Understood, adjusting course," Reeves replied, aiming the crippled shuttle toward the new coordinates. "I'm not sure we'll make it, though. It's like I'm flying a brick with wings."

"We'll make it," Kane replied, with surprising confidence. "The one thing the Bukkan know how to do well is build ships. If we'd been flying anything else, the blasts from that orbital platform would have already destroyed us."

Reeves made a few final adjustments, then turned and dove toward the ruined settlement. Dipping beneath the clouds, rain began to hammer down on the cockpit glass, impairing his visibility, while the storm-force winds buffeted the battered ship in all directions. Gritting his teeth, he held the control yoke steady, refusing to give in to the elemental forces that were now pulverizing the ship instead of the Sa'Nerran orbital platform. The metal of the substantial control column creaked and groaned and even began to bend from the strain, but Reeves' might was equal to the wrath of the storm.

"Hang on, this is going to be rough," he called out.

Seconds later, the shuttle smashed through the taller trees at the edge of the forest, decapitating them as effortlessly as dead-heading daisies. Lighting flashed all around them and the ship was struck, temporarily blinding Reeves and causing his muscles to flinch. The shuttle jerked in response to his involuntary input, then the nose dipped and dug into the stony ground on the hilltop. Reeves was thrown forward against his harness, the force of the impact stealing the breath from his lungs. Gritting his teeth against the pain, he strained to reach the thruster controls and threw them into reverse, but it was already too late. The Bukkan shuttle smashed against a cluster of rocks and cartwheeled back into the air, like a loose tire bouncing down a country lane. Reeves let go of the control column and gripped the sides of his bucket seat, no longer able to affect the course of the ship. It was now probability or a higher power that would determine their fate.

Out of the corner of his eye, Reeves saw Kane reach for a bank of physical consoles to her left. Incredibly, his XO still had the composure and wherewithal to act. She managed to turn a dial and immediately Reeves felt the forces acting on his body lessen. Somehow, Kane had managed to activate the inertial negation systems that were used to counteract the fierce accelerations and forces acting on the pilots during space flight. He was about to call out to Kane when the ship hammered into the ground for a second time, before crashing to its belly and tearing through the part-ruined buildings on the edge of the abandoned settlement. For several more agonizing seconds the shuttle continued to plough though the old, abandoned town until it finally came to a slow, grinding halt.

For a while, Reeves simply sat back in his seat in the smashed cockpit, chest heaving and heart thumping. The sides of the bucket seat where his hands were still gripped around the edges had been bent up so sharply, it look like he was cocooned inside it. Lightning still continued to flash outside, lighting up the dark night sky in moments of elemental brilliance. The rumbles of thunder and the sound of the rain hammering down on the cockpit drowned out the percussive chime of the reactor, which was cooling off in the aft section of the ship. Finally, he looked to his left to see Katee Kane already staring back at him.

"Are we still alive?" Kane said, her words tremulous and weak.

"I don't know, Katee," Reeves said, peeling his hands off the sides of the seat and flexing his fingers, which were almost entirely drained of blood. "This is kind of what I imagined hell to look like."

Suddenly, a new sound erupted from somewhere behind them, drowning out every other noise that was assaulting Reeves' ears. It sounded like the valve of a pressure cooker opening, and he suddenly realized what it was.

"We're venting reactor coolant," said Kane, beating Reeves by calling out the danger first. "We have to get out of here, now!"

The flood of panic in his gut convinced Reeves that he and Kane were still alive, and the imminent threat of death was enough to kick his muscles into gear. Tearing off the harness, he jumped up and ran to the rear of the cabin.

"We need grab whatever gear we can, and get off this ship fast," Reeves said, forcing open the door into the rear compartment. He was hit with a blast of hot air, and realized that the ship was on fire. "Just take whatever you can get your hands on. We have maybe a minute or two at most before this ship blows."

Kane staggered into the rear compartment, her own footing just as shaky and unsteady as Reeves'. Fighting against the heat and noxious gases, he grabbed two large holdalls of weapons and equipment then elbowed the emergency hatch release and threw them outside. Wind and rain howled through the opening, though this time he was glad of the bitter, wet air, which helped to cool his face and revive his senses.

"Let's go, Major, now, now, now!" Reeves said, urging his XO on.

Kane ran to the hatch, tossed out the large backpack that she'd hastily filled, then dove through the opening and onto the escape slide. Reeves followed barely a heartbeat behind her and thumped into the mud at the bottom. Grabbing his two bags, he glanced up at the ship and saw that the coolant venting was getting worse. Hauling the bags onto his shoulders, Reeves ran for cover, willing his aching body to move faster. Just shy of the broken door to the nearest ruined building, the shuttle exploded and the blast hurled Reeves the rest of the way inside. Coughing dust from his lungs, he climbed to his knees and saw Kane a few meters away, similarly dazed but also still conscious. His XO clawed dirt out of her mouth and spat the remaining wet grit onto the floor before shuffling closer to him and peering out at the burning wreckage alongside them.

"I told you the landing was going to be rough," said Reeves.

Out of all the things he could have said in that moment, his beleaguered brain had somehow decided to make a joke. However, unsurprisingly his XO seemed to appreciate it.

"That android had better be right about the Invictus being here," said Kane, flopping back against the wall and resting her head on Reeves' shoulder. "Because if it's not then you're in big trouble."

Reeves frowned and glanced down at his XO, though

he could only see the top her dirt-stained and smoke-scorched hair.

"Why would I be in trouble?" Reeves asked. "I didn't hide the damned ship here."

"Because if there's no way off this rock, I'm becoming a separatist and trading you in," Kane said, raising her muddy chin and smirking at Reeves. "Sorry, Devil's Blood, but that's the way it's gotta be."

"You're heartless, but I like it," snorted Reeves.

Through the door of the ruined building Reeves saw light climbing into the sky. Cursing, he rapped his knuckles against Kane's shoulder. "No rest for the wicked, Major," he said, pointing to the light outside. "They'll be coming for us soon, and I for one don't want to still be here when they arrive."

CHAPTER 13
MUD AND BLOOD

REEVES ACCEPTED the binoculars from Major Kane and examined their crash site through the powerful lenses. Since hurrying to their new hideout in the forest above the abandoned town, three shuttles had arrived to inspect the wreckage of the burning Bukkan ship. However, the occupants of the scout vessels were not members of Serena Shepard's New Earth Movement. They were not even human. They were Sa'Nerran warriors.

"I see six warriors around the crash site," Reeves said, adjusting the binoculars to give him some tactical information on the Sa'Nerran squads. "They're carrying standard Sa'Nerra plasma rifles plus the half-moon blades these psychopaths like to use. Two of them are using what look like hand-held scanners."

"Don't worry, our scanner jammers are working perfectly, so they'd need to have actual eyeballs on us to know we're here," said Kane, who was working on her buzz.

"Besides, their scans will also be affected by the lightning storms that appear to be the default weather on this horrible little rock."

Another rumble echoed off the hillside, but this time it wasn't a crash of thunder, but the roar of another approaching shuttle.

"We have a fourth craft inbound," Reeves said, adjusting his binoculars to get a closer look at the ship. "This one looks like a standard colony shuttle. It's unarmed and pretty beat up too, so I'd say its native to this planet."

Reeves continued to analyze the shuttle as it slowed and landed beside the three Sa'Nerran vessels. The side hatch popped open and three humans stepped out into the mud and driving rain. Reeves laughed bitterly as he recognized one of the occupants.

"What's so funny?" asked Kane.

Reeves sighed as he passed the binoculars to his XO. "See for yourself."

Kane frowned, but accepted the field glasses and began to scan the crash site again. It wasn't long before a curse escaped her lips.

"Serena Shepard?" she said, pulling the binoculars away from her eyes. "I can't believe she's allowed the Sa'Nerra to take refuge inside Bastion Federation space."

"Shepard told me the Sa'Nerra were helping her to establish a new human colony on Mars," Reeves said, thinking back to when the cult leader had deceived him and lured him to the Oasis Gardens to face the Imperator. "I assumed that the Imperator's price for his help was just my head on a plate. It looks like the leather-faced bastard got a much better deal than we first thought."

"We have to get word to the Bastion Navy," replied Kane. "Who knows how many ships and warriors they've already smuggled onto Thrace Colony, and other separatist worlds?"

Reeves could sense the fire building inside his XO's belly. Serena Shepard wasn't just a separatist and terrorist; she was traitor too.

"Let's worry about that later." Reeves stowed his compact binoculars in the purpose-designed pocket on his tactical vest. He was as eager to expose Shepard as Kane was, but they had more urgent priorities. "First we have to get off this rock alive, and to do that we have to find the Invictus."

Kane reluctantly returned to assessing the limited scan data provided via her buzz. She updated the readout to highlight their location relative to the coordinates Ambassador One had given them.

"We're about two kliks from Lone Water," said Kane, shifting position so that Reeves could see the map on her buzz. "We can follow the hills around the back of the town then sneak down to the breaker's yard. With any luck, the storm will last long enough to mask our approach."

Reeves huffed a laugh. "I never thought I'd be wishing for bad weather like this," he said, squinting up at the dark clouds above them, which were still being lit up by frequent flashes of lightning.

The roar of shuttle engines again rumbled across the

sky, and Reeves and Kane instinctively flattened their bodies to the sodden ground to reduce the chances of being seen. Peering through the tree canopy, Reeves saw that all four shuttles had blasted off, leaving their destroyed pirate vessel to burn. Shepard's shuttle, escorted by two of the Sa'Nerran craft, was heading toward Lone Water. The other two Sa'Nerran vessels flew over their heads and vanished behind the hills. Reeves checked his buzz to see if he could track the alien shuttles, but their own scanner jammers, coupled with the lightning storm, made tracing them impossible.

"Let's move out." Reeves pushed his face out of the mud. "But stay alert. This place could be crawling with Sa'Nerra for all we know."

Reeves took the lead, patrolling along the top of the hill and taking advantage of the cover provided by the thick forest of trees. The dense canopy overhead also helped to shield them from the worst of the storm, which raged harder the further they progressed toward Lone Water. Reaching a vantage point directly above the lake that nestled alongside the town, Reeves brought them to a stop and removed the binoculars again.

"I can see security lights on inside the breaker's yard, but it doesn't look like anyone is home," Reeves said, handing the binoculars to Kane.

"I can't see anything in that yard that's big enough to be the Invictus," Kane said, studying their destination through the lenses. "There are three ships under tarpaulin covers but, if the tactical overlay from these binoculars is correct, the largest is just under a hundred meters, and the Invictus is four times that size."

Reeves cursed. He hadn't thought to check the breaker's yard for the presence of the Invictus, and had simply assumed it was there. The android didn't seem like someone that would give faulty information.

"It's possible it was sold off, or carved up for parts years ago," Kane added, handing the binoculars back to Reeves. "Either way, it's definitely not in the yard."

Reeves checked again through the binoculars, but Kane was right. There was no chance that any of the tarpaulin-covered vessels in the breaker's yard could have been the Invictus.

"We should check out the yard, anyway," said Reeves, stowing the binoculars. "Maybe there's more to it than we can see from here. An underground garage or repair bay, perhaps?"

"Roger that," Kane said, though Reeves sensed that his XO considered the likelihood of finding a subterranean lair unlikely. "But even if the Invictus is a bust, we might still find a ship that can haul our asses off this forsaken planet."

Reeves drew his plasma pistol and was about to move out when the snap of wood from somewhere inside the forest to their rear caused him to freeze.

"That sounded like it came from that depression at eleven o'clock," whispered Kane, highlighting the direction with her hand.

Reeves spotted the dip in the terrain that his XO had indicated and thought he saw shapes moving through the trees. However with the near constant flashes of lightning that were popping off overhead, there were shadows that looked like Sa'Nerran warriors almost everywhere he looked.

"Cover me while I check it out," said Reeves, holstering his pistol and pulling out his plasma trench knife. If there was someone stalking them, he needed to deal with them quietly, so as not to reveal their position to the other warriors scouting the woods.

Kane nodded and moved into cover behind a cluster of moss-covered rocks. Reeves kept low and stalked toward the source of the sound, occasionally glancing down at his buzz in case its scanners picked up any movement. Unfortunately, his own scanner jammer was still rendering the device useless.

Ten meters from the depression in the terrain, Reeves heard another snap of wood. Heart racing, he moved into cover behind the trunk of a gnarled tree, whose spindly branches reached skyward like a wizard clutching a magical orb. He listened again for the sound and heard it closing in. Whoever he was stalking was stalking him too.

Knife poised and ready to strike, Reeves circled around the tree then sprang out to confront his quarry. A four-legged animal no larger than a pit-bull terrier stared back at him with wide, terrified eyes before darting into the darkness, shrieking like a stuck pig. Reeves laughed, more out of relief than amusement, then slumped back against the tree and closed his eyes, allowing the cold rain to refresh his face.

"Dalton!"

The cry from Kane woke Reeves' senses like a shot of

adrenalin to the heart. A Sa'Nerran warrior had rushed out of the tree line, aiming its rifle in the direction of the animal that had just bolted. The alien's bulbous yellow eyes then turned to Reeves, but he was already running and had shoulder-tackled the warrior before it could adjust its aim. Both Reeves and the warrior hit the ground hard and rolled down the side of the depression into the rain-filled bog below. Reeves still had hold of his knife, and pushing himself out of the mud he slashed the blade at the alien, but cut only air. The Sa'Nerran warrior pulled its rifle from the bog and squeezed the trigger, but the waterlogged weapon did not fire. Hissing wildly into the stormy night sky, the alien tossed the rifle and pulled its serrated, half-moon blade from its armor.

Another hiss pierced the air and Reeves saw a second warrior on the ridge. He cursed and looked for cover, but there was nothing but foul-smelling mud for ten meters in any direction. The warrior facing Reeves hissed at his companion and the alien took aim. Reeves shielded his face with his arms, hoping his energy absorption shield was still operating, then felt the blast thump into his chest. The mud anchored him to the spot and he was knocked to his back, the fall cushioned by the goopy bog water. Pressing his hands into the mud, he tried to push himself up again, but it was like being trapped in quicksand. The warrior facing him bared its jagged teeth then uttered another waspish cry to the Sa'Nerran on the ridge above them. Reeves checked his armor, but the initial blast from the alien rifle had already depleted his shields. A second blast would kill him.

Suddenly, Major Kane charged out of the trees and

flung herself at the warrior, deflecting the alien's aim at the last second. The blast thumped into the mud and coincided with a flash of lighting and rumble of thunder that entirely consumed the report of the weapon. His XO and the second Sa'Nerran tumbled out of view as Reeves struggled back to his feet. The warrior facing him had not squandered the opportunity to attack, and Reeves felt the alien blade rake across his chest armor before he was even upright. The vest was cut through, but the edge of the serrated weapon stopped short of slicing deeply into his flesh. Drawing the weapon back, the warrior went to strike again, but this time Reeves was prepared. Blocking the alien's blow with his left forearm, he swung his trench knife at the Sa'Nerran and pierced the alien's mud-covered bronze armor like an arrow. However, the bog water had caused the plasma-generator in the knife to sputter and fail, and without the benefit of its extra power, the alien armor was strong enough to repel his attack.

Before Reeves could yank the knife free and attack again, the warrior sunk its jagged teeth into his hand and bit down hard, like a saltwater crocodile. Screaming in agony, Reeves instinctively let go of the knife and withdrew his hand, leaving the blade impaled in the warrior's armor like a spike. The Sa'Nerran attacked again, stunning Reeves with a hard left jab then whirling the serrated blade at him like a scythe. Unable to move his legs more than a few inches, Reeves swayed back and the blade skimmed across his armor, carving another deep groove into the dense material. However, this time the blade did not cut through.

Shaking the pain out of his stinging right hand, Reeves met the warrior's eyes and gritted his teeth. Fighting with weapons and skill was one thing, but biting him like a rabid animal was an insult too far. Clenching his still-throbbing fist, Reeves invited the warrior to attack and waited for the alien to make its move. The serrated blade whirled at him again, but Reeves blocked the strike with such force that it shattered the Sa'Nerran's forearm. The alien hissed and the weapon fell from its limp fingers and was absorbed into the mud. Fist still clenched, Reeves struck the pommel of his trench knife, which was still impaled into the warrior's armor, and drove it fully into the alien's flesh, like a hammer striking a nail.

Reeves watched as the warrior attempted in vain to pull the knife clear. With the life already leaking from its body, he grabbed the back of the Sa'Nerran's leathery neck and buried its head into the vile bog water. The alien thrashed wildly, but Reeves maintained his hold, easily overpowering it. As the alien drowned, he considered ending its life more quickly, but the brutal and belligerent race had awakened something dark inside him. He knew that snapping its neck would have been the more humane thing to do, but in that moment he didn't care. He wanted it to suffer.

Eventually, the warrior stopped thrashing and Reeves pulled it out of the mud to retrieve his trench knife. Suddenly, the waspish hiss of the second warrior drifted through the air like the wail of a banshee. Fighting the weariness in his legs and the burning in his lungs, Reeves powered toward the sound of the struggle. He saw Kane on the ground with the warrior crouched over her, fighting to drive its blade into her neck. Blood oozed from wounds to Kane's thigh and arm, and it was clear she was losing the struggle. He felt rage pour out of him like blood from a severed artery and he stormed toward the Sa'Nerran, intent on tearing it limb from limb.

The warrior hissed and met Reeves' advance, lashing out at him with its blood-stained half-moon blade. Reeves blocked the strike, breaking the Sa'Nerran's wrist and sending the alien blade spinning into the darkness. The warrior hissed and clenched its injured arm, but this time Reeves wasn't interested in toying with his prey. Wielding the trench knife with all his might, he slashed the thick neck of the warrior. The Sa'Nerran clasped its long, leathery fingers to the gaping wound, but the blow had been delivered with such force that the alien's head was almost severed from its neck. With his XO looking on, her hand clasped to the wound on her thigh, Reeves grabbed the warrior's head and tore it from its shoulders, like twisting the cap off a bottle of beer.

Lungs burning so hot that his chest felt like it was about to explode, he tossed the severed head into the mud and met his XO's eyes. Her expression was a mixture of astonishment and disgust. The latter emotion, Reeves guessed, was likely due to the severed head that sat in the mud, staring at her blankly with dead yellow eyes.

"I might be wrong, but I think you got him," Kane said, grimacing as she tentatively kicked the warrior's head away with her good leg.

Reeves was so filled with venom and bile that nothing in that moment should have made him feel anything other than rage. However, his XO was always able reach him in ways that no-one else could. He shook his head then dropped to his knees beside her, still breathing heavily.

"Yeah." Reeves looked at the decapitated Sa'Nerran corpse. "I think I got him."

REEVES SNAPPED SHUT the lid of the medical kit then stashed the box back into Kane's rucksack. With shuttles circling overhead, there had only been time to hastily treat the worst of the cuts and bruises they'd sustained in the fight with the warriors. Kane had come off worst, but Reeves had managed to patch up the gash to her thigh and administer enough meds to make sure she didn't feel any lingering effects.

"I think it's fair to say they're looking for us," said Kane, peering up through the dense tree canopy at the lights of the shuttles above them.

"Check that your scanner jammer is still operating," Reeves replied, while performing the same check on his own systems. "They'll probably expect us to head away from the settlement, rather than toward it. So we should push on to the breaker's yard and look for any opportunity to steal some transportation en route."

"You've given up on finding the Invictus?" Kane asked.

"Even if it is still here, we're in no condition to find it now," said Reeves, replacing the emitter assembly in his plasma knife to make it functional again. "If the Invictus is on Thrace, we'll need time to figure out where, and what to do next. We can't do that while the Sa'Nerra are hunting us down."

Kane nodded then drew her pistol and took the lead. Their scanner jammers, combined with the dense tree canopy, were still doing an effective job of masking their movements. However, the storm was beginning to move east, taking with it the worst of the rain and cloud cover. And while this made for a more pleasant onward journey, Reeves knew it also made it easier for the Sa'Nerra to move up into the hills on foot looking for them.

Despite her injury, Kane was setting a furious pace and Reeves was struggling to keep up with her. He was coming down off a huge adrenalin rush and fatigue was setting in fast. Increasing the distance between them, Kane climbed over a rocky section of ground and dropped out of sight on the other side. Reeves heard her curse and his pulse quickened. Scrambling across the jagged rocks, scraping his hands and knees as he did so, he found Kane standing beside the corpse of an animal. The unfortunate creature looked like it had been torn apart by a pack of wild dogs.

"What the hell kind of beast could have done this?" said Kane, as Reeves slid down the bank and jogged to her side, struggling to regain his breath.

"I don't know, and I suggest we try not to find out," Reeves replied.

Reeves was used to the sight of blood, but even he was

finding it hard to look at the mangled corpse without scrunching his nose up in disgust. The animal was about the size of a cow or buffalo, but it otherwise bore no similarity to any creature Reeves had ever seen before. Its eyes and brain had already been clawed out and eaten, and its body had been savagely ripped open along the line of the belly. Reeves had no idea what internal organs the creature had originally possessed, but few of them remained. He could see nothing resembling a liver, kidneys or even a heart.

"Wasn't there a story about the Sa'Nerra preferring to eat live prey?" Kane said, raising an eyebrow.

Reeves snorted a laugh. "Yes, but I think this would be a tad excessive even for those barbaric bastards," he replied. Though, all he could now think about was a pack of Sa'Nerra, tearing into the dying animal and consuming its vital organs in some sort of feeding frenzy.

A shuttle buzzed overhead, reminding Reeves that there were other, more immediate dangers to worry about, besides the potential presence of a brutal apex predator. He circled around the dead animal then moved up to the tree line and looked down at the town of Lone Water. They were now only a few hundred meters away from the perimeter of the settlement.

"What do you make of all the fences and watchtowers?" said Kane, who had stealthily crept to his side. "I can understand why they'd have them around the breaker's yard, but they seem to surround the entire town too."

Reeves shrugged. "Maybe this whole place is some sort of low-security penitentiary, and the fences and guard towers are to keep people inside?" As soon as he suggested this, he knew it didn't sound right.

Kane then immediately came back with a more realistic, and ominous possibility. "Or maybe it's to keep whatever ate that creature out of the town." She sounded suitably disturbed by her own idea.

As if provoked by Kane's suggestion, a low growl suddenly rumbled through the trees from deeper inside the forest. It sounded like a pride of angry lions all snarling in unison, and was so powerful that Reeves physically felt the sound waves reverberate through his body. Kane was usually one to make a sarcastic comment in such circumstances, but even his glib XO was in no mood for joking around.

"I think we should pick up the pace." Reeves tightened his grip around his pistol and set out again toward a ridge near the edge of the town.

"Preferably in the opposite direction to where that noise came from," Kane added, only a heartbeat behind him.

Reeves heard the guttural growl rumble several more times before they reached the ridge above the breaker's yard. The sound appeared to be growing louder, but despite constant glances back, he couldn't see anything following them.

"Damn it, they're patrolling the yard now too," said Kane, peeking over the edge of the ridge then quickly ducking back into cover.

Reeves also chanced a look and saw four men moving through the yard, aiming the barrels of plasma pistols into every nook and cranny they could find. Each of them wore the familiar tan jacket that appeared to be the standard uniform of the New Earthers. Reeves cursed, but the words were drowned out by another ferocious roar. However, this time it was the exhaust of a shuttlecraft, and not some unseen predator that had startled him. The craft had swooped in over the hillside and was rapidly descending into the breaker's yard. Reeves watched it touch down, then two more New Earthers ran out to join their companions.

"There's our way out of here," said Reeves, again pulling away from the edge so that he couldn't be seen by the people below.

Kane scrunched up her nose then shrugged. "I don't like our odds of stealing that shuttle with six of Serena Shepard's zealots stalking around down there, but I don't have a better idea. What's our play?"

Reeves hadn't thought that far ahead, and took a moment to survey the edge of the breaker's yard in more detail.

"There..." Reeves said, pointing to a tattered-looking pre-fab office unit. "We can move along the ridge and scramble down onto the top of that building." He was formulating the plan on the fly as he spoke. "I say we then lob a couple of plasma grenades across to the far side of the yard. Then while all hell is breaking loose, we jump down, sprint for the shuttle and get the hell out of here, before anyone realizes what's happened."

"Sounds like a crazy-ass plan to me," Kane hit back, dryly. Then she smiled. "I like it."

"Good, because you're going first," Reeves said, returning his XO's audacious smile.

A raucous hiss pierced the air and Reeves turned to see a Sa'Nerran warrior at the edge of the tree line, close to the area he and Kane had emerged from only minutes earlier. Then a second warrior appeared out of the murky darkness, adding another hiss to the chorus of waspish sounds that were haunting the woods around Lone Water. Reeves froze, hoping the warriors hadn't spotted them, then the yellow eyes of the brutal alien fixed in his direction.

Kane was first to raise her pistol but was hit in the chest by a blast from the first warrior's rifle before she'd even leveled the barrel at the alien. The shot almost knocked her off the ridge, and Reeves had to move fast to catch her arm, and haul her out of the line of fire. Dislodged rocks rattled down the hillside to the breaker's yard below, alerting the New Earthers to their presence. Another blast raced over their heads and Reeves returned fire, driving the warriors into cover and buying them a few precious extra seconds.

"I'm okay, the absorption shield soaked up the worst of it," Kane said, wheezing the words out through gritted teeth. He could see where the blast had melted Kane's tactical vest. However, had it not been for the energy absorption shield, he knew that the shot would have gouged a hole into his XO's chest large enough to fit a bowling ball.

"Can you move?" Reeves said, firing more shots at the warriors, both of which were approaching along the ridge, using the jagged outcrops for cover.

"Do I have a choice?" Kane said, using Reeves as an anchor to help pull herself up.

Reeves threw his XO's arm over his shoulder and fixed his gaze on the opposite side of the ridge. He was about to move when he saw another warrior scrambling across the rocks toward him. Plasma blasts smashed into the rocks at his side and his face was pelted with fragments of gravelly dust that dug into his skin and stung his eyes.

"We're cut off!" Reeves called out, returning fire and hitting the warrior in the leg. A hiss erupted from the alien's slug-like lips, but still the Sa'Nerran came on. Reeves cursed, knowing that nothing short of blasting the warrior's leg off would halt its advance.

"Then we stand our ground and fight," Kane decided, slipping her arm off Reeves' shoulder and opening fire at the first group of warriors. One was hit in the chest, causing it to stumble and slip off the ridge. A wild hiss trailed behind it as the warrior fell the hundred meters to its death on the jagged rocks below.

Reeves felt a glimmer of hope as another of his shots also landed, blasting a hole into the second warrior's gut. However, no sooner had the first two warriors been dealt with than two more appeared out of the shadowy tree line. Reeves cursed bitterly and shook his head. He was used to fighting against the odds, but this time even he couldn't see a way out.

"Well, at least I don't have to worry about having flushed my Navy career down the can," Kane said, driving the Sa'Nerran reinforcements into cover. "We barely lasted more than a month in charge of Concord, never mind five years."

"Don't say I didn't warn you," Reeves answered, his

back pressed to the rocks to avoid a torrent of incoming blasts. "At least neither Shepard nor the Imperator will get the satisfaction of taking me out personally."

"We're not finished yet, Dalton," Kane said, for once forgoing sarcasm and replacing it with determination.

"If you have a plan then now's the time, Major," Reeves said, as more rocks exploded and peppered his face with coarse dust.

"We run for the ridge and take our chances," Kane replied, firing blind around the side of the rocks.

"That's a hundred-meter drop, Katee, we'd never survive," Reeves said. He was all for audacious escape strategies, but flinging himself off a cliff was a step too far, even for him.

"We won't survive up here, either," Kane countered. "At least this way, we have a chance, even if it's slim one."

Reeves cursed and was about to go along with his XO's ludicrous plan when another idea popped into his head. He cursed himself for not having considered it before.

"Wait, I have another idea," he said, clawing grit out of his eyes and nose. "Just trust me and follow my lead." Without waiting for Kane to acknowledge him, he stood up and thrust his hands into the air.

"Your idea is to set ourselves up for target practice?" Kane quipped.

"Just get off your ass, Katee and stand with me," Reeves said. He then tossed down his weapon and cleared his throat. "We surrender!"

Kane pushed herself off the rocks and cautiously

moved out beside Reeves, in full view of the advancing warriors. "Are you sure about this, Dalton?"

"The Imperator wants me alive, so if there's a chance I'll surrender, I'm betting these leather-faced bastards will take it," Reeves replied, asserting the statement confidently in the hope it would influence the gods of probability to smile on him.

"You're forgetting that these assholes don't speak English. They probably don't know what 'I surrender' means," Kane pointed out.

Reeves hadn't considered that possibility, but the fact he hadn't been blasted through the heart yet suggested his gamble was paying off. The closest warrior then hissed at him and removed a set of binders from its armor.

"What now?" whispered Kane

"Just get ready to rush them," replied Reeves, trying and failing to speak without moving his lips, like a bad holiday-park ventriloquist. "We'll figure the rest out as we go."

Suddenly, a growl thundered across the dark sky and reverberated through the rocky hillside like seismic waves. Reeves glanced beyond the approaching warriors and saw trees being toppled in the forest close to the ridge. The crack and creak of falling timber was as deafeningly loud as the roar that preceded it. The warriors also spun around, turning their attention away from Reeves and Kane to whatever was bulldozing its way through the forest. Then a cluster of smaller trees at the edge of the forest were bowled over, and a creature the likes of which Reeves had never seen or even imagined in his wildest dreams thundered into view.

"I think we've found our apex predator," said Reeves, watching the beast while staying perfectly still.

The creature had a horned head the size of a rhinoceros, but it was attached to a muscular, leathery body that more closely resembled that of a gorilla. The beast rested forward on claw-tipped knuckles that looked like they could have ripped open the hull of a battlecruiser, and peered at the warriors with glowing red eyes the size of tennis balls. Reeves was paralyzed with terror, but the Sa'Nerra showed no fear of the creature. Hissing wildly at it, the warriors turned their weapons away from Reeves and Kane and opened fire on the beast. Reeves watched in amazement as blast after blast thumped into the creature's hulking frame, doing little more than scorching its thick hide. The beast roared, and the power of its cry shook loose rocks and dirt from the hillside, sending them bowling over the ridge and crashing into the border fence surrounding the breaker's yard below. The warriors continued to fire, finally succeeding in penetrating the beast's dense skin, but the injuries only seemed to make the creature angry. Hammering its claws into the ridge like an angry bull stamping its hooves, the monstrous animal charged.

Crashing through the Sa'Nerra like a runaway train, it hammered the warriors into the hillside, which shook as if an earthquake had struck the town. One warrior was torn in half and tossed over the ridge, while a second attempted in vain to subdue the beast with its serrated, half-moon blade. The warrior that had cut off Reeves on the other side of the ridge raced past them, barging Reeves and Kane out of the way as it did so then firing at the creature at point blank range. A wound opened up in the monster's side, but again the beast only seemed to grow angrier. Swiping at the warrior with its claw, the Sa'Nerran was swatted over the ridge and sent crashing through a tarpaulin-covered shuttle inside the breaker's yard. The beast then turned its attention back to the sole remaining warrior and pinned the alien to the rocks with it claw. Opening its gaping jaws, the creature ripped the head off the Sa'Nerran warrior with a single, devastating bite. Blood, bone and brains oozed between the monster's teeth and ran down its jaws as it chomped down on the meal. Then it turned its red eyes to Reeves and Kane and roared again.

"Move, now!" cried Reeves, grabbing a stunned-looking Katee Kane and dragging her onto the ridge beside him.

"Move where?" Kane asked, still unable to tear her eyes away from the beast, as it continued to devour the warrior in enormous, savage bites.

"Anywhere is better than here, Major, now run, damn it!" Reeves ordered, dragging his XO along with him for fear she'd remain transfixed by the gory spectacle and become the creature's next snack.

Kane finally shook herself out of her stupor and ran. Reeves followed, but couldn't resist another look back. He wished he hadn't. The beast was coming for them, scrambling across the ridge using its claws to hook onto the rocks like climbing pitons.

"Hurry, it's coming!" Reeves called out to Kane, but his XO had stopped suddenly in front of him. Crashing into her back, he almost fell off the ridge before managing to grab a hand-hold on the rocks to steady himself. "Katee, what the hell..." Reeves called out, but then he saw why Kane had stopped. Clawing itself down toward the ridge from the hilltop opposite was another of the monstrous beasts.

"Dalton, what do we do?" Kane said, her voice shaky with fear.

Kane was practically pleading with Reeves for a solution, but this time he had nothing. Unlike the Sa'Nerra, there was no bargaining with these beasts. There was only dying.

The second monster roared and thumped its claws against the hillside, seemingly challenging the first beast for the prize of a meal. Reeves was forced to cover his head to fend off falling rocks and dirt, then the entire ridge shook as if a bomb had been detonated deep inside the hill. The dirt beneath his feet began to crumble, and Reeves lost his footing before the ground swallowed him whole, as effortlessly as the beast had devoured the warrior's head. Tumbling into blackness, he heard Kane crying out before he landed on something solid and his fall was brought to a sudden, sharp, and excruciatingly painful stop.

CHAPTER 15
TOMB OF THE UNCONQUERABLE

REEVES TRIED to push himself up but winced as pain shot through his body, paralyzing him to the spot. The rucksack he was wearing helped to cushion the impact of the fall, but it still felt like he'd been body-slammed through a solid wood table. Finally managing to sit upright, he peered through the hole in the hillside that he'd just fallen though. As the only source of light inside the cavern, it was like looking up at a stairway to heaven.

"Dalton, are you there?" Kane's voice emanated from somewhere in the darkness.

Reeves turned away from the light and looked toward the source of his XO's voice, but his eyes had yet to adjust to the darkness and he could see nothing.

"I'm here, Katee, and I'm in one piece, just about," Reeves called back. "How about you? Are you hurt?"

"There's nothing broken, but I have one hell of a headache," Kane replied.

Another spark of light then erupted inside the cavern

and Reeves saw Kane's face, illuminated by the light shining from her buzz. Reeves activated his own device then crawled across the surface he'd landed on to reach his XO's side.

"Where the hell are we?" Kane wondered, shining the light from her buzz around the cavern. The small communicator-turned-computer was able to function as a torch, but the beam of light barely penetrated the thick veil of darkness.

"Wherever we are, I already prefer it to where we were," Reeves said.

Reeves removed his backpack and fumbled around inside it for the more powerful torch he'd packed for just such a situation. The low growls and terrifying roars of the monsters above them were still filtering through the opening. Reeves didn't know and didn't care if the creatures were fighting each other or the Sa'Nerra; he was just glad to be out of their way. Finally rooting out a couple of torches, he fastened one to the shoulder of his tactical vest before handing Kane the second. Both torches switched on at the same time and the resulting flash of light was blinding.

"Quit shining that thing in my eyes," Reeves said, trying to shield his face from the intense glare of Kane's torch.

"Dalton, you need to see this..." Kane said. The way she spoke the words made it sound like she'd just discovered an ancient tomb.

"Take the torch out of my face and maybe I will," Reeves complained, still trying to claw the light out of his eyes.

Kane shifted position and Reeves was suddenly able to see again. It took several seconds for his eyes to compensate, then he understood why his XO had sounded so spellbound.

"I don't believe it. This is the Invictus!" Reeves found himself staring down at the dorsal hull of the thousand-year-old destroyer. The shape of the vessel was instantly recognizable even from such a close distance. However, even if he hadn't been familiar with the Marauder class, the design of the ship was clearly human in origin.

"Ambassador's One's coordinates were right, after all," said Kane. "The ship is exactly where she said it would be; it's the terrain that's shifted. This looks like a hangar that was part of a much older subterranean complex."

More growls filtered in from the hole above them and Reeves could also hear plasma weapons discharging. In the excitement of the discovery, he'd forgotten the planet was still crawling with humans and aliens that wanted them dead.

"We need to get this thing operational, fast." Reeves hustled along the hull, looking for an access hatch. "Assuming the Sa'Nerra don't all get eaten by those things outside, it won't take them long to figure out what happened to us."

"There's a scaffold on the port side," Kane called over. "I can't tell for sure, but it looks like the rear ramp is still lowered."

Reeves ran over to his XO, who was already descending a ladder that dropped down to a maintenance platform. The metal of the ladder was freezing cold and wet, and the entire structure creaked and groaned as it bore the weight of himself and Kane.

"This thing is more dangerous than the fire escape on my old apartment block, back when I was a cadet," Kane quipped. She dropped down to the maintenance platform and her right foot punched straight through the rusted metal.

"Try not to destroy this thing before we're on the ground," Reeves said, lowering himself to the platform with far more delicacy than his XO had displayed.

"I hope the Invictus hasn't rusted away like this scaffold has," Kane replied, making her way down the second ladder, this time taking more care. Suddenly one of the rungs collapsed and she slipped, barely managing to catch hold of the ladder with one hand.

"Hold on!' Reeves called out, dropping flat to his chest and managing to grab a fistful of Kane's backpack.

"Hold on? Are you kidding me?!" Kane cried out.

It wasn't unexpected for his XO to make a joke in the face of imminent death, but Reeves could hear genuine fear in her voice too. Beyond the penetrating glare of the torchlights, the cavern was still pitch black. Beneath Kane was endless darkness, like staring into black sea water in the dead of night.

"Get ready, I'm going to toss you across to the next platform along," Reeves said, taking the strain and rocking Kane from side to side, like the swing of a clock pendulum.

"That's a hell of a leap, Dalton, are you sure I can make it?" Kane replied, clearly doubtful of her chances of success.

"I could just drop you now?" Reeves hit back, drawing on his incredible strength to lift Kane higher with each swing back and forth.

"Fair point," said Kane. "Okay, I'm ready..."

Reeves gritted his teeth and threw everything into the last swing before releasing his hold on Kane's rucksack. She soared across the chasm between the two maintenance scaffolds and thumped into the lower level of the platform to his left. Kane rolled through the fall, but then the scaffold began to buckle.

"Katee, get off that thing!" Reeves called out, scrambling across the hull of the ship so that he was directly above where his XO had landed. "Katee?" There was no reply, then the scaffold collapsed and crashed into the darkness. "Katee!" Reeves called out, but the only reply was the echo of his own voice.

Cursing, Reeves ran back out across the hull of the Invictus, resuming his original idea of trying to locate an access hatch. Finding one, he tried to operate the hatch control panel, but it was completely without power. Instead, he tugged on the handle, trying to force the hatch open, but despite causing the handle to bow, the hatch would not budge.

Growing more desperate, he ran to the back of the ship and shone his light down onto the lowered rear ramp of the Invictus. Removing his backpack, he pulled out a length of rope and tied it on to the ship. He had belaying gear in his pack too, but there was no time to waste. Slinging the rucksack back over his shoulders, he grabbed the rope and threw himself over the edge. His hands were still wet from clambering over the hull and the rope slipped through his grasp as if it had been oiled. The skin on his hands began to burn from the friction and he tightened his grip, eventually slowing his descent to a safe velocity. A few meters from the ground, he let go and fell the rest of the way, hitting the ramp hard and tumbling to the cold, wet deck of the old hangar bay.

"Katee!" Reeves called out again, shaking the pain from his hands and running toward where he'd last seen his XO. He found the wreckage of the platform, with Kane twisted up amongst it.

"I told you that was a dumb idea," Kane groaned, while flailing around under the wreckage in an attempt to free herself. She then cried out in pain and held her left arm. "This time, something is definitely broken."

Reeves activated his buzz, switched to the medical diagnostic mode and held his hand over the injury to allow the computer to assess the fracture.

"It's okay, it's pretty clean," said Reeves, deactivating the buzz and removing his backpack again. "We'd best sort it now though, before we go any further."

Kane's face fell. "Ah hell, not the bone putty, I hate that stuff," she complained.

"I'm afraid I'm fresh out of tissue regenerators and bone fusion tools." Reeves flipped open the med kit and removed the requisite item. Kane glared at the syringe like it was a medieval torture implement.

"Someday, I'm going to enjoy sticking you with one of these things," Kane said, holding out her arm, turning away her head and squeezing her eyes shut.

"Don't be a baby," Reeves hit back, allowing a smirk to curl his lips, but only because his XO couldn't see his face at that moment. "Besides, my bone density is twenty times higher than yours, so I'm afraid you won't be getting your wish any time soon."

"Being a genetic freak has some benefits, huh?" Kane raised an eyebrow at Reeves.

"I guess so." Reeves positioned the needle, ready to inject the bone putty into Kane's arm. "On three, okay?"

Kane nodded and Reeves began the countdown, but stabbed the needle into his XO's arm at the count of two, rather than three. Kane cursed as he depressed the plunger, then was immediately paralyzed with pain as the bone putty compound was pushed into her body.

"It's okay, it'll be over soon," said Reeves, slipping the syringe back into the med kit, but also keeping hold of Kane with his other hand, more for moral support than for any other reason. Bone putty was an extreme treatment that regrew bone in a matter of seconds. It could be a literal lifesaver in the field, but it was also excruciatingly painful.

"I really hate that stuff," Kane said, once the agonizing effects of the treatment had finally worn off and she had stopped cursing Reeves' name.

"You'd like it better than a broken arm," Reeves replied, slipping on his rucksack again.

Suddenly the cavern was rocked by a distant explosion and loose debris rained down all around them.

"That sounded like a focused detonation; not a brute force blast," said Kane, getting to her feet.

Reeves nodded. "They must have found us and are

trying to blast their way through," he said, realizing the danger. "We don't have a lot of time. Let's get on board and see if this relic can still fly."

Reeves ran ahead and charged up the rear ramp of the Invictus into the cargo hold. He tried to activate a panel by the side of the ramp, but like the controls for the hatch he'd tried to operate, it was completely dead.

"The power is out, so our first job is to get the reactor back online," Reeves said, thumping a fist angrily against the wall.

"If the layout of this ship is anything like our destroyers, it should be somewhere between decks two and three, aft," Kane said, running ahead. She tried the door leading off the cargo hold, but it was also inactive. "Give me a hand with this," she called out, waving Reeves over.

Reeves ran to the door and began to force it open, then another focused detonation echoed through the cavern.

"They're getting closer," Kane said, slipping her fingers into the gap between the doors and lending her own efforts to the endeavor.

"You might have to hold them off while I try to at least get the backup cells online," Reeves replied, overpowering the door and slamming it into its frame. "I already tossed my weapon."

"I'm not sure what good a pistol will do against what's coming, but I'll do my best," Kane said, drawing her sidearm and moving back toward the ramp.

Suddenly, lights powered on inside the cargo hold, and the hum of energy reverberated through the deck plates and walls. It was like someone had just strummed the E-string on a gigantic bass guitar.

"You are not One," said a voice. Though quizzical, the voice was open and friendly, and also somehow familiar, Reeves thought.

"No, but if you mean Ambassador One then she sent us," Reeves replied, directing his answer to a random spot on the ceiling.

"I find that unlikely," the voice said. "One has held many titles, but never that of ambassador."

"A lot has changed over the last few hundred years," Reeves replied, anxiously looking out toward Kane, who was crouched by the rear ramp, aiming her pistol into the darkness.

"Has it been that long?" the voice replied. "I am currently unable to synchronize with the Bastion central computer, while I remain in low power mode."

"Look, whoever you are, we're about to be overrun by Sa'Nerran warriors and a bunch of angry humans who want to use my intestines as skipping ropes, so can we save the chit-chat till later?" Reeves said.

Another blast rocked the cavern, and this time Reeves could tell that whoever was laying the charges had broken through.

"Another lie..." the voice replied, growing less friendly and more skeptical by the second. "The Sa'Nerra have not been seen since the end of the war. One and I spent more than century looking for them to no avail."

"If you don't close that ramp and power up soon, you'll get reacquainted with the Sa'Nerra far sooner than you realize," Reeves said. Kane opened fire into the darkness, the blasts from her plasma pistol lighting up the cavern like flares. "Just use your eyes, or scanners or whatever, and you'll see they're coming!"

The voice was silent for a moment, and Reeves was about to abandon the conversation and run to Kane's aid, when it spoke up again.

"Go the rear ramp, and I will provide you with a weapon."

Reeves thumped his fist against the wall jubilantly then sprinted across the cargo hold.

"What the hell are you doing back here?" Kane said, firing into the darkness again, as blasts raced back in the opposite direction.

"I spoke to what I think must be the ship's computer," Reeves said, ducking instinctively as blasts flew high over his head. "It said it would help us."

Suddenly, blast doors sprang out of the deck and ceiling and thumped together, sealing off the cargo hold and trapping Reeves and Kane outside the ship.

"Somehow, I don't think that's going to help us very much," quipped Kane, raising an eyebrow at Reeves.

Reeves hurried to the blast doors and thumped his fists against the thick metal partition. "What the hell are you doing?" he yelled at the ship. "You said you'd help us!"

"I do not know who you are," replied the voice of the computer. "And there are no Sa'Nerra coming for you; only humans. I surmise that you are criminals, looking to steal this vessel. You will not succeed."

"Damn it, how can a genius, artificially-intelligent starship be so stupid!" Reeves yelled, still thumping his fists against the wall.

"Hold it right there!" cried another voice. "Throw down your weapons or we will kill you."

Reeves spun around to see a squad of ten armed men and women in tan leather jackets standing at the foot of the ramp. Kane had pressed herself into cover and was looking at Reeves, waiting for his command.

"Give it up, Major, they win this round," said Reeves, meeting his XO's eyes.

Kane cursed then tossed her pistol out onto the deck before moving in to the New Earthers' line of sight, with her hands raised. Reeves slowly walked up by her side, when another figure appeared out of the darkness. This woman, however, Reeves already knew.

"Commander Reeves, what a surprise," said Serena Shepard. "Now, I wonder what brings the Devil's Blood to my little planet?"

CHAPTER 16
SAVED BY THE BUZZ

REEVES FELT the butt of a plasma rifle thump into his back and he was shoved inside a holding cell in Lone Water's sheriff's office. Major Kane was shunted into the cell moments later and the door was slammed shut. Reeves turned to face the New Earthers that had frog-marched him and Kane from the cave to the town and glowered at them with murderous eyes. However, at that moment he was still angrier at the stubborn computer system on-board the Invictus than he was at being apprehended by Serena Shepard's thugs. Had it not been for the paranoid AI's cynicism, they could have already been on their way back to Concord Station.

"I hope the accommodations are to your liking," Serena Shepard said, stepping inside the sheriff's office and locking eyes with Reeves through the cell bars. Resentment oozed out of her with every word, though from the cruel smile on her face the woman was clearly also enjoying having Reeves at her disposal.

"Go to hell, Shepard," Reeves hit back. It was petty and petulant retort, but he was in no mood to play games. "If you're going to kill us then just get it over with. If you're looking for us to beg or plea for your amusement then you're wasting your time."

"Oh, don't worry, Devil's Blood," Shepard hit back, stepping directly in front of the cell door, as if to demonstrate that she wasn't afraid of Reeves or Kane. "I'll get plenty of amusement from watching you die."

"You tried to engineer my death once before," said Reeves. "That didn't work out quite as you planned, though, did it?"

The corner of Shepard's mouth twisted up even further. "An error that will soon be rectified," she said, smugly. "In fact, the Imperator is already on his way."

Reeves snorted a laugh. "It seems that you and the Imperator have a good thing going on." He stepped forward and gripped the bars to the side of the door. All six New Earther thugs aimed their weapons at him as he did so, but Reeves ignored them. "I knew it had to be about more than just revenge. They're using you to set up outposts inside Bastion Federation Space, in return for helping the New Earthers recolonize Mars." Reeves snorted again. "And yet you think I'm the one who's a traitor to the human race."

"Bastion is a lie, founded on the bones of millions of true humans who perished because of the Omega Task-force," Shepard spat, risking taking another pace toward Reeves. "Humanity ceased to exist when your ancestors destroyed Earth, and it won't be restored until the true believers return home, to the solar system."

"And once the Sa'Nerra rip through the six realms, you think the Imperator will just leave you alone to play happy families on Mars?" Reeves hit back. The zealotry and small-mindedness of Shepard and her New Earth cult staggered him. "The Sa'Nerra will wipe you out too, and finish what they began a millennia ago."

Shepard shook her head and continued to regard Reeves as if he was a stain on her clothes.

"You're still so stuck in the past, Devil's Blood," Shepard said, sounding as staggered by Reeves' response and he had been of hers. "In some ways, it's a shame you won't live to see that I'm right. But the Imperator has other plans for you." She turned her disdainful gaze toward Major Kane. "This one, however, no-one gives a shit about."

Shepard stepped away from the cell door and snatched a plasma rifle from the hands of the nearest thug. Pressing the butt of the rifle into her shoulder, Shepard slipped her finger onto the trigger, and Reeves instinctively knew that the leader of the New Earth Movement wasn't bluffing.

"Kill her, and the Imperator won't get what he wants," Reeves said, stepping into the line of fire. "Remember, that asshole doesn't just want me dead; he wants to beat me first. Kill Major Kane, and I won't put up a fight. Then your precious Imperator won't be very pleased with you."

"Such arrogance," Shepard spat, again shaking her head at Reeves. "You think you're so important, don't you, Devil's Blood?"

"It doesn't matter what I think, it only matters what the Imperator wants," Reeves replied, coolly. The fact Shepard had hesitated meant he'd succeeded in planting a seed of doubt in her mind. "And I'm willing to bet you don't want to risk pissing him off. So if you want me to play ball, the Major stays alive."

"Fine, I'll let the Imperator decide what happens to her, once he's done with you," Shepard said, shoving the weapon back into the hands of the New Earther thug. "Like all the non-believers, she'll die anyway. It's just a matter of when."

Shepard turned to leave, but Reeves wasn't going to waste the opportunity to get some answers of his own.

"Just how did you get off Concord Station without being seen or monitored?" Reeves called out, asking the question with a casual nonchalance, as if he didn't really care about the answer.

"I could ask you the same question," Shepard replied. The leader of the New Earthers turned and folded her arms across her chest. The smug, cruel smile had returned. "Except, I already know how you got off Concord."

Reeves frowned then saw that Shepard was feigning a look of mock-surprise.

"You didn't really think you can do anything on that station without me finding out about it, did you?" Shepard sneered. "Between the New Earthers, Sid Garrett and just about the entire population of the station, there aren't many people on Concord who would shed a tear over your death, or think twice about informing on you for a few credits."

Reeves silently cursed the Bukkan trader that had set them up with the pirate shuttle. Besides him, Ambassador One and Chief Raspe, no-one else knew about the deal. And whereas at one time he might have suspected his chief engineer, after fighting side-by-side with the Bukkan, there was no longer a question mark over Raspe's loyalty.

"I must admit that I am curious about why you're here," Shepard continued, taking a few steps back towards the cell. "I was surprised when I received word that your stolen shuttle was heading to Thrace Colony. I'm guessing it has something to do with that ship we found in the cave?"

"I have no idea what that relic of a ship is," Reeves said, hitting Shepard with his best poker face. "I came here to gather intel on your New Earth cult, since Bastion cut me off from accessing their records. I wanted to find something I could use to get you off my station."

"You're a terrible liar, Devil's Blood," Shepard hit back. "But it doesn't matter now. Soon you'll be dead, and another loser just like you will be sent to take command. Concord will get back to normal, and the true children of humanity will return home."

"You keep believing that fantasy, Shepard," Reeves said, stepping away from the cell door. "But if you believe anything that yellow-eyed alien says, you're no worse than the turned traitors that betrayed humanity a thousand years ago."

Serena Shepard's jaw tightened, but this time the leader of the New Earth Movement didn't take the bait.

"Watch them, and no matter what, don't open this cell until the Imperator arrives," Shepard said, addressing one of her followers. "If either of them cause trouble, hurt her as much as you like, until the Devil's Blood behaves," she continued, pointing to Major Kane. "He must be left untouched. The Imperator wants our esteemed commander to be nice and fresh, ready for slaughter."

Shepard left and was followed by four of her armed cultists. The remaining two backed away from the bars and sat down at a small wooden table opposite the cell. One removed a dog-eared pack of cards from his pocket and began dealing. Neither spoke, or even met Reeves' eyes. It was like they were programmed, brainwashed servants, no different to the mind-altered humans that the Sa'Nerra used in their war against humanity a millennia ago. This time, however, the indoctrination was self-inflicted and not the result of neural manipulation. To Reeves, this made the New Earthers much worse than the turned human traitors his ancestors had faced. Shepard and her cohort were will ingly betraying their own kind. And they had to be stopped.

"How long do you think we have before the alien-in-chief gets here?" asked Kane. She had turned her face away from the guards and kept her voice low in an effort to disguise the fact she was speaking.

Reeves was about to answer when a bright flash lit up the dark sky outside the barred cell window. The lighting storm had long-since moved on, which meant the flash had been caused by something else.

"I have a feeling that our esteemed guest might have just arrived," replied Reeves, covertly checking his buzz. "I'm picking up a spike in surge energy. That flash could have been an aperture forming in low orbit."

Kane also covertly checked her buzz. Thanks to the stealthing technology that Lieutenant Curio had embedded into the devices, Shepard's thugs had not found them when he and Kane had been searched after their capture. And with their tactical vests and scanner jammers removed, the devices were now able to provide a comprehensive scan of the area.

"You're right, I'm picking up some residual surge energy," Kane whispered, deftly lowering her palm to her side.

"Keep quiet!" barked the closest of the two guards. The man was now on his feet, aiming his rifle into the cell. "And keep apart from each other. One of you at each side of the cell. Now. Move!"

Reeves smiled at the guard and made a show of complying with the command by briefly separating from Kane and strolling to the other side of the cell. Before long, the guard had returned to his seat and resumed the card game with his companion.

"What's our play?" whispered Kane, who was also trying to appear nonchalant.

Reeves wished he had a plan, but the truth was they were in a bad spot. Glancing out of the window again, he could now see a light moving across the sky, far brighter than any star or other planet in the Thrace system. Briefly checking on the guards to make sure they weren't watching him; he tapped a sequence of commands into his buzz then cursed under his breath. The flash of light had been a Sa'Nerran Battlecruiser surging into the system, and it had already launched a shuttle toward the planet.

"We fight and take our chances," Reeves said, resigning himself to the fact there was no easy escape from their predicament. "I'm going to try to crack the lock in the cell door. Be ready to move and improvise."

Reeves casually moved away from Kane, aware that one of the guards was watching him out of the corner of his eye. As soon as the New Earther returned his attention to his hand of cards, Reeves quickly switched modes on his buzz and began scanning the cell's locking mechanism. The facility was timeworn and poorly-maintained, and he considered that his chances of hacking the lock were good. Anxious seconds ticked by before the buzz bleeped softly, indicating that it had begun working on the mechanism. Reeves cursed and pressed his palm tightly to his thigh, trying to muffle the sound. He hadn't expected the device to make a noise, and in the deathly quiet of the cell block, the chirrup seemed as loud as a dinner gong.

"Hey, what was that?" The guard closest to the cell stood up and aimed his rifle at Reeves. "You've got something in there. Show me, now!"

Without warning, Kane threw herself to the ground and began writhing in agony close to the bars. At first, Reeves felt his heart thump, fearful that his XO had sustained an internal injury that his earlier medical scans had missed. Then he saw her subtly wink at him while rolling around on the floor, and the penny dropped.

"She's dying!" cried Reeves, thinking on the fly and trying to sound convincingly distressed. "She took a hit to the body before you captured us. It's internal bleeding."

"Do I look like an idiot?" the guard snapped. The second guard had also now approached, and was peering at Kane, seemingly trying to work out if she was faking it.

"You heard what Shepard told you," Reeves said, not allowing either guard time to think. "It's up to the Imperator to decide what happens to Major Kane. Do you want to explain to your boss how you let her die?"

"I heard her tell me to keep this cell door shut, no matter what," one guard retorted. The man then wafted a hand at Kane. "If she bleeds out and dies, I don't give a shit."

Reeves checked on Kane in his peripheral vision. She had maneuvered herself close enough to be able to reach the through the bars and grab one of the guards. Then his buzz bleeped for a second time.

"There it is again!" the guard said, stabbing his rifle barrel through the cell bars at Reeves. "You have something in there; a communicator or a scanner."

"You got me," replied Reeves, holding up his hands and showing the buzz to the guard. "I'll take it off and let you have it."

"Slowly, asshole," the guard hit back, still aiming his rifle at Reeves.

Kane then grabbed the ankle of the second guard through the bars and began pleading with him to help her. Her performance was good enough that it almost convinced Reeves.

"Let go of him or I'll shoot," the guard in front of Reeves yelled, now turning the weapon onto Kane.

Reeves saw his chance. Barging open the now unlocked cell door with all his strength, he hammered the metal bars into the New Earther's head, hitting the man with such force that he was propelled all the way across the room.

The second guard tore his leg free of Kane's grasp and raised his rifle, but Reeves was already on top of the man. Yanking the weapon out of the New Earther's grasp, he thumped a hard right cross into the man's face, cracking bone and flattening the guard's cheek like it was made of paper. The New Earther's body went limp and he fell heavily, cracking his head open on the hard stone floor.

"That was the easy part," said Reeves, grabbing one of the rifles and handing it to Kane, who had made a sudden and miraculous recovery.

Kane took the weapon, then there was a sonic boom outside and Reeves peered through the window to see a Sa'Nerran shuttle hurtling toward the town of Lone Water.

"There are three shuttles on the deck outside," Kane called out. She was looking out of the barred window on the opposite wall. "The launch keys are likely in this office somewhere. I say we take one and get clear of this shitty town. We can figure out the rest from there."

"If we leave now, we'll never get the Invictus," Reeves said, turning his gaze toward the hillside behind the breaker's yard, which was barely a hundred meters from where they were.

"We'll find another ship," Kane hit back, pushing away from the window and moving in front of Reeves. "Dalton, come on. Even we manage to reach it, that ship's asshole AI won't even let us on board."

Reeves gritted his teeth and peered out of the window again. The Sa'Nerran shuttle was circling around the town and preparing to land. He knew Kane was right, but he had a strong gut feeling that the Invictus was important.

"Ambassador One specifically wanted that ship, Katee," Reeves said, making his decision. He turned back to his XO and held her eyes. "If there's something special about the Invictus, we can't let the Sa'Nerra get hold of it. We have to try. We won't get another shot at this."

Kane also gritted her teeth then let out a curse. "You're one infuriating bastard, do you know that?"

"I'm guessing that's why no-one likes me," Reeves hit back, managing a weak smile.

"Fine, we go for the Invictus," Kane said. She knew that when Reeves had made up his mind, there was no changing it. "But assuming we can even get out of this building, we're going to need one hell of a distraction to make it all the way back to that cave without being spotted."

"I do actually have an idea about that," said Reeves, raising an eyebrow.

"Am I going to like it?" replied Kane, raising an eyebrow of her own.

"No, I'm pretty sure you won't."

CHAPTER 17
RUN FOR THE HILLS

REEVES EDGED OPEN the door that led from the main cell
block into the sheriff's office and peeked through the crack.
Shepard and the other New Earthers had gone, but Reeves
knew they would soon be back in force once the Imperator
had arrived. Waving his XO on, he crept inside the office
and immediately spotted their confiscated gear shoved into
the corner of the room.

"Jackpot..." Reeves muttered, setting down the plasma
rifle he'd taken from the guard onto a desk and pulling on
his tactical vest.

"They still have power too," said Kane, grabbing her
own vest. "I'm activating the energy shield and scanner
jammers now."

"Hold off on the scanner jammers till we need them,"
Reeves said, catching Kane's hand before she could activate
the system. "If we kick out a ton of jammer interference
now, it could tip off Shepard that something's wrong."

Kane nodded and pulled on the jacket followed by her

rucksack before recovering her sidearm, which was on a table beside a metal storage cabinet. Reeves then heard his XO let out a long, low whistle. Turning to see what had attracted Kane's interest, he found her holding an enormous plasma rifle and an equally enormous power cell.

"What the hell is that thing?" said Reeves, checking out the weapon more closely. It was twice the size of the plasma assault-rifle he'd appropriated from the New Earther guard.

"I don't know what it's called, but I'm guessing they keep these bad boys around to deal with those creatures that lurk outside the fence," replied Kane, sliding the weapon onto the desk then stowing a couple of regular energy cells into pouches on her vest.

Reeves slung his assault rifle then picked up the heavy weapon and slapped the energy core into it. The weapon hummed dangerously, as if it were a bomb that might go off at any moment.

"It's not those creatures I'm worried about right now," Reeves said, pressing the butt of the rifle to his shoulder and testing his aim. Due to its size and weight, the weapon would have been cumbersome for most people to use, but thanks to his unusual strength, Reeves found that he could aim it with comfort. "But this thing could certainly come in handy."

Suddenly, the loose ornaments and untidy stacks of documents on the desks started to shake and rattle. A coffee mug vibrated off a counter top and smashed onto the floor, spilling its murky brown contents onto the stone slabs like black blood. Reeves ran to the window and cautiously peered outside, careful not to be seen by anyone who might have been lurking nearby.

"The Sa'Nerran shuttle has touched down," said Reeves, watching the craft become consumed in the cloud of dust its thrusters had kicked up to arrest its descent.

"Then it's time to hear your genius plan for getting out of here, Commander," Kane said, moving up beside Reeves and also peeking out of the window.

"It's simple, really," replied Reeves, trying to convey a suitable degree of certainty, without coming across as over-confident. His statement wasn't technically a lie; the plan was simple, but that didn't necessarily mean it was easy. "We head out of here then make a run for the border fence at the foot of the ridge, blast through and work our way back into the hills."

"I could have come up with that idea on my own," Kane hit back, sounding distinctly unimpressed. "Where's the part about creating a distraction to stop the Sa'Nerra and New Earthers from hunting us down like Bastion elk?"

"Those horn-headed monsters is what will stop them, not us," Reeves said. He was now getting to the part he knew Kane wouldn't like.

"And what's to stop those horn-headed monsters just choosing us for dinner instead?" asked Kane, still sounding unimpressed.

"They won't bother with us, if they have more tempting prey," Reeves replied, remaining confident. "After we blow through the border fence, we have to make it more attrac-tive for the beasts to enter the town than to come after us."

Kane winced. "Go on..." she said, cautiously.

"That means we string up some fresh meat on the fence to lure those monsters inside," Reeves replied, as coolly as he could manage, considering the gruesome nature of the suggestion he'd just made. "If we can get a few of those beasts to enter the town, Shepard and the others will be too busy dealing with the havoc they're causing to worry about us."

"Damn, Dalton, you do have a dark side," said Kane, peering at Reeves with a mixture of reverence and revulsion.

"Do you have a better idea?" Reeves hit back.

Kane shrugged. "I prefer the idea where we just steal another shuttle and get the hell out of here." Reeves scowled at his XO, but Kane raised her hands and headed him off before he could argue back. "But since we're going after this mythical thousand-year-old ship with an attitude problem, stringing up a New Earther on the fence sounds like a solid plan."

"I'm glad we're agreed, Major," said Reeves, hauling the massive rifle over his shoulder then heading for the door. "Scanner jammers on," he added, while enabling the stealth system on his own tactical vest. "Let's go beast hunting..."

Reeves threw open the door to the sheriff's office and was immediately confronted by a man coming in the opposite direction. The two locked eyes, each equally surprised to see the other. There was a tense pause then the New Earther reached for a pistol. Instinctively, Reeves deflected the barrel of the weapon and the pistol discharged, thumping a blast into the roof of the sheriff's office and causing plaster to rain down on their heads. Striking the New Earther with the butt of the massive rifle, Reeves drove the man back, giving him enough space to aim the huge weapon. Pulling the rifle into his shoulder, he squeezed the trigger and shot the New Earther in the chest. The report of the weapon sounded like the crack of thunder from a nearby lightning strike, and the result was even more shocking. The powerful weapon had blasted a hole clean through the man's chest large enough to fit his entire head inside. Suddenly, shouts and the scuffle of boots echoed along the streets outside and Reeves cursed, knowing that any element of surprise they might have had was already lost.

"Let's go, Major!" Reeves said, ushering Kane outside. "You head for the fence and I'll cover you."

Kane ran, weapon raised and with a steely look of determination on her face. As usual, when it was game time, any hint of the irreverent and sarcastic Katee Kane vanished, and all that was left was Kane the soldier. Pausing at the corner of the sheriff's office, Kane dropped to one knee and aimed her rifle along the street toward where the shuttle had landed.

"We have six New Earthers heading this way," Kane called out, while laying down fire at the incoming contacts.

Reeves moved up to her side then peeked around the corner. "Go, I'll cover you," he said, readying the massive weapon.

Kane made a dash for the building across the street and Reeves took up her previous position, blasting the leg off an advancing New Earther above the knee. His XO had already taken out two of the cultists, but the remaining three were still advancing fast. Behind then, Reeves could see more moving into position. Then there was a sharp hiss of escaping air, as the ramp of the Sa'Nerran shuttle began to open. Moments later, six warriors in dark red armor stormed out, followed by the massive seven-foot frame of the Imperator.

Cursing, Reeves stayed focused on the New Earthers and saw one of them drop into cover and open fire on Kane. The man was shielded from him by the corner of the building, but the New Earther hadn't accounted for Reeves' new weapon. Taking careful aim, he squeezed the trigger, blasting through the bricks and mortar and taking the man's head clean off.

"Go!" Kane called out from across the street.

Reeves ran while his XO suppressed the remaining New Earthers. In his peripheral vision, he could see that Imperator and its honor guard were advancing toward his position. To make matters worse, the Sa'Nerran warriors that were already on the ground were also closing in.

"There are too many of them, just run to the fence and don't stop!" Reeves called out, firing shots blindly down the street toward the incoming hoard. A blast thumped into his back and though his vest's energy shield absorbed the impact, he was still knocked off balance and fell. Moments later he felt hands grabbing around the straps of his vest and he looked up, bleary eyed, to see Kane dragging him to safety.

"Damn it, Dalton, you weigh a ton," Kane said, ducking

into cover as blasts began to obliterate the wall of the building they were hiding behind.

"I'm just big boned, now run, damn it!" Reeves hit back, slapping his XO on the shoulder and giving her a gentle shove toward the border fence.

Reeves knew that their only hope now was to get outside the perimeter, and hope that the planet's native predators chose the richer pickings of the town instead of a couple of morsels like himself and Kane.

Thumping a volley of blasts down the street, Reeves killed two more New Earthers and a Sa'Nerran warrior, forcing the others to take cover. He knew it was only a temporary reprieve, but he was willing to take any advantage he could get. Turning and sprinting for the fence, he caught up with Kane and slid to a stop on the stone road. Aiming his rifle at a fence post, he was about to squeeze the trigger when blasts of plasma rained down all around them, tearing up the road and smashing through the buildings to their side. Grabbing Kane, he pulled them both back just in time to avoid being strafed by whatever weapon had unleashed red hot fury on them.

"Was that a ship?" Kane said, spitting dust and debris from her mouth.

Reeves chanced a look over what remained of the corner of the building and saw what had attacked them.

"No, it's a damned guard tower," Reeves replied, pulling back into cover as more blasts began to tear up the building. "There's one New Earther up there with a heavy cannon that looks big enough to take down a pirate raider."

"Do we go back?" asked Kane, reloading her rifle with a fresh cell.

"There's no time, I'll have to take it out," replied Reeves. "Though don't ask me how."

"I'll create a distraction," Kane said, jumping up and running out of cover along the line of the fence.

"Katee!" Reeves called out, trying to grab her vest and haul her back into cover, but his agile XO was had already out of his reach.

The guard tower opened fire, strafing the road and the fence in an attempt to mow Kane down. Reeves cursed and moved out from behind the partly demolished wall. The New Earther in the tower saw him and began to adjust the cannon's aim, but Reeves had the advantage. Holding down the trigger of the massive rifle, he obliterated the floor beneath the heavy weapon, causing the tower to collapse and crash to the ground, smashing through a wide section of fence as it did so.

Turning toward Kane, he saw his XO on the floor about twenty meters away and ran to her. She still had all of her limbs, which was enough to let Reeves know that she'd somehow managed to evade a direct hit from the guard tower. However, she was also twisted up in the remains of the border fence that had been mangled by the heavy cannon before Reeves had taken it out.

"Katee, get up, we need to move," Reeves said, hauling the large chunks of debris away as if they were mere Styrofoam blocks

"I take it my distraction worked?" Kane groaned, untangling herself from a mass of wires.

"Yes, but I think you used up one of your nine lives doing it," Reeves replied, keeping half an eye out for New Earthers or Sa'Nerra. "Though we now don't have a fence to string up our bait on."

Kane smiled, but her expression immediately hardened again. Quick-drawing her pistol, she opened fire, sending blasts racing past Reeves' head so close he could feel the heat of the shots. Spinning around, Reeves saw two Sa'Nerran warriors lying dead behind him, but three more were advancing fast. All of them were holding serrated half-moon blades, rather than plasma weapons.

"Why aren't they shooting at us?" grunted Kane as she scrambled the rest of the way out of the debris and clambered over the mass of tangled metal to the open ground outside the town.

"The Imperator wants me alive," Reeves said, blasting one of the advancing warriors in the gut. The power of the shot severed the alien in half. "For once I'm not complaining, if it gives us a chance to escape."

Reeves and Kane continued to scramble over the wreckage of the fence until they were at the foot of the hills. The Sa'Nerra continued their pursuit, hissing angrily as shots from Kane and Reeves continued to thin their numbers. Then the warriors suddenly halted, and their egg-shaped, yellow eyes looked beyond Reeves and into the hills behind them.

"Why have they stopped?" Kane called out, pulling into cover behind a cluster of jagged rocks.

"I don't know, but keep moving," Reeves replied, dragging one tired leg in front of the other and continuing to climb up the steep incline. Then he saw why the warriors had halted their advance. Staring down at him was one of the horned-headed beasts that had laid waste to the hillside and Sa'Nerra before they were captured. The creature snorted at Reeves, blowing a plume of hot mist from its nostrils, before stomping its claws into the ground and releasing a thunderous roar.

Heart-thumping hard in his chest, Reeves raised the heavy rifle to his shoulder and fired. The blast thumped into the beast's thick hide and burned a cavity into its chest. Roaring again the creature charged, giving Reeves barely a split-second to fire a second shot. This time the blast hit the monster full in the face, opening up its skull and melting its brains. The beast fell and tumbled down the hillside like a boulder. Reeves dove out of its path, narrowly avoiding being crushed, and the creature eventually slid to a stop in front of the waiting pack of Sa'Nerra. Heart still in his mouth, Reeves clambered to his feet and aimed toward the horde, but still the Sa'Nerra were not advancing.

"Dalton..."

Reeves turned to Kane, but her eyes were fixed on the hillside above them. More thunderous roars pierced the air and Reeves stared, wide-eyed along the path to the ridge. Four more of the beasts were slowly stalking toward them, hungry red eyes fixed on him and Kane. Pulling the butt of the rifle into his shoulder, Reeves took aim at the closest beast and squeezed the trigger, but nothing happened. Cursing, he checked the weapon and pulled the trigger again, but it didn't fire. The power core was dead.

Two more of the massive, claw-wielding predators

appeared up the hillside, and suddenly blasts of plasma were racing over Reeves' head. He ducked down and peered toward the town. A cluster of New Earthers had taken up positions in the streets and on rooftops, while others were rushing to man nearby guard towers. A strident alarm sounded, wailing out from towers dotted all around Lone Water. Reeves felt a chill run down his spine as he realized that the beasts were not only approaching from the path above him, but from all around the town. He knew they couldn't go forward, but going back seemed like a death sentence too.

"Dalton, what's our move?" Kane called out. She was still hunkered down behind the jagged rocks, eyes wide with fear.

Before Reeves could answer, the beasts on the hillside let out a colossal, synchronized roar that was so loud his ears rang. Moments later, a reply thundered around the town, reverberating off the hillside like the sound of an avalanche. Then, in unison, the monsters advanced, not just from on the hillside above him, but from all around Lone Water. Reeves knew the decision had been made for him. Going forward was suicide, but so was going back. The only way they were getting off Thrace Colony alive was if they could reach the Invictus and convince its paranoid AI to take them in.

REEVES AND KANE dove for cover as one of the horn-headed beasts leapt over their heads and crashed through the forward line of Sa'Nerran warriors, scattering them like ten pins. The surviving warriors slashed their serrated blades at the creature's flesh and blasted it at close range, but their efforts did little more than graze or scorch the monster's skin. Spotting an opening, Reeves tried to push himself up, but Kane pinned him to the ground. Moments later, two more of the planet's apex predators charged down the hillside, bulldozing through what remained of the Sa'Nerra and stampeding into the town of Lone Water.

"Thanks..." said Reeves, as Kane finally lifted herself off him.

"Don't thank me yet," replied Kane, her eyes fixed on the land rising up toward the ridge. "I think we just stirred up a hornet's nest."

Reeves scanned his eyes across the hillside and saw dozens more of the creatures, spread out all around the town's perimeter. Glancing back into Lone Water, he saw the town's inhabitants rushing from their homes and into underground shelters. Others slung rifles over their backs and joined the first group of defenders, climbing into guard towers or onto rooftops. The Imperator's shuttle remained parked in the center of the town square. Reeves couldn't see the leader of the belligerent alien race, but the Imperator's soldiers were everywhere, their bronze armor sparkling under the searchlights.

"We need to find the cave entrance and reach the Invictus," said Reeves, still keeping a careful eye on the beasts above them. "That ship is our only route off this rock."

"Then we'd better hope the ship's computer is in a better mood," replied Kane, ramping up the power setting of her pistol to maximum. Then a smirk curled her lips. "At least we got that distraction we were looking for."

Reeves huffed a laugh. "And it didn't involve stringing anyone up either," he replied, secretly grateful for that. "Right now the New Earthers are far too busy to worry about us."

"I don't think it's the New Earthers we need to worry about," said Kane.

There was dark, foreboding tone to her voice, and Reeves saw that she now had her focus turned to the hillside below them. Reeves rolled on his back and peered toward the smashed fence and guard tower that he'd destroyed. A squad of Sa'Nerran warriors was advancing toward their position. Most were bloodied, while others clearly had broken limbs, but none showed any pain and weakness, and all of them were focused on Reeves and Kane.

"These bastards have no quit in them, I'll give them that," said Reeves. He pushed himself to his feet and prized a Sa'Nerran half-moon blade from the long fingers of a warrior who had been trampled flat into the ground. "But if they're still insisting on taking me as a prize for their master, that gives us the advantage."

Kane made a show of pointing to each of the warriors in turn, counting out loud as she did so. "Seven, eight, nine..." she continued, before turning to Reeves. "I'm not sure how nine on two gives us the advantage."

"Because they won't shoot me, but I *will* shoot them," said Reeves, advancing down the hill toward the aliens.

"They might not shoot you, but there's nothing to stop those leather-faced assholes shooting *me*," Kane complained, though she was still by Reeves' side, weapon raised.

"I suppose there has to be some advantages to being the Devil's Blood," Reeves hit back. He then sucked in a deep breath and steeled himself for the fight. "Aim for the head and make every shot count."

A warrior with a smashed ankle dragged itself up the path and tried to grab Reeves. Kicking the warrior's hand away he dropped low and sunk his serrated blade into the back of the alien's neck, driving it deeper until the spinal column was cut in half.

"That's one..." said Kane before blasting a warrior in the face and sending it cartwheeling to the smashed fence below, "That's two. Only about a hundred more to go..."

Reeves ignored Kane's quip; the blood was already thumping through his veins, and he could feel anger swelling inside his gut. There was something about the Sa'Nerra that brought out the more animalistic warrior inside him. Fighting Shepard's thugs and Garrett's goons felt different somehow, but while in the past he was reluctant to embrace this darker side of himself, now he knew he'd have to rely on it to survive.

Blasting the head off a warrior with his pistol, Reeves picked up speed and barged through a second alien before it was able to swing its blade at him. The warrior tumbled down the hill, taking two more off their feet in the process. Kane advanced behind him, steadily picking off the warriors farther down the hill, while behind them and all around the town of Lone Water, the roar of the horn-headed beasts continued to rumble off the rocky terrain.

Reaching ground level, Reeves slashed open the throat of another warrior then scrambled across the wreckage of the fence. Kane worked her way down, methodically picking off more of the alien soldiers before covering Reeves with her pistol.

"Can you see the cave entrance?" Kane called out, ejecting an expended power cell and slapping in a fresh one.

Reeves looked to the ridge where he and Kane had fallen through the hillside and landed on top of the Invictus. Tracing a line down, he saw a patch of rock and fresher, darker soil. The fence opposite was already warped out of shape, as if Shepard had forced it open in order to reach the mouth of the cavern.

"I see it, but we'll have to go through the town to reach it," said Reeves, returning his gaze to the streets around him. The first batch of warriors had fallen, but he knew that dozens more still remained in the town.

"If we stick to the back streets, we might be able to reach the cave without being seen," replied Kane, stepping over the broken fence and working her way toward Reeves.

Suddenly, heavy plasma fire began to thump into the walls of the building next to them, and Reeves and Kane both took cover.

"Why the hell are they shooting at us?" Kane yelled, shielding her head from falling debris.

"They're not," said Reeves, feeling a lump tighten in his throat. "They're shooting at those."

Three horn-headed beasts stormed down the hillside and tore though the remaining sections of fence at the edge of the town. A guard tower fifty meters inside the perimeter opened fire again, and one of the creatures took the full force of the blast. Chunks of flesh were savagely burned and melted and within seconds the creature had collapsed. The remaining two continued on, one leaping over Reeves and Kane and clawing itself across the rooftop of the building they were hiding behind. The second rushed the guard tower and rampaged through it, sending the tower and the three New Earthers inside crashing to the road below.

"Let's move, Major, before there's nothing left of this town to move through," Reeves said, brushing the larger chunks of brick and mortar off his shoulder.

Reeves took the lead with Kane covering their rear. At

least twenty of the horned monsters were now inside Lone Water, and Reeves could see at least six more dead on the ground. Flashes from plasma weapons were popping off throughout the town, like a constant volley of fireworks. Guard towers and New Earther militia sprayed panicked blasts in all directions, most missing their targets and dealing as much damage to the buildings and infrastructure as the creatures themselves were. Buildings were crumbling and many more were on fire. It felt like they were in a war zone.

Sticking close to the perimeter fence, Reeves broke cover and made a dash across a road. Glancing left, he could see warriors racing toward him from deeper into the town. He fired randomly in their direction, but despite the blasts flashing between the warriors and coming desperately close to hitting, none of the aliens flinched. Still racing toward cover on the opposite side of the road, the ground suddenly began to shake beneath his feet. Two horn-headed beasts crashed through the building in front of him, smashing the corner off the structure like it was a sandcastle. Reeves slid to a stop, but his feet slipped from under him, and he crashed hard to the ground. Kane's arms were soon around him, hauling him up, but he could barely make her out through the clouds of dust and smoke that were billowing out from the smashed building.

Plasma blasts flashed overhead and Reeves could see the red eyes of the beasts through the dust as the two creatures fought each other, demolishing what remained of the building and blocking Reeves' path to the cavern. Cursing, he looked left and saw more shapes approaching through the clouds of dust. Serrated blades reflected the flashes of plasma, and soon the leathery faces of six Sa'Nerran warriors were in front of him. Five wore the familiar, bronze-colored armor that Reeves was used to seeing, but the lead warrior was different. This alien wore the crimson red armor of the Imperator's honor guard.

Raising their pistols, Reeves and Kane opened fire on the squad. Reeves focused on the honor guard, but the warrior had already hunkered down and was deflecting the blasts using an energy shield that was being emitted from the bracers on his armor. Three of the regular warriors fell to Kane's blasts, before Reeves finally turned his focus away from the honor guard. He managed to kill one of the warriors before his pistol fizzed and spluttered in his hands. Inspecting the pistol, he saw that it had taken damage and overloaded. Tossing the weapon, he swapped the Sa'N-erran half-moon blade to his right hand and waved the honor guard warrior on.

The elite warrior advanced with surprising speed, managing to slash its blade across Reeves' chest before he could dodge away. His tactical vest was ripped open from the strike and he felt the sting of the blade on his skin. A second strike whirled toward him a split-second later, and he parried before thumping a fist into the alien's face. It staggered back and spat dark-crimson blood onto the dusty ground, but unlike the regular warriors, Reeves could see this bigger, stronger alien could take more punishment. The darker side of him was glad; he wanted the Sa'Nerran to suffer.

To his right, Kane blasted one of the two remaining

warriors, but was then tackled to the ground by the final alien. In a one-on-one versus a Sa'Nerran warrior, only the most skilled and determined fighters could come out on top. Kane was on her own, but he wasn't concerned. She was as tough as they came.

Hissing wildly at Reeves, the elite warrior activated a device on its left pauldron, and Reeves watched as a length of wire unfurled. Suddenly, the wire electrified and crackled with energy and the warrior came forward, baring its jagged teeth. Reeves backed away as the alien whipped the energized cord at him, catching him across the forearm. The snap of the cable combined with the jolt of heat and electricity was almost crippling, and the warrior wasted no time in pressing its attack. Reeves barely managed to dodge the swing of its blade, before the warrior lashed him again with the energized cable. This time the cord wrapped around Reeves' forearm like a boa constrictor. The pain was excruciating, and only grew more intense as the warrior began to reel him in like a fish.

Feeling his strength begin to ebb, Reeves brought his own serrated blade down hard across the warrior's elbow. The crimson armor refused to be cut, but the force of the strike was still enough to shatter bone. The alien released its hold on Reeves and staggered back, clutching its broken arm, but Reeves knew better than to give the honor guard warrior even a second to recover. Charging toward it, Reeves drove the serrated blade into its forehead. The now-blunted blade acted like a hammer, smashing the warrior's cranium and spilling its brains out over its startled face. Reeves left the blunted blade lodged inside the alien's head then kicked it away. Retrieving the honor guard's blade from the floor, he turned to Kane and found her still locked in a struggle with a warrior. He was about to run to her aid, when Kane slipped underneath a wild swing from the alien and hammered her elbow into the back of the warrior's neck, crushing a vital nerve cluster. The warrior's body jerked chaotically then it fell to its face, quivering as if it was being electrocuted. Kane picked up the alien's serrated blade and stood over the warrior, about to put it out of its misery, but Reeves called out to stop her.

"Leave it," Reeves said, causing Kane's eyes to meet his own. They looked uncertain, and uncomfortable. "Leave it to suffer."

Kane frowned. "Dalton, that's not you talking," she replied, still poised, ready to strike.

"Maybe it's time I stopped pretending, Katee," Reeves said, walking over to the crippled alien and placing his boot on the back of its quivering neck. "The Omega Taskforce won because they were just as ruthless as the Sa'Nerra. If we don't start acting the same way, we won't make it."

"I don't believe that, Dalton, and deep down I don't think you do either," Kane hit back.

Reeves held his XO's eyes for a moment, before peering down at the warrior and flipping it over with the toe of his boot. He was still wracked with doubt and filled with bile.

"Look at this thing, Katee," Reeves continued, aiming his serrated blade at the alien. Despite its crippling injuries, the warrior was still hissing wildly, and trying desperately to claw at Reeves with what little strength it had left. "The

Sa'Nerra won't show us mercy. Why should we be any different?"

"Because we *are* different," Kane said, holding her ground. "We're better than them. You're better than them. So be better."

Reeves exhaled heavily and continued to watch the struggling alien. Despite all hell breaking loose around them, in that moment only one decision mattered.

"Be better than them, Dalton," Kane said again. "You can be the 'Devil's Blood' without becoming the devil."

Reeves shook his head then rolled the alien onto its side. He dropped sharply, using his weight to drive the blade into the warrior's neck, severing the nerve cluster and killing the alien in an instant. Rising to his full height again, Reeves locked eyes with his XO.

"I hope you're right, Katee, I really do," Reeves said. He wanted to believe her, but the darkness inside him had already awoken and he feared it was already too late.

"Come on, let's get off this shithole of a planet," said Kane, thumping Reeves on the shoulder.

Forging ahead, with blasts still flying across the town in all direction, Reeves and Kane made it to the cavern that Shepard had blasted open. Checking quickly to make sure he wasn't being followed, he took a step toward the dark mouth of the cave, but then immediately froze as he saw something emerging from it. His gut tightened into a knot as the Imperator marched into view, flanked by two of his honor guard.

Without hesitating, Kane raised her pistol and squeezed the trigger, but the weapon did not fire. Cursing, she released the expended cell and went to slap in another, but before she could reach the fresh power module a dozen more warriors ran out behind them and fenced them in. A raucous chorus of hisses assaulted their ears like a million angry rattlesnakes.

"This is one situation we can't shoot our way out of, Katee," Reeves said, grabbing Kane's hand to stop her reloading the pistol. "The Imperator came for me, and I'm going to give it what it wants."

CHAPTER 19
ROUND TWO

REEVES WATCHED the Imperator advance toward him as more Sa'Nerran warriors arrived to fence off and defend the position against the beasts that were ravaging the town. Behind the Imperator were its honor guard warriors, standing to attention like sentries, blocking the entrance to the cave and Reeves' only hope of escape – the Omega Taskforce warship called the Invictus.

"What brings you to this world, descendant?" the Imperator said, while continuing to take slow, measured paces toward Reeves.

"I could ask you the same thing," Reeves replied, cagily.

They were trapped and at the mercy of the alien leader, but Reeves figured that if he could at least keep the warrior talking, he might be able to think of a way out. However, surrounded by dozens of Sa'Nerra and with their only exit blocked, the situation seemed hopeless.

"I came here to kill you," the Imperator replied, stopping a few paces short of Reeves. Again, he was struck by just how massive the alien warrior was, especially compared to its foot soldiers.

"I meant why are your warriors here, playing house with the New Earth separatists?"

"I know what you meant, human." The alien leader glanced over its muscular shoulder toward the dark mouth of the cave behind it. "The ship in there; what is its significance?"

Reeves was surprised that the Imperator did not know the Invictus, considering his detailed familiarity with the Omega Taskforce. He expected that a vessel which had played such a pivotal role in the destruction of his own planet and civilization would have been as famous to the Sa'Nerra as it was to the humans of the Bastion Federation.

"What ship?" Reeves replied, offering the Imperator a casual shrug.

The alien leader shook its head at Reeves, though the gesture was so slight it was almost imperceptible.

"You will tell me, descendant," the Imperator hissed.

Reeves had been in the warrior's presence enough times to recognize when it had grown angry. The alien's slug-like lips pressed together more tightly and the skin around its leathery brow became even more deeply wrinkled.

"I came to Thrace to learn about the New Earth move-ment, and its leader," Reeves, continued, offering the Imperator a slice of the truth. "I didn't expect to find your warriors camped out here, and I don't know anything about a ship. My vessel was shot down by your illegal weapons platform." Reeves took a step closer to the Imperator, which held its ground imperiously. "I wonder what the Bastion Ambassador would think about the Sa'Nerra stationing forces inside federation space?"

"Your attempt to manipulate me is futile," the Imperator hit back. It then gestured to its honor guard warriors, two of which began to march toward Reeves and Kane. "Humans, however, are easy to control."

The two soldiers in crimson armor seized Major Kane and dragged her away from Reeves. Kane fought back, hammering elbows and kicks into the warriors. Reeves tried to help her, but a dozen warriors rushed out of the circle and aimed plasma rifles at him, forcing him to give up his efforts.

"If I hurt this human female, you will tell me what I want to know," the Imperator continued, nodding to the warriors holding Kane.

One of the honor guards drew its serrated blade, pushed it against the side of Kane's face and gradually began to draw the blade down. Kane cried out and Reeves instinctively tried to run to her aid, but the dozen warriors to his rear dragged him back. He gritted his teeth and fought them, but there were too many to overpower. All he could do was watch helplessly as the honor guard continued to draw Kane's blood.

"Tell your warriors to let her go and I'll talk," Reeves said, turning back to the Imperator, whose thin lips had curled into a sadistic smile. "And I don't just mean let her go so you can kill her later. I mean let her walk out of this circle. This is between you and me."

"I care nothing for this human," the Imperator replied,

coldly. It nodded to its honor guard, who dragged Kane toward the edge of the circle and threw her onto the dirt.

"I'm not going anywhere," Kane growled, clawing grit out of her mouth.

Suddenly, Kane sprang up and stole a serrated blade from the armor of one of the honor guard warriors. However, before she could use the weapon in anger, she was hammered across the side of her face by a vicious punch that knocked her flat on her back.

"Major Kane, get out of here, that's an order," Reeves barked, conscious that the Imperator and the honor guard warriors would only tolerate her protests for so long.

"That's a shit order, Dalton, and you know I won't follow it." Kane dabbed blood from the corner of her mouth with the back of her hand.

"You'll follow it, Major, even if they have to drag you away," Reeves snarled. Then he took a deep breath and tried to soften his tone, realizing that his anger would only serve to inflame Kane's. "You can't do any good here, Katee. Don't be a fool."

"It's not going to happen, Dalton," Kane hit back, doubling down on her decision. "I go where you go. That's the deal."

Reeves cursed, realizing that Kane wasn't going to back down no matter what he said or did. Ironically, his enemy was now the only option he had to save his XO's life.

"Whatever happens to me, she walks, understood?" Reeves said, still trying to negotiate with the Imperator on behalf of his stubborn XO. "If you agree to that then I'll fight you to the death, if that's what you want."

The Imperator glowered at Reeves. The muscles in its leathery face had become taut, which only accentuated the fierce intensity of its hateful stare. Reeves could see that it was on the verge of losing control.

"Tell me what the significance of that ship is and I will consider it," the Imperator hissed.

"Damn it, it's the Invictus," Reeves replied, deciding to answer rather than further anger the Imperator and put Kane at more risk. "I would have thought that name meant something to you?"

The Imperator recoiled a little, and regarded Reeves with its distrustful, yellow eyes.

"That is impossible, that vessel no longer exists," the Imperator replied, its eyes narrowing.

Reeves could hear the doubt in the Imperator's voice. More than that, for the first time he also detected fear. He silently cursed himself for revealing the secret. He hadn't realized that the Invictus would hold such power over the alien leader, and now he had put the vessel at risk too.

"Look, I've answered your question now release my officer, and let's settle this between us," Reeves said, trying to move the subject away from the ship.

"Neither of you will leave this world," the Imperator hissed, with quiet menace.

Suddenly Kane was hauled to her feet and Reeves turned in time to see a warrior plunge its serrated blade into her side. The weapon's razor-sharp edge penetrated the seam of Kane's tactical vest and sank deep into her flesh. Kane cried out as the warrior twisted the blade before pulling it out and flinging her body onto the rocks. At first,

Reeves was too shocked to act or even to speak. He simply stared at Kane, open mouthed, watching her blood paint the stones and gravel red. Reeves closed his eyes. He'd seen enough battlefield injuries to know that her wound was serious, probably fatal.

Anger was now swelling inside Reeves, like a tornado building in speed and ferocity. Adrenalin surged through his hyper-dense muscles and he shook off the warriors that were restraining him then charged at the Imperator. His attack was clumsy and driven by blind rage, and the Imperator evaded it easily, striking Reeves to the back and sending him face-first into the dirt. The honor guard warriors moved to intervene, but the alien leader hissed at them and immediately they all fell back to rejoin the circle. Reeves scrambled to his feet and tried to compose himself. Then he again saw Kane's body, her life essence leaking from the savage wound, and rage overcame him.

"Your ancestors cared nothing for the lives of their subordinates," the Imperator said, dodging another wild swing by Reeves and countering with a powerful backhand that staggered him. "Perhaps you are not as strong as they are?"

Reeves roared as he charged at the Imperator again, driving a shoulder tackle into the alien's gut. The warrior dug in its heels and used its own considerable strength to gut-wrench Reeves off the ground and slam his body into the rough, stony dirt at their feet. Reeves cursed and gritted his teeth, yet despite the punishment he was taking, he felt no pain. With each strike from the Imperator, the darkness inside him grew stronger.

"I expected more from you, descendant," the Imperator continued, launching a kick into Reeves' side that sent him tumbling toward the mouth of the cave.

Reeves dragged himself off the ground, hands clawing the dirt so forcefully that he crushed the loose stones into dust. Suddenly, he felt the alien's long fingers around his throat and the Imperator hauled him up by the neck, so that the balls of his feet barely touched the soil.

"Now, descendant, you will die," the Imperator hissed into his face.

Reeves grabbed the Imperator's hand and prized the alien's finger away from his throat. Eyes widening with surprise, the warrior clutched Reeves with its other hand and tried to intensify its choke hold, but to no avail. Reeves had now been consumed by the darkness inside him. With a burst of raw power, he broke the Imperator's hold then hammered a right hand across the side of the alien's jaw. The strike rocked the Imperator, causing it to stagger away, dark crimson blood leaking over its thin lips. Reeves again saw Major Kane on the ground. She wasn't moving. Whatever was left of Dalton Reeves in that moment vanished, and was replaced by the individual the Imperator had come to fight – the descendant of the Omega officers that had ended the Sa'Nerran war. The Devil's Blood.

Surging toward the Imperator, Reeves hammered punches into the alien's face and armored body, denting metal and cracking bone. The Imperator closed its guard, managing to block or deflect some of the blows, but the sheer relentless fury of his attack was unstoppable. Finally, the alien leader was caught flush to the face and it went down hard. Incredibly, despite their leader lying bleeding and prone on the ground, none of the Sa'Nerran warriors moved to intervene. Whatever contest the Imperator had instigated, it was between them and them alone.

Reeves moved in for the kill, but suddenly the ground shook so violently that he could barely remain on his feet. Dropping to one knee, Reeves turned to see rocks and dirt pouring down from the ridge above them. Then the side of the hill exploded like a volcanic eruption, pelting the shield wall of Sa'Nerran warriors like cannon fire.

The Imperator's honor guard rushed in and dragged their leader to safety. For a moment, Reeves considered pursuing the red-armored warriors and finishing what he'd started, but then he saw Kane, blood still oozing out of her. Sprinting over to his XO, Reeves hauled Kane over his shoulder and dove into the shelter of the cavern as rocks continued to rain down all around them.

Then a thunderous roar resonated off the hills surrounding what remained of Lone Water. However, this was not the roar of a beast, but the roar of starship engines. Bursting from of the summit of the ridge like a nuclear missile launching from a hidden silo, the Invictus raced overhead, engines burning brightly. Reeves looked up, shielding his eyes from the rocks and dirt falling all around him, and watched in stunned astonishment as the ship turned sharply and descended over the town, crushing buildings under the immense mass of its dense armor and hull. The vessel spun around, smashing more buildings in the process, and its lowered rear ramp was inched toward him.

"Get on board, Commander Reeves," boomed the voice of the Invictus' computer, amplified through unseen speakers.

Reeves didn't think; he just acted. Hauling the dying body of Katee Kane back over his shoulder, he climbed over the rocks and scrambled across the scarred landscape as fast as he could before leaping onto the waiting ramp. Immediately, the ramp began to whir shut, sending Reeves and Kane tumbling to the deck inside the cargo hold. He lay there next to his unconscious XO, chest burning and muscles aching. There should have been a million questions racing through his thoughts, but in that moment, there was only one thing on his mind; saving the life of Major Katee Kane.

CHAPTER 20
FLIGHT OF THE INVICTUS

HEART STILL POUNDING in his chest, Reeves scrambled beside Kane and checked her wound. It was deep and she'd already lost a lot of blood. Her lips were turning blue and he could feel that the skin on her face was cool and clammy. He felt for a pulse and found one, but it was weak and getting weaker by the second.

"Katee, can you hear me?" Reeves called out, gently slapping his XO to the side of her face in an attempt to rouse her. She mumbled incoherently and her head lolled to one side. "Katee, I need you to stay awake, okay? Stay awake while I patch you up."

Removing his backpack, Reeves tore open the flap and tipped the contents onto the deck. Finding the med kit, he tore away the metal lid of the box and searched for the items he needed. Forcing his breath into a calmer rhythm, he tried to focus his mind and remember what he needed to do. Ripping off Kane's bloodied tactical vest, he tore back her shirt, then opened a hemostatic wound dressing using his teeth. Placing the patch over the wound, the dressing automatically adjusted to the correct size and shape and attached to Kane's skin like a limpet.

Suddenly, the ship was rocked hard and Reeves detected the change in the forces acting on his body, which indicated the ship was maneuvering hard. While the inertial negation systems compensated for the rapid acceleration, he'd experienced enough ship-to-ship combat to know the Invictus was under attack.

Returning to the med kit, Reeves cursed realizing the equipment he'd tipped onto the deck had now rolled away. Scrambling across the cold metal decks plates, he hastily tried to gather up the life-saving equipment. Then the large double door leading off the cargo hold swooshed open. Instinctively, Reeves reached for his weapon before remembering he no longer had it. Then he saw a medical stretcher hover into the cargo bay, suspended on anti-gravity repellers.

"Do not be alarmed," the voice of the computer said, its tone friendly and reassuring. "Please place her onto the stretcher."

Reeves peered around the cargo hold, but the voice surrounded him, as if a thousand mouths had spoken the words at the same moment.

"Why, where are you taking her?" Reeves called back, aiming his question at a random spot on the ceiling of the cargo hold.

"I will tend to Major Kane's injuries," the computer replied, still calm and friendly. "However, I require your assistance on the bridge. This vessel was not designed to operate purely autonomously."

"What does that mean?" replied Reeves, while lifting Kane's body onto the gravity stretcher. Retaining straps automatically sprang out from underneath the stretcher and wrapped themselves around Kane's shoulders, chest and legs.

"It means that I require a captain," the computer said. "Or, to be more precise, a companion."

"I'm not good company right now, but I can certainly be your captain," Reeves said.

"Thank you, Commander Reeves," the computer answered, cheerfully. "Please follow the stretcher."

With Kane now secured to the gravity stretcher, the device hummed away and quickly exited through the still open double doors. Reeves did as the computer instructed and followed the stretcher until it reached a bank of elevators. The doors of two separate elevators swung open and the stretcher containing Kane hummed inside the nearest car. Reeves followed, but the computer spoke again to call him back.

"Please enter the second elevator," the computer said. "It will bring you directly to the bridge." Reeves hesitated, still staring down at Kane's dying body. "Do not be concerned for your friend," the computer added, softly. "I will take good care of her."

Curiously, the computer's words of reassurance gave Reeves comfort, despite the fact he had no idea what sort of medical skills the AI had, or even if it had a medical facility suitable for treating humans. Yet there was something about the way the computer talked – a familiarity that he couldn't quite place – that meant Reeves instinctively trusted it. Stepping out of the elevator car, he watched Kane until the doors shut, before entering the second elevator.

"We are under attack from three Sa'Nerran Hornet-class attack shuttles," the computer said, as the elevator rapidly ascended to deck one of the compact, Marauder-class Destroyer. "Many of my systems are still resuming from hibernation, and I require your assistance."

"Why don't you just surge?" said Reeves, waiting for the doors to open before hurrying into the corridor outside. He turned right, intuitively knowing where the bridge of the warship was, then pressed on into the command center of the Invictus.

"I lack sufficient fuel to break orbit and there is not enough power to charge the surge field generator," the computer replied. "We will need to subdue the Sa'Nerran threat, then find a place to land."

Reeves moved into the center of the bridge, but it was an eerily empty space where the walls were covered in strange geometric shapes, like the inside of an anechoic chamber. There wasn't even a viewscreen so that he could see where the ship was headed.

"What the hell do you expect me to do in here?" Reeves called out, throwing his hands out wide. "There isn't even a seat."

"Standby, Commander Reeves, I am about to scan your mind," the computer replied, calmly.

"What?" Reeves hit back, shouting up at a blank space

on the ceiling, since there was no focal point to direct his anger toward. "You can stay the hell out of my head. I've studied enough human history to know that sort of tech doesn't end well."

"This is not neural control, Commander," the computer said, again speaking in a calm, reassuring voice. "I am simply analyzing your brain to determine the most suitable environment."

Reeves continued to look around the bizarre space, anxiously waiting for something to happen. He'd expected an evil-looking probe to fly out and stab him with a needle, or for something to drop down from above and clamp itself around his skull, like a medieval head crusher torture device. Suddenly, the bridge began to reconfigure itself. The bizarre geometric shapes morphed into walls with computer consoles and duty stations that Reeves was instantly familiar with. A seat materialized underneath him, scooping him up like a giant hand and molding itself around his body. Finally, the entire front third of the bridge became smooth and curved, like the inside of a concave lens, before the material melted away and was replaced by a panoramic view of the planet. Reeves fought to overcome dizziness and nausea as the ship raced through valleys and across rolling hills, like a jet fighter.

"It seems that you have everything under control, computer, so what do you need me for?" Reeves said, gripping the arms of his seat. The entire experience, while unsettling, had also highlighted just how advanced the Invictus was, and how unnecessary to its functioning Reeves appeared to be.

"I was configured to work in tandem with another mind," the computer said, while powering up a mountainside and blasting over the snow-capped peak. Flashes of plasma from the pursuing Sa'Nerran Hornets zipped past them and Reeves felt another hard impact rumble through the ship. "Your mind is strange, yet familiar. You may take the helm, while I devote my currently limited resources to defensive systems."

Manual controls grew out of the arms of the seat and Reeves suddenly felt like he was back in the cockpit of a fighter training program at the naval academy.

"Are you sure this is a good idea?" Reeves queried, tentatively taking the controls into his hand. "I have no idea how to fly this thing."

However, even as he spoke the words, Reeves realized they weren't true. Everything about the controls that had sprouted around him were familiar, but they were more suited to a twenty-meter-long heavy fighter than a four-hundred-meter destroyer.

"Trust your instincts, Commander," the computer replied, again somehow managing to instill Reeves with more confidence than he had any right to feel. "I will manage the weapons systems. You have control."

"I have control?!" Reeves cried out.

Suddenly, the Invictus lurched downward, and Reeves found himself staring at the icy blue water of an enormous lake.

"I would suggest pulling up," the computer said, though this time Reeves noticed a hint of anxiety in its voice.

"I don't even have any instruments!" Reeves yelled, staring at the controls and trying to switch his brain into fighter-pilot mode.

"Apologies, Commander, look now," said the computer.

Reeves brought his eyes level with the panoramic viewing window and all of the readouts he'd expect to see on a helm control station were now visible. Grabbing the controls, he pulled up hard, cutting a groove through the water as if a giant whale had just breached.

"Where are the readouts coming from?" Reeves said, quickly waving a hand in front of his face. They didn't appear to be holographic in nature.

"I am generating them directly through stimulation of your optic nerves," the computer replied, cheerfully.

Reeves was ready to complain about the computer's continual invasion of his body and mind when two hard thumps rocked the bridge. Looking at his miraculous new scanner readout, he saw that his dallying had allowed the Sa'Nerran Hornets to close on them.

"Shields holding at twenty-one percent," the computer replied. "I suggest we destroy the Hornets as quickly as possible. My energy reserves are approaching critical."

Reeves pushed any further questions or concerns out of his mind, and focused on the imminent danger, not only to the ship, but to his XO, who was still gravely wounded. He flexed his fingers, took hold of the controls and focused ahead.

"Then I guess it's time we find out what a thousand-year-old starship can do," Reeves said, before blowing out a low slow breath and taking control.

Reeves turned the Invictus hard to port and swooped down through a valley. Incredibly, the destroyer handled with the dexterity of a Jinx-class heavy fighter, and the rate of his turn surprised him. Compensating, he threw the Invictus into another turn, cutting through a narrow valley then looping back in an attempt to get on the tail of the Sa'Nerran fighters. The alien vessels had clearly also been surprised by the unfeasible agility of the Invictus and were caught out of position. Reeves powered in behind the nearest fighter, then a reticule appeared over the vessel, as if he had locked on to the ship merely through force of will.

"I have a good lock," said the computer. "Firing..."

A rapid pulse of tightly-focused plasma raced out ahead of the Invictus, and each bolt struck the Sa'Nerran fighter cleanly. There was an intense flash of light as the Hornet exploded, and Reeves turned away to avoid colliding with the debris. However, he then realized there was no debris; the hornet had been all but vaporized.

"Very good, Commander, I believe you're a natural," said the computer. The jovial tenor to its voice then changed to a darker, more ominous tone. "Reserves at seven percent. I am only able to remain in flight for another sixteen minutes. Less if we are required to expend excess energy destroying the remaining fighters."

"I get the message," Reeves said, jinking the ship to throw off one of the two remaining Hornet fighters, then climbing sharply and braking hard to cause the alien vessel to overshoot them. "Just stick to shooting, and let me handle the flying."

"I have forgotten how disagreeable humans can be," the computer replied, huffily.

However, Reeves had stopped listening. Far from the strange and alien-feeling environment that he'd walked into, the Invictus now felt as familiar as an old pair of boots. Even more, he was actually starting to enjoy himself.

"Get ready to fire, I'm going to put this alien asshole right in front of us," Reeves said, weaving a chaotic path through the dark skies of Thrace Colony.

Their trajectory had taken them into the middle of a raging lightning storm, but even the planet's destructive weather was less violent than the Invictus, especially with Reeves at the controls.

"I have a lock," the computer said, as the alien fighter appeared dead ahead, exactly as Reeves had promised. More flashes of plasma raced out and immolated the Sa'N-erran Hornet.

"The final fighter is making a run for it," said Reeves, turning to pursue.

"The storm is disrupting its communications," the computer replied. "It is attempting to get clear so that it can relay our position."

Reeves brought the Invictus level, directly on the Hornet's tail, but he was unable to gain on it. "I need more thrust," he called out. "It's getting away."

"I must reserve engine power to find a suitable landing spot," the computer replied.

"But it's getting away!" Reeves argued. "If that ship exits the storm, it'll just tell the Imperator where we are."

"It will not get away," the computer replied, calmly.

Reeves was about to ask how when a column of energy erupted from the nose section of the Invictus, carving a path across the sky and slicing the Sa'Nerran fighter in two.

"Beam cannons too, I'm starting to like this ship," said Reeves, turning sharply and heading back into the heart of the storm to remain hidden.

"Thank you for the compliment, Commander," the computer replied, cheerfully.

Reeves frowned, wondering what the relationship between the computer and the Invictus was, and whether in essence they were one and the same thing.

"There is a large cave overhang in the mountains north east of our current heading," the computer added. "In addition to my own stealth systems, the metal orcs in the rock will act as an effective shield against orbital scans."

Reeves saw a waypoint marker appear on his nerve-stimulated scanner, and he maneuvered the ship on course. Spotting the location the computer had highlighted, he brought the ship lower and prepared to slot it inside the cave. There was barely enough room for the Invictus, but according to the scans, the Marauder would just about fit inside.

"If you prefer, I will assume piloting duties again," the computer said. To Reeves' ear, it sounded anxious to take back controls.

"No, I've got this," said Reeves, keen to explore just how intuitively the unique controls were. "You relax computer, you've earned it."

"There is very little room for error," the computer replied, now clearly on edge. It was like a driving instructor taking a student out for his very first lesson behind the wheel.

"Relax, computer, I've been flying ships for years," Reeves hit back, beginning the delicate landing maneuver.

"And I have been flying this particular vessel for almost a millennium," the computer answered, more than a little haughtily.

"Then you could use a break, right?" Reeves said.

Their success in destroying the Hornets had given his confidence levels a huge boost, but he was also eager to prove the computer wrong, and show it that he could pilot the ship just as well as the AI could.

"Ten meters..." the computer said, as Reeves teased the vessel deeper inside the cave structure. "Five meters... two meters..." the computer went on, sounding more stressed with each passing second.

Reeves felt a light jolt of feedback through the controls in his chair as he set the ship down and deactivated the engines and thrusters. He checked the close-range scanners and winced.

"I may have dinged the fender a little bit," Reeves said, taking his hands off the controls.

"It is nothing that cannot be hammered out," the computer replied, continuing the analogy. "I am actually impressed. You handled the Invictus with great skill."

Reeves pushed himself out of the seat and peered around the transformed bridge, which appeared to be an amalgamation of all the favorite parts of all the different fighters, corvettes and destroyers that he'd either flown or commanded.

"It's strange, it's like I've known this ship my whole life," Reeves said. He then frowned and stared up at a random spot on the ceiling. "You're not still messing with my mind, are you?"

"I was never messing with your mind, Commander," the computer replied. "In truth, I was glad to escape your thoughts. They reminded me of another, darker time."

Reeves' frown deepened into a scowl, and he was about to question what the computer meant when he suddenly remembered about Kane.

"Wait, how is Major Kane?" Reeves said, hurrying toward the door. "Is she okay?"

"Major Kane's heart stopped beating sixteen seconds ago," the computer replied. This time the AI's voice contained no cheerful nuances; it had spoken the words plainly and without emotion.

Reeves staggered back and just managed to catch the arm of his seat to stop himself falling. He tried to speak, but no words came out. There was just an agonizing pain in his chest, as if in that moment, his own heart had stopped beating too.

CHAPTER 21
RESPIROCYTE TRANSFUSION

IT HAD BARELY BEEN sixty seconds since the computer had dropped the bombshell about Kane's heart stopping, but as Reeves ran out of the elevator toward the medical bay, it felt like hours had already passed. Guided by lights at floor level, he rushed to the medical bay and found Kane lying on a bed in the center of the room. She was surrounded by robotic medical arms and automated instruments that had sprouted from the ceiling and the floor. The rest of the room was barren and resembled the inside of an egg shell, with smooth, curved walls that were so stark it hurt Reeves' eyes to look at them. Kane was lying perfectly still, like she was on a mortuary slab, and he feared the worst. Edging closer, he then heard the familiar bleep of an ECG and was overcome by a wave of relief, realizing that his XO was still alive.

"I am stimulating Major Kane's heart to keep it beating, but her injuries are serious, and she has lost a considerable amount of blood," said the computer. The voice again surrounded him as if the words had been spoken directly into his mind. "This vessel has not carried organic beings for centuries, so I lack the compounds needed to synthesize her lost fluids."

"There must be something you can do?" said Reeves, inching as close to Kane as he could get without interrupting the work of the medical robots.

"There is, though it is a technological, rather than biological, solution," replied the computer.

"I don't care if you use black magic, just do whatever it takes to keep her alive," Reeves hit back. "She's only out here because of me, and I'll be damned if she's dying on my watch."

"Very well, Commander Reeves, I will do what I can," the computer said.

Reeves noted that the AI had come across sounding more serious, like a surgeon who had agreed to perform a delicate and dangerous procedure. The medical bay began to reconfigure itself and Reeves found himself being drawn away from Kane. Confused, he looked down to see that the floor was moving and taking him along with it.

"I am creating a sterile environment around the medical bed," the computer said, as the floor tile below Reeves stopped moving. "Please remain where you are to avoid contamination."

"Just what are you planning to do?" asked Reeves, growing concerned that the computer might actually be acting on his suggestion to use arcane means to save his XO.

"I am replacing Major Kane's blood with a synthetic

fluid containing customized respirocytes," the computer replied.

"I'm not a doctor, so what does that mean in English?" Reeves said, not even bothering to hide his irritation. Tech speak annoyed him, especially when it was slipped in casually, as if he was stupid for not understanding.

"In essence, I am giving her a transfusion of artificial blood," the computer replied, apparently taking no offense at Reeves' snippy comeback. "It will not only save Major Kane's life, but also provide her with a significant advantage over other organic beings. The respirocytes are able to transport orders of magnitude more oxygen around the body than blood, which means that Major Kane will not tire. She will even be able to hold her breath for hours, potentially, with no adverse effects."

Reeves raised an eyebrow toward the ceiling. "She'll be able to hold her breath for hours?" he said, deeply skeptical. "Hours, not minutes?"

"Yes, hours," the computer answered, cheerfully. "Assuming she survives the procedure, of course."

"She'd better survive, because she's only in that bed because you shut us out and threw us to the wolves," Reeves hit back. The casual way in which the computer had described Kane's likelihood of surviving had pissed him off.

"I apologize for the misunderstanding earlier," the computer said, sounding genuinely sincere. "It was only after I finished analyzing your DNA that I realized who you are, or more specifically who you are a descendant of."

"I could have told you that if you'd asked," Reeves said,

still angry at the AI. "Now about Katee's chances of survival; just how bleak are they?"

"If it helps to set your mind at ease, Commander, I estimate a ninety-four-point two percent chance that Major Kane will make a full recovery," the computer answered.

Reeves felt the tension in his muscles ebb, like an over-inflated airbed that was slowly being let down.

"You could have started with that, computer," he said, before breathing out a long slow breath.

The medical robots continued to work, during which time Reeves barely took his eyes off his XO. He and Kane had been in more fights than he could count, and while both of them had suffered injuries, neither of them had ever been wounded seriously. As he watched the living ship replace Kane's blood with a synthetic substitute that would give her super-human abilities, he realized he'd never even considered that either of them might die. Fighting and living to tell the tale had given him a feeling of invincibility. Yet, unlike the ancient AI and Ambassador One, Reeves and Kane were moral, and the Imperator had reminded him of this fact in the most brutal manner possible.

Soon, the rhythmic, mechanical hum of the life support machines and medical robots began to have a soporific effect on Reeves. Combined with the come-down from the massive adrenalin rush he'd experienced; he was feeling weary and tired. Sliding his back down against the smooth, egg-shaped wall, the sound of the machines slowly drifted into the background, like white noise, and he found his eyes starting to close.

"Dalton?"

The voice jolted Reeves awake and he opened his eyes to see Kane standing in front of him. She was dressed in a dark grey uniform, not dissimilar to a Bastion Navy uniform, but without any rank insignia or identifying badges.

"Katee, are you okay?" Reeves said, rubbing his eyes. He realized that the floor and wall that he'd rested against had become soft and were constantly adapting to the shape of his body, like memory foam. "I guess I must have dropped off there for a minute or two," he continued, groggily climbing out of the strange bed that had helped accommodate his need to rest.

"You were asleep for four hours, Commander Reeves."

Reeves turned to the source of the voice and saw another figure standing in the room, dressed in a similar, dark gray uniform to Kane's. The figure was clearly humanoid, but its skin was a matte bronze color, and it was not obviously male or female. The head of the figure resembled that of a shop mannequin, with smooth, sculptured lines and a soft sheen, like marble, that only accentuated the being's shimmering golden eyes.

"Excuse me for being blunt, but who the hell are you?" said Reeves. He'd had enough surprises in the last few hours to last him a lifetime, and this new shock to his senses was not welcome.

"I am Three," the figure answered, cheerfully. "In essence, I am the Invictus."

Reeves rubbed the aching muscles in his neck and shoulders, and briefly considered if Kane and the shimmering android were hallucinations, or if he was still asleep and they were just part of some messed-up dream. Then Kane placed a hand on his shoulder and gently squeezed it, and Reeves knew he was awake, and that they were real.

"Thanks for pulling me out of there, I owe you one," said Kane, smiling at Reeves. She then turned to Three and gave the android a respectful nod. "I owe you as well, though probably a lot more than one. I don't know what you did to me, but somehow I feel fitter and stronger now than ever."

"You are welcome, Major Kane," said Three, returning the gesture of respect. "However, we are still in grave danger. Our priority is to refuel the Invictus so that we are able to return to Concord Station."

Reeves frowned, wondering how the computer knew where they were heading, but Kane was quick to fill in the blanks.

"While you were asleep, I briefed Three on the mission and why the ambassador sent us," Kane explained.

"And you're on board with all this?" asked Reeves.

Reeves hadn't accounted for the fact the Invictus itself would be a unique intelligence, and as such didn't want to assume he could requisition the vessel and its operator without its permission or approval.

"The Sa'Nerra never stopped being a threat, Commander Reeves" Three replied, suddenly taking on a more ominous tone. "One and I searched for them for a long time without success, but Shadow Space was always the one frontier we could not traverse. If the Imperator is being truthful, and these events are guided by the hand of the Progenitors, it is more than just humanity that is at risk. All sentient organic life is under threat."

If the android's speech had intended to refocus Reeves' mind on the mission and motivate him to get back on-task, it had succeeded.

"So, how do we go about refueling the ship if we're stuck inside this cave?" Reeves asked.

"I have a shuttlecraft," Three said, inviting Reeves and Kane to walk with it, before heading out of the medical bay into the similarly anonymous-looking corridor outside. "My scans detected a fuel depot about four hundred kilometers south west of this location. While compact, the shuttle's cargo bay can store enough fuel to allow the Invictus to reach Concord Station."

"What's the catch?" said Kane, beating Reeves to the punch.

"The depot appears to be heavily defended," Three said, confirming Reeves' suspicions. "You will need to employ stealth and subtlety in order to succeed."

Reeves wasn't sure whether this remark was a veiled snub on the less-than-subtle tactics he and Kane had employed while attempting to escape from Lone Water, however he decided to let it slide.

"Are we dealing with just the New Earthers, or are the Sa'Nerra defending the depot too?" asked Kane.

"My scans indicate there are no Sa'Nerra in the vicinity," Three replied. "Though should you attract undue attention to yourself, they will no-doubt make an unwelcome appearance."

"I get it, we have to use stealth," Reeves said, finally

giving in and responding to the AI's implied criticism of their escape plan. "Besides, I'm sure you'll be there to remind us, should it look like we might get trigger-happy."

"I am unable to leave the Invictus," Three, surprising Reeves with its response. "I am an integral part of this vessel, and cannot be separated from it."

"That must get a little claustrophobic?" replied Reeves, continuing to follow the android through the stark white corridors of the thousand-year-old ship.

"Not at all," the android said, charting a course through the ship without even looking where it was going. "This ship is my body, and the entire galaxy is my domain. In fact, I feel sad that organic beings are restricted to the confines of mere planets, unable to experience nebulae and dark matter and the heat of a star as you fly past it."

Reeves snorted a laugh. "Now that you put it that way, I guess it doesn't sound so bad," he admitted.

The android finally led Reeves and Kane into a small shuttle bay. A sleek-looking craft about seven meters long sat on the landing pad. To Reeves' eyes, it looked brand-new, despite the fact it was in all likelihood as ancient as the Invictus was.

"I have programmed the coordinates of the fuel depot into the navigation computer," said Three, as the side hatch of the compact craft hissed open.

Reeves peered inside, finding the interior of the shuttle to be as blank and formless as the bridge of the Invictus had been, prior to the android scanning his brain. He was about to ask how to reconfigure the interior to something he could actually operate, when the shuttle began to reorganize itself.

Kane let out a long-low whistle as the cockpit was generated before their eyes, taking only a matter of seconds to complete.

"That's a neat trick," said Kane, leaning inside the craft and checking out the new interior. "It looks like the cockpit of a Falcon-class attack shuttle," she added, smoothing her hand along the fabric of the seat. "That's so weird, because I was just thinking that this looks about the same size as a Falcon." Kane swung her head out of the shuttle and smiled at Three. "It's like you read my mind."

"It's funny you should say that..." Reeves quipped. His response caused his XO's brow to furrow.

"It is important to note that there are differences between this craft and the vessel Major Kane referred to," said Three, continuing before Kane could ask what Reeves found so amusing.

The android slid into the pilot's seat and activated the reactor start sequence. The shuttle powered up in an instant, and the sudden thrum of its engines caused Reeves to jolt back in surprise and crack his head on the door sill.

"A little warning next time?" Reeves complained, rubbing the fresh bruise.

"A feature of this vessel you may find useful is its stealth field," Three went on, ignoring Reeves' complaint. "When activated, it will manipulate the electromagnetic fields around the vessel in order to obfuscate sensors and remain undetected."

"So it's like our scanner jammers then?" asked Kane.

"Similar, but while it is possible to detect the use of a scanner jamming field, the method used here is harder to uncover," the android replied. "In addition, the shuttle's stealth field is able to manipulate the visible light spectrum, essentially making the vessel difficult to see."

Reeves was impressed, but also wary. "How come no-one else has seen this sort of technology before?" he asked. "Stealth capabilities like this could have been a game-changer in a dozen wars and conflicts over the last few hundred years."

"The computing intelligence required to continually manipulate the EM fields in order to preserve the illusion is far beyond what exists in any of the six realms," replied Three. "While the shuttle itself is not sentient, the fragment of my programming it contains is sufficient to operate a stealth field."

The AI's statement would have sounded arrogant coming from a human, but Reeves detected no pride in the android's voice.

"Basically, you mean our computers are too stupid to make this tech work?" said Kane, smirking.

"Artificial intelligence is common, Major Kane, but true machine sentience has only been achieved a handful of times," the android said, sounding suddenly wise, like an old sage. "First there was One. I am Three."

"What happened to Two?" asked Reeves, though he admitted to being more than a little wary of what the answer might be.

"The second was never given a name, but in any case, it no longer exists," the android said, its tone now colored with a touch of melancholy. "You may have known it by the name, 'Obsidian Soldier', though this entity was unique amongst those creations."

Reeves let out a heavy sigh. Just as everyone on Bastion knew the story of the Omega Taskforce, even if most considered the stories to be mere legends, everyone had also heard of the Obsidian Soldiers. Created to fight the Sa'Nerra, the artificially-intelligent robot soldiers evolved and eventually rebelled against the Omega Taskforce. Reeves recalled that one of these robots had become uniquely self-aware and had challenged Ambassador One, but was defeated. In the years that followed the end of the Sa'Nerran war, an uneasy peace had existed between the remaining Obsidian robots and the emerging Bastion civilization. Then the Obsidian Uprising led to humanity and the remaining robots going their separate ways. It was these events that had prompted the Bastion Federal Government to cease the use and development of all artificial intelligences; a directive that existed to the present day.

"Should your efforts to remain undetected fail, I should also highlight that the shuttle's offensive capabilities are also considerable," Three added, distracting Reeves from thoughts of psychopathic robots. "Its weapons systems are roughly equivalent to the Hornet-class Sa'Nerran fighters we recently encountered."

Three slid out of the cockpit and Reeves dropped into the pilots' seat, which automatically adapted and adjusted to his body, to create a supremely comfortable fit.

"I would encourage you to refrain from employing destructive means, however," the android added. Though the entity lacked eyebrows, Reeves felt sure it would have raised one had they been present.

"Will you stop banging on about us not being stealthy?" Reeves hit back. "We can do stealth, isn't that right, Major?" he added, turning to his XO to back him up.

Kane scrunched up her nose and shrugged. "To be honest, stealth isn't really our forte," she said, shooting the android an apologetic look.

"I see," said Three. Reeves felt sure he saw the android roll its golden, glowing eyes, but he could have been imagining it. "In that case, I will monitor the location of the depot for catastrophic explosions, and assume that if one is detected, you are on your way back."

REEVES AND KANE hunkered down on the on the cliff edge and peered through binoculars at the fuel depot, twenty kilometers away on the valley floor. The depot sat on the outskirts of a small town, which was surrounded by tall mountains like the one they'd landed the compact shuttle on.

"The depot is outside the town's perimeter fence, but security still looks pretty tight," said Kane. "I'm seeing ten guards patrolling the fences and one in each of the four watch towers."

"People must really have a thing for stealing fuel on this planet for there to be security like that," said Reeves, examining the site though his own binoculars.

"It's probably more to stop those horn-headed beasts from breaking in and picking off the workers for lunch," replied Kane. She lowered her binoculars and held out her buzz so that Reeves could see the screen. The display showed a topological map of the area, which was covered with red dots. "Each of these markers is one of those creatures."

Reeves sighed and nodded. With everything else that had happened, the marauding, flesh-eating creatures had slipped to the back of his mind. He counted fourteen red dots on Kane's screen before deciding not to go any further.

"At least it's daytime, not that you'd really know it, and those creatures seem to mostly come out at night," said Reeves, peering up at the grey sky with its angry, swirling, black clouds. Daylight on Thrace was still barely brighter than twilight on Bastion. "I was going to suggest we wait till nightfall to make our move, but you've just changed my mind,"

Kane sat down on the rocks and thrust her legs out in front of her. "Honestly, I don't think it makes a difference what time of day we do this. I can't see how we're getting inside that depot without making a scene."

Reeves used his binoculars to examine the town instead of the depot. A bustling bar on the outskirts of the settlement caught his attention. As he watched, a ground transport trundled through the security gate around the town and swung past the bar, where it briefly stopped to allow its passengers to alight. Reeves enhanced the image and saw that most of them appeared to be wearing the same dark-blue overalls and yellow high-vis jackets as the workers inside the depot.

"I think I might have an idea," he said, hatching the plan on the fly.

"Does it involve stealth?" asked Kane, doubtfully.

"Actually, it does," replied Reeves, surprising even himself with the answer. "It also involves going to a bar."

Kane raised an eyebrow. "Ooh, I like this plan already," she said smiling. "I like the part that involves a bar, anyway. I'll reserve full judgement until you've told me the rest."

As if on-cue, a fuel transporter began to head out of the depot, suspended on powerful anti-gravity repellers, before it turned along a slip-road and accelerated along a highway that cut through the mountains to the north.

"Those transporters carry enough fuel blocks to power the Invictus on a round-trip around the galaxy," Reeves said, pulling the binoculars away from his eyes. "If we can appropriate the clothes and IDs of a couple of those depot workers, we can sneak inside the depot and hijack one of them."

"By 'appropriate', I assume you mean we knock a couple of workers out and steal all their stuff?" said Kane, smiling.

"Yes, but 'appropriate' makes it sound a little less criminal, don't you think?" replied Reeves, also smiling.

"I like your thinking, Dalton, especially the part about going to a bar, but those fuel transporters are hardly inconspicuous," Kane hit back. "There would be a dozen police patrols on our ass long before we got anywhere near the Invictus."

"That's why we're not bringing the transport to the Invictus," said Reeves, feeling smug that he'd already thought of a solution to the flaw Kane had rightly pointed out. "We fly the shuttle down to the valley floor and hide it by the roadside. Its stealth tech means someone would have to actually walk into it to know it was there. Then we roll up in the tanker, quickly fill the shuttle's hold with as many fuel blocks as we can and haul-ass." Reeves smiled and threw his hands out wide, in a 'ta da' moment. "We get the fuel and no-one gets blown up or shot!"

Kane scrunched up her nose and appeared to be in a state of deep contemplation. Eventually she shrugged and smiled.

"Hell, it might actually work," Kane admitted. "But ten credits says that it all goes to shit and we have to blow something up before the day is out."

"I'll take that bet, Major," Reeves said, remaining confident in his plan. "And I'll gladly take your credits too."

Reeves and Kane shook on the wager, like a couple of sports fans betting on which player would score the first points in a game.

"Let's get to it," Reeves said, jumping up and turning back to the shuttle. However, the vessel had gone. "Where the hell did it go?" he called out, his pulse climbing at a rate of knots.

"It's camouflaged, remember?" replied Kane, hurling a rock past Reeves' ear. It struck the stealthed shuttle and the shimmering outline of the vessel became visible for a fraction of a second before it again disappeared.

"How the hell are we supposed to remember where we parked this thing?" said Reeves, tapping a command into his buzz to de-stealth the ship.

"We'll have to set it down somewhere memorable," replied Kane, who was again studying the settlement through her binoculars. "There's a small commercial airport a couple of klicks south of the town. We can set down there with the stealth-field activated then steal a ground transit to reach the bar. It's a straight run from the fuel depot back to the airport."

Reeves switched back to the topological map of the area on his buzz and plotted a route from the depot to the airport. Kane was right on the money, as usual.

"Incredibly, this might actually work," Reeves said, not quite believing it himself. "And I'm definitely looking forward to part one of this scheme."

"That's the part where we hit the bar, right?" said Kane, hopefully.

"More specifically, it's the part where you buy me a drink," Reeves replied, grinning at his XO before sliding into the pilot's seat of the shuttle and powering up the engines.

CHAPTER 23
THE HIGH RIVER HEIST

REEVES CAREFULLY SET down the shuttle behind a disused hangar at the edge of the small airport and powered down the engines. He'd timed his approach to coincide with the arrival of a light air freighter, which had landed on the far runway. The roar of the old and well-used freighter's landing thrusters had more than masked the sound of the shuttle's sophisticated anti-grav repellers. As such, Reeves felt confident that their decent had been stealthy enough to impress even their android friend, Three.

Checking through the cockpit glass to make sure no-one was looking, Reeves grabbed his pistol then popped-open the gull wing door and moved out. Kane jumped out a second later and stashed her pistol into the pocket of her new grey tunic, before closing the door. The shuttle shimmered like a mirage, then vanished before their eyes.

"I think I probably blend in okay around here, but you

look like my old academy commandant," Reeves said, scowling at Kane's uniform.

The one thing they hadn't considered was what they were wearing. Reeves was still in the civilian clothing he'd changed into before heading to Thrace Colony, though it was now scuffed and dirty. Major Kane, however, was wearing the smart, military-style uniform that Three had fabricated for her, after she had recovered from her miraculous, life-saving surgery.

"There's no way your academy commandant looked this good," said Kane, smoothing down the front of her tunic and striking a pose like a catalogue model.

"You're missing the point, Major," replied Reeves, taking a suitably sterner tone. Though, he had to admit that the quality, cut and fit of the uniform was step above the Concord Station garb. "You might look good, but what you need to look is inconspicuous."

"It'll be fine, we can just say I work for the fuel company," Kane hit back, wafting a hand at Reeves dismissively. "Maybe I'm from headquarters, touring the facility to inspect working conditions and employee satisfaction, or some bullshit like that."

"I hope your acting skills are better than your ideas," Reeves commented, reluctantly admitting that they really didn't have a choice. "First things first; we need a ground transit, because I'm sure as hell not walking into town."

Reeves glanced up at the sky, which was still as dark and ominous as it had been before they'd departed the clifftop, twenty kilometers away. However, time had moved on and it was now well into the evening, closer to when the horn-headed beasts preferred to prowl the landscape.

Kane began to walk away, moving out of the cover provided by the disused hangar and into full view of anyone who might have been looking.

"Katee, where the hell are you going?" Reeves called out, speaking in urgent but hushed tones.

"To requisition a transit, of course," Kane replied, frowning at his stupid question. "Just act natural and follow my lead, and no-one will suspect us."

Reeves cursed under his breath then stashed his pistol down the back of his pants and strolled out in pursuit of his smartly-dressed XO, trying to act casual. Suddenly, a small ground transit turned off the main road, kicking up a plume of dust as it did so. A security barrier raised and the transit rolled inside the airport grounds, heading straight for them. Reeves froze but saw that Kane had continued without a care in the world. He followed her, despite his instincts telling him to run for cover. The transit swung around the back of the hangars then pulled into the small parking area that Kane seemed to be heading toward. Heart rate climbing, as if he were about to charge into battle, Reeves drew up alongside his XO as the door to the transit swung open. A middle-aged woman in a suit got out and looked at them.

"Can I help you folks?" she asked, pushing the door of the transit shut. Reeves saw that it had the words, 'High River Airport' written on the side.

"I'm from corporate HQ, here to inspect the facility with my assistant." Kane casually hooked a thumb toward Reeves. "So far, I'm very impressed with your operation, but I thought I'd check out the town and transport links too. It looks like you guys could do with some more investment."

The woman's eyes widened and her cynical glower transformed into a beaming smile. "Oh, well that's great to hear," she said, inspecting Kane's uniform before turning her gaze to Reeves and scrunching up her nose a touch. "We obviously lost a lot of off-world trade after we declared for the separatists, so a cash injection would be welcome. Well, at least until we all ship off to Mars anyway!"

The woman laughed and Kane joined in, though Reeves saw nothing amusing about their situation. However, after Kane gently nudged him with her elbow, he reluctantly added his own brand of strained and obviously faked mirth to the mix.

"Well, if you want to check out the town, you can borrow this transit," the woman said, handing Kane the ID key. "Pass this back to me when you return and I'll sign it back in."

Reeves had to stop himself from shaking his head in disbelief. Kane's easy charm and bluster had actually worked.

"Thanks, I'll be sure to do that," Kane said, still smiling innocently at the woman. "What's your name, for the report I'm writing?"

The woman appeared to grow an inch taller, as if she'd just been bestowed with an honor by the Bastion Federation President himself.

"I'm Hilary Nox, Safety and Compliance Manager

here at High River Airport," the woman announced, proudly.

"Nice to meet you, Hilary, I'll be sure to put in a good word with the board," said Kane. She then breezed past the woman and opened the door of the transit, before turning to Reeves with an expectant look on her face. "Come on then, snap to it," she said, in a bossy, schoolteacher-like tone. "We don't have all day."

Reeves' scowl was now so deep it was hurting his face. "Yes, I'm just coming," he replied, as humbly as he could manage, though he was aware he sounded more peevish than obedient.

Moving around to the opposite side of the transit, Reeves pulled open the passenger door and slid into the seat. Kane dropped into the driver's seat a moment later and slammed the door. She was the personification of smugness.

"Go on, I know you're dying to tell me how good I am," she grinned.

"Okay, that was pretty good," Reeves admitted. "I can't believe Hilary just went along with it, though."

"This part of the airport is cordoned off with a security fence," said Kane, inspecting the transport's controls in preparation to drive away. "The shuttle's stealth tech got us in undetected, making it look like we'd already passed the relevant security checks, so Hilary had no reason to suspect we weren't legit." She shrugged. "Plus, I'm a great actor."

"Great liar more like," Reeves hit back, huffing a laugh. "But if you really want to impress me, let's see you talk your way into that bar without anyone suspecting us."

"Are you proposing another wager?" Kane replied, looking at Reeves with hungry eyes, as if he was an easy mark, rich for the picking.

"Another ten credits?" Reeves said. Sense told him that the bet was a bad one, but he couldn't back down now.

"You're on," replied Kane, still beaming at him.

She started the transit's motor and accelerated out of the airport like she was a bandit on the run from the law. A plume of chalky dust billowed up from the rear of the vehicle, slowly floating across the airport before consuming the Safety and Compliance Manager of High River Airport, as she merrily waved them goodbye.

CHAPTER 24
KATEE KANE'S CON

KANE HID the transit down a side street a block away from the bar, in the event that Hilary Nox worked out she'd been duped and sent the local law enforcers looking for it. Walking the rest of the way to the bar, Reeves was aware that his XO was drawing curious and often mystified looks from passersby on account of her unique outfit. The stares only became more intense as Kane pushed through the door to the bar and strolled inside as if she owned the place.

"Fancy dress day is tomorrow, sweetheart," one of the patrons at the bar called out, to a muted ripple of laughter from other drinkers nearby.

Reeves studied the heckler, taking an instant dislike to him. The man appeared to be in his mid-thirties, though his thin, weaselly face and scraggy hair made him look older.

"Or maybe you were looking for the posh bars here in Tanker's Gulf?" The weaselly man added, before snapping his fingers. "Oh, wait, there are no posh bars in this shithole town!" There was another ripple of laughter, this time a little louder.

"I'm right where I'm supposed to be," said Kane, retaining her bright, cheerful expression despite the passive-aggressive comments from the heckler. "Assuming this is the bar where the workforce from the fuel depot come to drink, right?"

"No, sweetheart, I just like to wear these overalls for fun," the weasely man replied, gesturing to his dirty blue boilersuit and high-vis vest. The reaction to this latest quip was even more energetic. He appeared to be feeding off the crowd and growing in confidence.

"That's a shame, because if you don't work at the depot then you won't be getting the bonus payout I'm putting through for the workforce of Tanker's Gulf," said Kane, in a casual, off-hand manner.

Reeves raised an eyebrow then watched his XO turn to the barman and tap a finger on the counter. The barman, who was a bald-headed titan of a man with a face that could sour milk, frowned at Kane before snatching a dark brown bottle of ale from a fridge. The man tore off the cap with his hands and slammed it down on the counter in front of her.

"What bonus payout?" said a thin man standing to Kane's other side. The mention of money had silenced the jeers and cackles like a gunshot being fired into the ceiling.

"The payout for the hardest working site in the region," replied Kane, answering the question as if it was obvious. "I've inspected the depot in Tanker's Gulf and looked at your records, and you folks have been doing great work."

"And who might you be, miss?" the thin man continued. He was older than the worker who had chosen to be an asshole, and when he spoke, the others quietened down and listened.

"I'm Paige Turner, Senior VP of Human Resources," Kane replied, keeping a perfectly straight face, despite the ridiculous made-up name. "I'm going to run this by corporate comms and make sure the entire organization knows that hard work pays off."

Encouraged by Kane's early success, and intrigued to know where she was going next, Reeves sidled up to the bar a few meters away, giving Kane room to work her audience. He hadn't pegged her as someone who could play a con, but at that moment Kane almost had him convinced she was a fuel company exec.

"Just how much of a bonus are we talking about?" the thinner man continued. The worker still sounded suspicious, but it was clear to Reeves that Kane had hooked her fish.

"An extra twenty percent, backdated for the last quarter," Kane said, before taking a swig from the bottle of ale. A murmur went up from the workers in the bar, though instead of unkind laughter, this was a wave of cheers.

"Well, that's good to hear," the thin man replied, sounding more enthusiastic despite still not smiling. "I've been telling management for months that they either need to cut us some slack, or pay us for all the extra work. Since breaking off from the Federation, interstellar trade has fallen off a cliff and fuel demand has plummeted. They let twenty-five percent of my guys go last week, and increased the shifts for the others, without adding extra paid overtime."

There was chorus of agreement from the drinkers in the bar. Kane had inadvertently struck a chord with the workers, and seemed to be pulling off her ruse. Quite where she was going with it, however, Reeves still had no idea.

"If you don't mind, though, I'd like to confirm this story of yours," the thin man added, remaining cagey. "If you don't mind me saying so, lady, it sounds a little too good to be true."

"Of course, you got it," replied Kane, throwing up her hands and smiling at the man as if his request was no big deal. "I've got a transit parked a block away. If you fancy taking a ride, I'll run you up to local management now, so you can see that this is all above board."

The thin man scowled at Kane for a few seconds, chewing the inside of his mouth as he did so. "Okay, let's take a ride," he said, sliding off his stool. "And if this checks out, the next round is on me."

There was another cheer from the drinkers in the bar, and Reeves watched as Kane followed the thin man toward the exit.

"I'll leave my associate, Mr. Dingwallace, here while we're gone," Kane said, pointing to Reeves while strutting away from the bar.

Reeves scowled back at her. She was clearly enjoying herself, though the use of farcical names risked exposing her ploy, and he for one didn't want to get stranded in a bar full of angry fuel depot workers.

"In the meantime, open a tab on the company, and enjoy yourselves!" Kane added, shouting the invitation loud enough that everyone in the bar could hear her.

There was another roar of approval as Kane disappeared out of the door, flashing her eyes at Reeves. He cursed under his breath, realizing that while Kane had caught herself a fish, he'd been left to find his own way to snag himself a worker's uniform.

"What a crock of shit," the weaselly man suddenly called, though he'd now lost the support of his audience, who were busily ordering drinks. "That fancy tart won't get us squat from the company. It's just some PR bullshit, if you ask me. Us drivers haven't had an extra credit on our paychecks for years."

The weaselly man was jostled and jeered for his pessimistic suggestion, causing the worker's mood to sour further. Cursing and muttering under his breath, the man huffily slipped off his stool and shoved past Reeves, making a bee-line for the rest-room. Ordinarily, Reeves would have taken umbrage with someone so rudely barging him out of the way, but he'd just found a reason to like the disagreeable, weasel-faced worker. The man had identified himself as a transporter driver.

"I'm going to the can to work on something more important," the weaselly man announced, while pushing open the rest-room door, though no-one was now listening to him.

Reeves had sized up the worker as he'd jostled past. The man was a little taller than he was, but the boiler suits were loose fitting enough that the difference wouldn't be noticeable. He then realized that the worker had left his wallet on the counter in front of his bar stool. Reeves made sure no-one was looking – which was helped by the frantic scramble to order more drinks – then slipped the wallet off the bar, removed the man's credits payment card, and pocketed the rest. Suddenly, the hulking, bald-headed frame of the barman appeared in front of him, and Reeves' heart-rate spiked, fearing that he'd just been caught red-handed.

"I'm going to need some kind of down-payment to cover all these drinks, pal," the barman said, glowering at Reeves in the particular manner that only veteran bar owners can achieve.

"Put this round on my personal account," Reeves replied, slapping the stolen payment card onto the counter. "I'll just head out to my transit and grab the company card for the rest."

The barman scowled, but took the card, and Reeves didn't hang around to make sure it worked. Jostling his way through the advancing horde of fuel depot workers, he pushed through the door to the rest room, nodding and smiling to a worker who was already on his way out. Dropping to a crouch, he then checked underneath the doors of the cubicles, spotting only a single pair of feet, surrounded by a crumpled mass of blue fabric. The unmistakable sound of straining was emanating from the occupied cubicle. The grunting and groaning noises were only slightly more palatable than the smell, which rivaled the stench of a Sa'Nerran warrior's breath.

Snapping the handle of the door to the rest room, Reeves marched in front of the cubicle and launched a kick at the feeble-looking lock mechanism. The door flew off its hinges and smashed into the weaselly worker, first crashing into the man's knees then clubbing him over the head a millisecond later. Reeves picked up the now dented slab of metal and wedged it between the end cubicle and the rest-room door, jamming it shut in the process.

"I'm afraid you won't be getting your bonus, asshole," Reeves said to the unconscious worker, as he slipped the overalls out from beneath the man's feet.

Suddenly, Reeves heard the sound of another door swinging open. Cursing, he jolted out of the cubicle, but his makeshift barricade was still in place.

"What the hell is going on here?" a voice boomed into the room.

Reeves spun around to find a barrel-chested man with a beard as long as his forearm standing at the other end of the restroom. It was only then that he noticed there were two entrances into the room, and that he'd missed the one leading into the main saloon.

"I asked you a question, shithead," the man continued, stomping toward Reeves, fists clenched.

The worker was a solid six-five, Reeves guessed, and easily three-fifty pounds, even without the added mass of the man's beard.

"I'm just inspecting the rest-rooms," Reeves said, though he was painfully aware that his ability to invent lies on the spot was sorely lacking compared to his creative XO. "And I've discovered that you have a quite significant blockage."

Reeves pointed to the unconscious man, who was now

partly wedged inside the toilet bowl, and the huge worker's eyes widened. The weaselly man would have simply looked like he'd passed out drunk while sat on the toilet, were it not for the fact he was bizarrely naked, bar his socks and a grubby white undershirt. The bearded man's eyes returned to Reeves before spotting the bundle of clothes he was still carrying.

"So you think you're a funny guy, huh?" the worker said clenching his fists and taking another pace toward Reeves. "Let's see how funny you find this..."

The man swung a massive right hand at Reeves, but what the worker possessed in strength, he lacked in finesse. Reeves dropped the overalls and caught the punch with his left hand then squeezed the worker's fist as hard as he could. The crack of bone and cartilage was masked by the man's howls, which were quickly silenced as Reeves countered with a punch of his own. Striking the goliath in his sizable gut, Reeves sent the man down, kneeling at Reeves' feet like a worshiper praying at an altar. He picked up the overalls and was about to leave, when we realized he hadn't yet obtained one of the high-vis jackets. Pulling the bright orange vest over the head of the man at his knees, Reeves added the garment to the bundle then made a hasty exit through the door to the saloon. Another worker was already heading toward the rest-room, but Reeves grabbed the man's shoulder and stopped him in his tracks.

"I'd give it a few minutes, if I was you," said Reeves, shooting the man a serious look. "Trust me, you don't want to go in there."

The worker scowled at Reeves, but he didn't allow time

for the man to question him, before setting off at a rapid pace toward the exit. Pushing through the main door and onto the street outside, Reeves heard shouts and cries rise up inside the bar, and he cursed, realizing his handiwork had been discovered. He looked around for Kane, but his XO was nowhere to be seen. Suddenly, the double doors to the bar flung open and a mob of fuel depot workers stormed outside. Reeves immediately recognized one of them as the man he'd tried to stop from entering the rest-room.

"That's him, he's the one who did it!" the worker yelled, stabbing an angry fist at Reeves.

Reeves counted at least a dozen workers already outside, and knew there was no way to subdue them all, or outrun them on foot. Reaching behind his back, he closed his hand around the grip of his plasma pistol, which was still tucked down the back of his pants.

"Sorry, Three, but it looks like I'm going to have to make a scene, after all," he said out loud, pulling the pistol out of his waistband. However, he was more bothered about losing the bet and the credits to Kane than he was about proving the sentient AI correct.

The workers advanced and Reeves was about to fire a warning shot into the air, when the roar of a motor drowned out the shouts from the angry mob. A ground transit sped around the corner, clipping the side of another parked transit as it did so, before pulling to a stop next to Reeves. The door flung open and he saw Kane in the driver's seat, already wearing blue overalls and a high-vis vest.

"Need a ride?" said Kane, smiling at Reeves.

Reeves turned and dove inside the transit as the workers descended on the vehicle like a pack of hungry wolves. Hands grabbed at his feet and ankles, but Reeves managed to kick them away and pull the door shut. Suddenly, the barman stepped out into the road, holding what looked like a traditional firearm. It was the size of a rifle, but had two enormous barrels as wide as eyeballs.

"Get down!" Reeves yelled, grabbing Kane and dragging her head out of the firing line. The windshield of the transit smashed and fragments of glass rained down over him. Kane shot up then floored the accelerator, ploughing the little transit through the barman and sending the man's hulking frame clattering over the roof and onto the street behind them. Bottles were flung at the transit, but they all smashed harmlessly into the road as Kane wrestled the vehicle down a side street and out of sight of the mob.

"I think that went quite well, all things considered," said Kane, ruffling her hair to shake loose the fragments of glass that were lodged in it.

Reeves laughed. "I guess we didn't blow anything up, so we're still sort of acting stealthily," he said, though he doubted Three would have agreed with him.

"I'd get changed quickly," Kane added, patting her hand onto the bundle of clothes that were sprawled out inside the cabin. "We're going to need to hijack a transporter soon, before that mob comes looking for us or raises the alarm."

Reeves grabbed the boiler suit then slid into the rear seat and began to remove his tattered civilian clothes.

"You owe me ten credits, by the way," Kane added, peeking at Reeves in the rear-view screen.

"You got lucky this time," Reeves replied, slipping off his pants. Kane wolf-whistled as he did so. "Besides, it's Mr. Dingwallace that owes you the credits, not me."

Kane snorted a laugh then looked over her shoulder and beamed a smile at Reeves. "Admit it, my plan worked," she said, slowing the transit to a more sensible pace and heading for the security gate that led out of town.

"Getting these outfits was the easy part," Reeves replied, zipping up the boiler suit then sliding back into the front seat. The depot was already visible in the distance, and the sight of it sobered him up in flash. "The hard part is what comes next."

CHAPTER 25
DANGEROUS DRIVING

Reeves glanced anxiously at the fuel depot, which was just over fifty meters away from where they'd stopped the transit by the side of the road, feigning motor trouble. Katee Kane was sprawled out on the floor inside, head tucked underneath the driver's side console with her feet pushed up on the seats. She'd already stripped part of the trim away and was busy working on the mass of circuits and wires beneath it.

"How much longer is this going to take?" Reeves asked his XO.

"I should be done in a minute," Kane called back, her voice strained from the effort of maintaining her contorted position.

"And you're sure this will work?" Reeves added, returning to anxiously scanning the border fence of the fuel depot.

"It'll work, alright," Kane replied, sliding herself out

from inside the footwell. "I just hope it doesn't take the whole damned depot out with it."

Reeves helped extricate her from the transit then she stood next to him, blowing out her cheeks and dusting off her hands. Through the window of the transit, he could now see the fruits of her labors.

"We only need to create a distraction, not an extinction level explosion," Reeves said, waiting for Kane to catch her breath.

"It will be distracting, that I can promise," Kane replied, smiling.

Reeves could see that a couple of the guards on the border fence had gotten together. One appeared to be looking at them through binoculars, while the other was speaking into a comms handset.

"I think we've been noticed, so let's head out before they decide to send a security patrol to check on us," said Reeves. "We need to get as close as we can to the main gate, before springing our little surprise."

Reeves and Kane set out on foot toward the fuel depot, leaving their transit by the roadside, with the hood still popped open. The vehicle used a variant of the fuel cells that he and Kane needed to steal from the depot in order to replenish the Invictus. The cells were ordinarily robust and resilient to physical damage, fire and other dangers. However, with the correct know-how, it was possible to wire the power section in such a way as to cause the cells to fail, often with catastrophic results.

"Now?" asked Kane, as they advanced to within twenty

meters of the barrier. Reeves could now clearly see the armed guards on the fence watching them closely.

"Not yet, wait till we're almost at the checkpoint roadblock, just before the main gate," Reeves said, turning his attention away from the guards and inside the main yard behind the fence. Three fuel transporters were waiting inside. One appeared to be fully loaded, while the other two had returned empty.

"I hope we don't have to run. These boiler suits chafe like a bitch," said Kane, filling the tense silence with her usual brand of sardonic humor.

"Just make sure you can still reach your pistol easily," Reeves answered.

The checkpoint control post in front of the main gate was now directly ahead of them. The guard on duty was looking at Reeves and marching out to head them off.

"What are you two doing outside on foot?" the guard said, dispensing with any pleasantries. "You know that workers have to enter and exit using the official transits. Unless you want to get eaten by one of the horns."

"We're inspectors from out of town," Reeves replied, telling the guard the story that he and Kane had agreed while traveling to the depot. "Our transit cut out a couple of hundred meters away," he added, hooking his thumb in the direction of the vehicle. "We're expected, though, so if you'd just let us through, we'll be on our way."

"I'll have to clear it," the guard grunted. His tone and body language were aggressive. "And I'll need your IDs." He held out an outstretched hand toward Reeves, while plucking a comms handset out of the guard tower with the other.

"Now?" asked Kane, with hopeful eyes.

Reeves nodded. "Now..."

Kane activated her buzz and entered two quick commands. A second later the ground transit that they'd sabotaged and abandoned detonated. Kane had not been exaggerating when she'd said the explosion would be distracting. The fireball alone would have consumed the entire bar in the town they'd just left, while the shock wave was powerful enough to blow back Kane's hair, like she'd been hit by a strong gust of wind. Dust and smoke billowed out from the detonation site, and Reeves and Kane used the cover it provided to slip around the rear of the checkpoint. The guard had already forgotten about them, and was speaking urgently into his comms handset, while shielding his eyes from the noxious cloud enveloping him. Alarms began to wail inside the depot then, as expected, the gates began to trundle open. The sound of sirens was added to the wail of alarms, then a fire truck hummed through the gate and began accelerating toward the burning transit.

"Now, let's move," Reeves said, slapping Kane on the back.

Reeves set off at a sprint, though the smoke in his lungs was making it harder to run. Kane, however, appeared to be barely affected by the cloud of dust and noxious gases, and made it into the compound in half the time it took Reeves to struggle inside.

"That techno-blood the android pumped you full of

seems to be doing the trick," Reeves observed, coughing and wiping dark mucus onto his sleeve. There was chaos inside the depot, and no-one seemed to have seen them run through the gates.

"Now I know how it feels to be super-human, like you," said Kane, smiling.

"What the hell are you two doing?"

Reeves spun around to see a gruff-looking older man standing behind him. Unlike the blue boiler suit that he and his XO were wearing, this worker's overalls were a dark red color.

"And where the hell are your hard hats?" the man added. A secondary explosion from the burning transit then caused the man to flinch and curse out loud. "Never mind, just get inside with the others."

The older worker ran outside the gate and joined a group that appeared to have congregated to assess what had happened. The gate slowly began to trundle shut again.

"So far so good," said Reeves, glancing further into the compound at the three waiting fuel transits. "Now we just need to steal one of these things."

"I'm driving..." said Kane, beating Reeves to the loaded transport.

"So long as you know how to drive this contraption," Reeves called after her, still struggling to run due to the smoke in his lungs.

"I can fly a space fighter; how hard can it be?" Kane hit back, jumping up on the transport's side sills then pulling open the door.

Reeves ran to the passenger side door and climbed inside the cabin. Slamming the door shut, he skimmed his eyes across the console and realized that he didn't have the first clue how to operate the truck-sized vehicle. Glancing over to Kane, it was clear that she was equally clueless.

"I'll figure it out," Kane blustered, hurriedly examining the controls and switchgear in front of her.

Two workers outside appeared to notice Reeves and Kane inside the transport and began jogging over to them. Both wore the same dark red overalls as the older man they'd met earlier.

"Figure it out quickly," said Reeves, as the men ran up to the side of his door and hammered their knuckles onto it.

"We're on alert, you can't take this out!" one of the men yelled at Reeves through the window. Reeves pretended that he couldn't hear him, which only encouraged the man to step onto the sill and pull open the door. "I said get the hell out of this transport and get inside. You know the rules!"

"Ah, I've got it!" Kane shouted, turning to Reeves with a broad smile on her face. "But I think we need a key."

"Are you morons deaf?" the man in the red overalls growled. "Get out now, or I'll have security drag you out!"

"I'm sorry," said Reeves, shuffling in his seat so that he was facing the man.

"You'll be sorry when you lose your job!" the worker yelled, going increasingly red-faced to match his uniform.

"No, I'm sorry for this," Reeves replied, before kicking the man hard in the chest.

The worker was propelled off the door sill and sent cannonballing through his co-worker. Both men ended up in a crumpled heap on the ground alongside one of the empty transporters. Slamming the door, Reeves rummaged inside his overalls for the wallet he'd stolen from the weaselly transport driver in the bar. He flicked through the contents, which included three calling cards for local 'massage therapists', two used toothpicks, an old motel-room key and a receipt from a burger bar for two double cheeseburgers with extra pickle and no cheese. Shaking his head at the sheer stupidity of the weasel-faced man, he finally found an ID card and handed it to Kane, before tossing the wallet to the rear of the cab.

"Try that," Reeves said, as Kane took the card and scowled at it. "I took it from a guy in the bar who said he was a transporter driver."

"Do I want to know how you got this off him?" Kane asked, eyebrow raised, while looking for somewhere to slot in or press the card to.

"I followed him to the rest room and kicked in the door while he was taking a crap," Reeves answered, straight-faced.

Kane laughed before realizing that he wasn't joking. "I thought we weren't supposed to be creating a scene," she retorted.

"I think it's a little late for that." Reeves watched the plume of smoke from the burning transit car billowing into the murky-grey sky.

Kane pushed the ID card into a slot on the console and the dashboard powered up. "Bingo!" she called out, before hitting the start button to bring the huge transport's powerful motor online. "How do you propose we get out of the compound?"

Reeves sucked in a deep breath and sighed. "Like you said, it's a little late for not making a scene," he said, staring at the gate directly ahead. Then he turned to Kane and smiled. "Floor it..."

Kane returned Reeves' smile then gripped the wheel of the transit and fixed her eyes on the road ahead. Reeves pulled his plasma pistol out of his overalls then gripped the grab-handle on the A-pillar. Kane pressed the accelerator to the floor and the transit lurched forward, accelerating at a rate that belied its hulking size. Fuel depot workers frantically waved their hands before running or being forced to dive out of the transporter's path. Reeves gritted his teeth and moments later the vehicle crashed through the gate, smashing it open like it had been made of aluminum foil and breadsticks. Reeves and Kane were bounced and jostled around in the cabin as the transporter raced over the remains of the gate, which thumped and scraped against the undercarriage of the vehicle's gravity-repelling propulsion system. Once the ride had smoothed out again, Reeves wound down the window and craned his neck outside. The rush of cold air across his face was a welcome tonic, but he knew it was too soon to celebrate. They may have successfully broken out of the compound in a fully-loaded fuel transporter, but now every law-enforcement officer in the town of Tanker's Gulf, and perhaps beyond, would be coming for them in force.

"We've already got company..." Kane called out,

looking at the rear-view screen that showed a panoramic image from the back of the transit.

"That was quick," said Reeves, again craning his neck out of the window to get a better look. Cursing, he saw two drones buzzing after them. "They're going to try to get ahead of us and drop gravity stingers on the road ahead."

"If they do that then we're dead in the water, and we still have a couple of kliks to go before reaching the shuttle," Kane called back. The transport was already traveling so fast that the cabin was shaking and juddering, like a car driving over a cattle guard.

"Stay on course, I'll take them out," said Reeves, tightening his hold on his pistol then throwing open the transporter's door. Forgetting his strength, the door was ripped off its hinges and went cartwheeling along the road behind them.

"That's not going to be cheap to fix," quipped Kane. Because of the juddery ride it sounded like someone was drumming fists onto her back.

"Just hold it steady," Reeves replied, climbing out onto the sill and aiming his pistol at the drones.

Reeves' strength allowed him to keep a steady hold on the handrails, but the buffeting effect of the air rushing past still made it difficult to aim. Squeezing the trigger, he sent a blast sailing past the lead drone, which jinked in an effort to avoid the shot. Cursing again, Reeves adjusted his aim and fired a second shot, this time striking the flyer dead in its center. It exploded like a firework and sent a stream of fiery debris crashing down on the road.

"Nice shot!" Kane said. She was watching in the rear-view screen. The broad smile hadn't left her face since the moment she'd started up the huge transporter.

Reeves shot at the second drone, but this too jinked out of the way then put on a rapid burst of speed. Adjusting his already precarious position on the door sill of the trans- porter, Reeves tracked the flyer and fired again, but his shot sailed wide.

"Dalton, it's gotten ahead of us," Kane called out.

"I can see that," Reeves hit back, though he was frus- trated at missing his shots, rather than at Kane stating the obvious.

Reeves aimed and fired a third shot at the drone, but this too sailed wide, missing by mere inches. Then the flyer opened a compartment on its belly and Reeves cursed again.

"Veer right!" Reeves yelled, as the drone dropped a gravity stinger onto the road directly ahead of them.

The transporter lurched to the right, catching Reeves off guard. His foot slipped off the door sill and instinctively he dropped his pistol to grab hold of another handrail on the side of the cab. The vehicle then swerved left, completing it high-speed jink, and Reeves was sent thumping into the side of the cabin. The motor faltered and Reeves felt the far side of the transport drop and grind across the road before suddenly righting itself again.

"That was close," Kane called out, breathless. The stinger disrupted the repellers, but didn't disable them.

"Next time we won't be so lucky," Reeves replied, pulling himself inside the cab as the drone hovered away.

Kane seemed to notice that Reeves was no longer

armed and took one hand off the wheel in order to remove her own pistol. Her knuckles were almost completely drained of blood from the pressure of steering the transit at high-speed.

"That's our only weapon, so don't lose it," she said, her expression suddenly deadly serious. The near-miss had wiped the smile off her face.

Reeves grabbed the pistol then pulled himself back out onto the door-sill. The remaining drone was still following them, and he guessed it was reloading, ready to deploy a second stinger. Taking aim at the flyer, he squeezed the trigger and blasted the drone out of the sky.

"It would have been nice if you'd done that thirty seconds earlier," Kane said, eyebrow-raised but eyes still fixed on the road.

"Just concentrate on driving, and let me do the shooting," Reeves hit back.

Then, far ahead of them, Reeves saw red and blue flashing lights pulsing against the angry sky. Ducking back into the cab, he quickly checked his buzz.

"Damn it, that's a police interceptor," Reeves said, while dialing the power level of the pistol up to maximum. "How far are we from the shuttle?"

"I'd say it's about a hundred meters or so past where we're going to meet that interceptor," Kane replied, her eyes flicking from the road ahead to the nav map on the dashboard in rapid, staccato movements.

Reeves saw on his buzz that the interceptor had armed its weapons. He had no idea what kind of laws were in force on the separatist planet of Thrace Colony. However, it seemed clear that stealing a transporter containing fuel cells worth a quarter of a million credits was not considered a trivial crime.

"I think it's time we made another scene," said Reeves, grabbing the hand-rail, swinging out onto the door sill and aiming his pistol at the Interceptor. "Whatever happens, keep that accelerator floored."

"Aye, sir..." Kane replied, pushing the transport as hard as it could possibly go. Her whole body was shaking and her eyes had grown wide with fear. He'd seen a similar look before, when they were about to crash-land the Bukkan pirate shuttle on the planet. They'd survived that event by the skin of their teeth, and they were about to roll the dice again.

Reeves squeezed the trigger and sent a blast racing toward the interceptor. It struck the police cruiser on the nose and he saw the vehicle veer to the side. He fired again, hitting the interceptor for a second time, causing electrical sparks and debris to rain down from the flying vehicle. The interceptor returned fire and the transport was hit hard below the windscreen. Kane wrestled with the wheel as the vehicle began to fish tail along the road. Screens and consoles blew out on the dashboard and Reeves could feel the transit bottoming out on the road as the repellers faltered.

Gritting his teeth, he waited for Kane to regain control, then squeezed the trigger three times in rapid succession. The first two blasts hit the interceptor, dealing significant damage, but the third melted the barrel of the pistol, which was glowing red hot. The heat rapidly spread into Reeves' hand and he dropped the weapon over the edge, cursing and shaking the pain from his throbbing palm. The first two shots had been enough to put the interceptor out of commission, and it was going down. However, before it crashed into the side of the road, the police vehicle managed to get off a final shot. The blast thumped into the side of the cabin and Kane was rocked hard. Reeves felt his gut tighten into a knot as her head thumped into the steering column, but then breathed a sigh of relief as she pulled herself up, blood leaking from a cut above her eye.

"We're losing power," Kane called out. "That interceptor hit us hard."

"Keep it going for as long as you can, the airport is just up ahead," replied Reeves, pointing at the cluster of hangars, behind which the Invictus' combat shuttle was hidden in stealth mode.

"We won't have long to transfer the cells over and get the hell out of here," Kane said, steering the near-crippled transport toward the airport.

"We only need enough cells to get us off this rock and back to Concord," replied Reeves.

Alarms began to wail inside the cabin. He tried to find the cause of the alert, but with the majority of the screens and indicators on the dashboard already smashed and burning, there was no way to tell. Then the transporter began to stutter, like a car on the verge of stalling, and he knew their journey was coming to an end.

"Turn off the road, now," Reeves said, reaching across Kane and fastening her harness.

"We're not at the airport turn-off yet," Kane said, eyes still fixed ahead.

"We won't make the turning," Reeves answered, fastening his own harness. "Just make your own road, while we still have power."

Kane nodded, blew out her cheeks and swerved the massive transporter in the direction of the hangars. Smashing the through the barriers at the side of the road, the vehicle flew through the air for a few seconds before thumping into the grassland on the other side. The repellers just managed to give the transport enough lift to prevent it from burying itself in the dirt, but Reeves could feel that the machine was dying. Less than fifty meters from the hangar, the repellers failed, plunging the nose of the vehicle into the hard, stony ground. Kane pumped the brakes, but it was no use; the course of the transporter was now governed purely by the laws of physics. Reeves grabbed the handrails again, while Kane braced herself against the wheel as the transport ploughed through security fences then into one of the hangars. Metal and girders punched through the windshield, almost spearing Reeves like a fish. Then the vehicle lolled to the side, groaning like an old ship, and came to rest.

For a few moments, Reeves and Kane just sat in the cabin, breathless, motionless, as glass rained down around them. Then dust began to settle on the shape of a spacecraft, parked achingly close to them. He met Kane's eyes, and there was an instant understanding between them.

They'd diced with death and won, and now they had to capitalize on their victory as swiftly as possible. Without another word spoken between them, they both threw off their harness, jumped outside and started to the load the precious fuel cells onto their shuttle.

CHAPTER 26
SIX ON ONE

REEVES RESTED against one of the Invictus' front landing struts and blew out a weary sigh. Thanks to the shuttle's stealth tech, they'd made it back to the Marauder-class Destroyer without being detected, despite twenty more police interceptors joining the hunt. However, manually unloading and replacing the spent fuel cells in the Invictus was a task he hadn't counted on. Even his genetically-enhanced muscles were tired, but the work had knocked the wind out of him more than it had made his muscles ache. Major Kane, on the other hand, showed no signs of fatigue, thanks to the respirocytes in her synthetic blood. And Three, being a sentient android, naturally did not tire at all. It was almost unheard of for Reeves to be the physically inferior member of any group, whether human or alien, but at that moment, he felt beat.

"Congratulations, the fuel cells you managed to retrieve are sufficient for the return journey to Concord

Station," said Three, standing at the base of the Invictus' rear ramp.

"I don't suppose you still have showers on this ship?" Reeves said, pushing away from the landing strut and turning to the android. "I could really use a wash and a change of clothes."

"Yes, the secretions from your eccrine and apocrine glands have combined with the bacteria on your skin to produce an unpleasantly pungent odor," Three replied.

Kane, who was reclined in the pilot's seat of the shuttle, snorted a laugh. "In other words, you stink," she called out, grinning.

"Thank you for that assessment, Major."

Unfortunately, Reeves knew that any attempt to assert his authority while wearing torn and sweat-stained clothing and stinking to high-heaven was pointless.

"To answer your question, the Invictus no-longer contains liquid water showers, though I will endeavor to fabricate some," Three said, cutting back in. "I will first need to create a sustainable water-production facility, which I will do once I am restored to full power on Concord Station."

"How about a new set of clothes then?" Reeves asked, determined to find some way to update his disheveled appearance. "Something slick, like the major is wearing."

"I will fabricate you some new clothes, and also sanitize your body prior to you putting them on," Three replied.

Reeves scowled at the android, curious and also more than a little concerned to learn how it planned to 'sanitize' him. However, before he could ask the question a roar began to thunder down the valley. Reeves ran out from underneath the ship and saw three Sa'Nerran Skirmishers pass overhead in a vee formation.

"It's a good bet they're out looking for us," Reeves said, watching the alien craft bank right and begin another sweep of the area.

"That is correct," Three said, appearing beside Reeves, along with Major Kane, who was no longer smiling. "I estimate that they will discover our location in approximately nineteen standard minutes."

"Then we'd better get moving," said Reeves, turning back to the android.

"I concur," Three replied.

At the same time, the shuttle's gull-wing doors closed and the craft began to pilot itself back inside the Invictus. Reeves wondered if it could have been Three doing the piloting remotely; the nature of relationship between the android and the ship was something he still hadn't quite gotten his head around.

"Sometimes, I don't know where you start and the ship ends," said Reeves, watching the shuttle thread itself though unfeasibly narrow spaces inside the cave to reach its destination.

"I am everything you see here, Commander Reeves," Three replied, while inviting him and Kane to climb the ramp into the cargo hold. "When you operate the controls, it is me. When you sit in a seat or sleep in a bed, it is me. When you breath the air, it is me."

"I'm not sure I like the idea that I'm ingesting you every time I breath," Kane said, though she was smiling again.

They followed the android through the ship, which was now humming with energy. Reeves could feel the beat of the ship's reactor. It was like a heartbeat, feeding the Invictus with the precious life blood it needed to survive and thrive. He closed his eyes and listened to the pulse of the ship, feeling it resonate through his body.

"I have fabricated a uniform for you," said Three, snapping Reeves out of his meditative state.

"Great, thanks," he replied, following Three out onto deck one of the Invictus. "Do I need to head to one of the crew quarters or stores to pick it up?"

"No, it is already waiting for you on the bridge," said Three, cheerfully. The door swished open and the android led them onto the ship's command center. "Here it is," Three added, picking up the bundle of clothes that was waiting on a pedestal that had sprung up from the deck.

"I'm going to need somewhere private to change into this," said Reeves, subtly trying to indicate that there wasn't a chance in hell of him stripping off in front of Kane and the android.

"No, need, I can complete the sanitization process here," Three replied.

Reeves and Kane both frowned at the machine, then their frowns deepened as the android took two measured paces back. Kane followed the android's lead, moving away from Reeves as if he was a stick of dynamite with a fuse that was running short.

"Whatever you're about to do, I don't like it," Reeves said.

Suddenly, a column of bright yellow light rose from

beneath Reeves' feet, entirely consuming his body. There was a faint smell of burning and he felt his skin tingle, as if he'd been submerged in a weak acid solution. Then as quickly as it had appeared the light vanished and Reeves was left temporarily blinded and disorientated.

"Oh my god..."

The astonished cry came from Kane, though Reeves still couldn't see her. He rubbed his face and eyes, trying to massage some sensation back into them. Then he realized he felt cold all over.

"Your vision will return momentarily, after which you can dress," said Three.

Reeves could make out the shapes of the two figures on the bridge, though one of them appeared to have their hands on their head, as if they'd just bet everything on black and lost.

"Where do I put the old clothes?" Reeves said.

Then the realization of what had happened hit him like a cold shower. The android hadn't just sanitized his skin; it had literally burned the clothes off his back too.

"Damn it, Three, is this some kind of joke?" Reeves yelled, grabbing the uniform and pressing over his exposed private parts. His eyes had now adjusted and he could see that it was Kane who had her hands on her head. She looked like she'd just seen her parents making out in the kitchen.

"If the process was amusing then it was unintentional," Three replied. The android's androgynous face had emulated a look of confusion and embarrassment perfectly.

"Haven't you heard of privacy?" Reeves complained,

turning his back on Kane and the android and hurriedly pulling on the new pants.

"Ah, yes, I apologize, Commander Reeves," Three said. "I admit to being unfamiliar with the emotional foibles of organic beings."

"Well, get familiar with them fast," Reeves snapped. He noticed that Kane now had her hand covering her mouth, but it was clear to him that she was only doing so to stifle a laugh.

Suddenly, the ground shook and Reeves heard the distant clunk of objects striking the exterior of the ship. Everyone fell silent. Then the ground rumbled again and more thuds echoed around the ship.

"They have discovered us," said Three.

The panoramic viewscreen activated and Reeves watched as blasts of plasma rained down from the sky and thumped in the valley beyond their cave. Reeves cursed and finished fastening his tunic before grabbing the new pair of boots off the top of the plinth.

"There are now five Skirmishers circling the valley, and a single Sa'Nerran heavy cruiser in orbit," the android added. Three was peering up toward the ceiling as if it could see directly into space.

"Tell us what you need us to do," said Reeves, fastening the boots as the plinth was slowly reabsorbed into the ship.

"I will pilot the Invictus," Three said, turning and marching toward the helm control station. "I suggest Major Kane controls the weapons systems."

"And what about me?" asked Reeves, standing tall again and smoothing down his tunic. The uniform fitted like a glove, while the 'sanitization' process the android had subjected him to had left him feeling fresh and revitalized. He was ready for battle.

"You are the commander, are you not?" Three said, turning a quizzical eye to Reeves. "You will command."

Reeves didn't need asking twice. He stepped onto the command platform and dropped into the captain's seat. It molded around him then sprouted controls that were all perfectly positioned for him to use. As before, display screens appeared in front of him, projected directly onto his retinas, so they persisted no matter where he looked.

"Is there any way to reconfigure this to a more conventional console layout?" Reeves asked. Having the readouts beamed directly onto his eyes was effective, but also a little unnerving. "Call me old-fashioned, but I prefer it that way."

No sooner had Reeves said the words than his captain's seat reconfigured itself again, adopting a new layout that was exactly what Reeves had wanted.

"Thanks, it's like you read my mind," Reeves said, examining his revised seat configuration.

"I did," replied Three, smiling softly at Reeves.

Reeves huffed a laugh then glanced at Kane. "Red alert, all weapons and shields to maximum," he called out, feeling electricity tingle through his body. To him, the thrill of combat never diminished.

"Engines report ready, Commander," said Three, adopting the professional tone of a Bastion naval officer.

"Take us out," Reeves ordered, gripping the arms of his personalized seat tightly.

Under the intuitive control of the android, the Invictus lifted off and exited the narrow cave with laser-precise accuracy. The main engines ignited and the ship rose above the valley, sending another rumble of thunder across the land as the sound barrier was penetrated. Reeves' consoles updated, showing the six Sa'Nerran contacts that were circling the valley. All of the alien Skirmishers were heading straight for them. Reeves targeted two of the enemy vessels to their rear, operating the controls just as intuitively as the android had.

"Lock on with the aft torpedoes and fire," Reeves called out to Kane.

"Aft torpedoes away," Kane replied, smartly. "Wow, I didn't expect that..."

"Didn't expect what, Major?" Reeves asked, fearing the worst.

"I didn't expect them to be plasma torpedoes," Kane said, raising an eyebrow at Reeves.

Part of the viewscreen switched to show the targeted Skirmishers. Reeves watched in amazement as the torpedoes raced toward the enemy vessels, accelerating at twice the rate of the conventional weapons the Bastion Navy employed. Within seconds the alien ships had been annihilated.

"Targets destroyed," Kane said, though the confirmation was hardly necessary.

"That's an understatement," said Reeves, still awestruck by the power of the attack.

Plasma blasts then thudded into the ship from multiple

directions, shaking the deck and causing Reeves' grip to tighten further.

"Shields holding at eighty-nine percent," Kane said, working her station with composed fluidity. "The three remaining Skirmishers are targeting our engines."

"As much as I'd love to stay and fight, it's time we kissed this sorry planet goodbye," Reeves said, turning to Three. "Set a course for Concord Station and prepare to surge."

"Aye, Commander," the android replied. "If it makes things easier, you can refer to me as 'Ensign' while I am in control of the helm."

"Understood, Ensign Three," said Reeves. He admitted that it did sound more comfortable to address the station using a rank, even if the rank was arbitrary.

"Direct hit to aft shields," Kane called out, as the Invictus was rocked again. "No damage, but they're punching through."

Reeves targeted all three ships on their tail then fixed his gaze on Kane. "Fire torpedoes, Major. Let's swat these bugs."

"Aye sir, torpedoes away," Kane replied, executing the command.

The torpedoes again raced toward the Skirmishers like ethereal, glowing arrows, but this time the Sa'Nerra were ready. Point defense cannons engaged the torpedoes, destroying two of the three weapons before the third snuck though, forcing the central craft in the formation to disengage.

"One down, but the rest are still coming for us," Kane confirmed, bracing herself against her console as more blasts thumped into their shields. "A section of our aft shields are buckling. I'm rebalancing to compensate."

The starry blackness of space was now enveloping the ship, but the advanced warship maneuvered like it was still in the atmosphere. Reeves checked his readings then decided the Invictus needed a little more shakedown time, before they surged out of the system.

"Come about Ensign Three," Reeves said, locking onto the reactors of the remaining two Skirmishers. "I want to see what else this ship can do."

"Aye, Commander, coming about, attack pattern Keller Three," the android said, maneuvering the ship into a high-power turn.

"What's pattern Keller Three?" asked Kane, beating Reeves to the question.

"It is an older style of flying," the android replied. "From this vessel's Omega Taskforce days."

Reeves and Kane exchanged intrigued looks, then he saw the attack pattern flash up on his screens.

"I think that attack pattern violates the laws of physics," Reeves said, though the android remained calmly confident.

"It more bends them than breaks them," Three replied, cheerfully. "Stand by with pulse cannons and beam cannons."

"Targets locked, standing by," Kane replied.

Now flying toward the Skirmishers, the Invictus suddenly began a vertical climb, as if it had been fired out of an ejector seat. The move was so sudden and ferocious that the inertial negation systems failed to compensate for it fully, pressing Reeves into his seat like he was on a roller-coaster ride.

"Engaging beam cannon, now!" Kane called out, the stress of the maneuver showing in her voice.

An intense beam of energy raced out from the Invictus and cut through space, slicing through the hull of one of the Skirmishers and causing it to detonate ferociously. Three dived toward the remaining Skirmisher like a hunting hawk and swooped in behind it before it even realized what had happened.

"I have a good lock," said Kane, working her console. "Firing on the final Skirmisher."

A ripple of rapid, tightly-focused plasma blasts erupted from the Invictus' main cannons. The aft shields of the Skirmisher were pummeled and collapsed, and sparks and explosions popped off across the hull of the alien vessel.

"Incoming torpedoes from the cruiser!" Kane called out, but it was already too close to evade, and the weapons thumped into their forward shields. "Shields buckling; we've taken minor damage," Kane continued, assessing the readouts on her damage control panel. "I'm compensating."

"Let's finish this, Major," said Reeves, as Ensign Three weaved the ship through space to get on the heavy cruiser's tail. "Target their reactor and fire."

"Aye, sir... locked on and firing," Kane called back.

Flashes of plasma again pierced space, striking the larger alien vessel across its belly. The cruisers shields collapsed and the remaining bolts of energy tore through its hull and speared its main reactor. The enemy ship detonated like a nuclear bomb, leaving nothing behind but smoke and ash.

"All enemy vessels destroyed, sir," said Kane.

His XO sounded surprised, and with good reason. They had just taken out an entire Sa'Nerran taskforce single-handed, a feat that would have required half-a-dozen or more Jinx-class heavy fighters or a bare minimum of three Bastion Navy Destroyers.

"I think I'd call that a successful shakedown test," said Reeves, peeling his fingers off the arms of his seat and pushing himself up. "I take it this ship has independent surge capabilities, Ensign?"

"It does, Commander, and the course to Concord Station is already laid in," the android replied. "It will require two standard surges, though I can attempt it in one, if you prefer?"

Reeves snorted a laugh. "I think we've bent the rules of physics enough for one day, Ensign," he said, smiling at the android. "Even two standard surges from this distance is a hell of a lot quicker than I'm used to."

"Very well, Commander," Three replied, bowing its head graciously. "The surge field generator is charging."

Reeves' console then chimed an alert and he dropped back down into his seat to check it.

"I'm reading a surge field forming, dead ahead," said Kane, who had apparently monitored the same alert.

"I take it this field is not being generated by us?" Reeves asked. The giddy feeling that came from being victorious in battle was rapidly fading.

"Negative, Commander, it is another ship," Three replied.

A flash of light illuminated the viewscreen and a ship five times the size of the four-hundred-meter Marauder appeared from out of the surge dimension.

"One Sa'Nerran Heavy Battlecruiser just came onto the board," Kane said as scans of the vessel flooded onto Reeves' console. "It's the Imperator's ship, and it coming in hot, gun ports open."

Reeves pushed himself out of his seat again and stepped closer to the viewscreen. His heart told him to stand and fight, but his head told him to return to Concord and continue their mission.

"Tactical analysis, Major," Reeves said, pressing his hands to the small of his back.

"It's a brute, sir," Kane replied, shaking her head. "Without going into specifics, that cruiser has more fire-power than three Bastion Destroyers combined."

"What about us?" Reeves said, directing the question as much to Three as to Kane. Kane rose an eyebrow and deferred to the android.

"We could stand toe-to-toe with the Sa'Nerran battle-cruiser, but neither ship would escape without taking significant damage," Three replied, coolly.

Reeves' console chimed another alert, but this time he could guess the nature of the update.

"The battlecruiser is hailing us, sir," said Kane.

"Get ready to surge on my order," Reeves said to his android pilot, before turning to Kane. "Put the asshole-in-chief through."

A holo image of the Sa'Nerran Imperator appeared in front of Reeves, life sized. He could see that the alien leader had not bothered to heal the burns to its face, and was instead wearing the scar like a badge of honor.

"I had you beaten," the Imperator said, fixing its yellow eyes onto Reeves.

"Yet, here I am," replied Reeves, throwing his arms out wide. "That means you failed, Imperator."

"A mistake I am about to correct," the Imperator hissed.

"Weapons lock detected," Kane said, her voice rising in intonation. "They're about to throw the kitchen sink at us."

"Not today, Your Majesty," Reeves said, remaining focused on the alien leader. "Initiate surge."

The muscles in the Imperator's leathery face tightened and it bore its jagged teeth at Reeves. Then the holo image vanished, along with the space outside the Invictus, followed by the bridge and finally Reeves himself, until the entire ship had been consumed by the surge dimension and had begun its journey to Concord Station.

CHAPTER 27
ABYSS SQUADRON

REEVES COULD ALWAYS REMEMBER the first time he'd experienced a surge. It had been terrifying and unsettling, like his body had been disintegrated, leaving him trapped in an inter-dimensional gulag of the mind. Now, hundreds of jumps later, traveling through the surge dimension was an almost Zen-like experience; an opportunity to pause and reflect. The surge dimension had a way of bringing a person's greatest hopes and dreams to the forefront of their mind, but it could also surface their deepest fears and anxieties. Unfortunately for Reeves, the two long surges that the Invictus had been required to complete to reach Concord had been as far from Zen-like as he'd ever experienced.

During the first surge from Thrace Colony, Reeves' thoughts had been filled with the Imperator and the alien's obsession with defeating him in single combat. The contests that he and the alien leader had already fought were replayed as if he were observing the battles through his own eyes. Then there were fights that had not taken place, yet still felt just as vivid and real. He had no idea if his mind was just inventing the brawls or whether the surge dimension was tapping into the future, and showing him contests that were still to come. Either way, it was not an enjoyable experience.

The second surge to Concord Station had been worse. Reeves' thoughts had been polluted with images of war. He saw battleships and outposts burning in space, and human and Sa'Nerran soldiers lying dead and mutilated on the decks of vessels and littered throughout the smoldering remains of scorched cities. It was only after the surge had completed and Concord Station had burst into being that Reeves realized that he'd been experiencing memories of the Sa'Nerran war that could not have been his. They were ships, soldiers, and cities from a time long before he'd been born. How he was able to see and experience the suffering of these long-dead people, Reeves didn't know. Yet deep down in his gut, he had a feeling that it was all about to happen again, and the prospect of that terrified him.

"Surge complete, Commander," said Ensign Three from the helm controls. "Concord Station is directly ahead, range one hundred kilometers."

Suddenly, there erupted a chorus of alerts from Reeves' and Kane's stations.

"I'm picking up four Sa'Nerran warships between us and Concord, sir," Major Kane called out. "Three Skir- mishers and what looks like a heavy destroyer."

"Tactical analysis, Major, what are we dealing with?" Reeves said, putting an image of the alien taskforce on the panoramic viewscreen.

"The heavy destroyer is approximately one-point-two kilometers long," Kane began, as the tactical data was overlaid onto the viewscreen. "It's packing four heavy plasma cannons and a beam cannon, plus multiple forward and aft torpedo launchers."

"Is this something you've come across before, Ensign?" Reeves said, hoping that the android's superior knowledge of the Sa'Nerra could help to determine how much of a threat the vessel was.

"The vessel bears some similarities to the heavy destroyers that fought in the human-Sa'Nerran war," Ensign Three replied. "They were crewed by only the most dedicated and fanatical warriors. Conditions on board were cramped and harsh, even for the Sa'Nerra, so that every square meter of the vessel could be honed for war."

"So, no big deal then?" quipped Kane.

Reeves shot his XO an admonishing look; now was not the time for jokes. His console then chimed another alert, and Reeves saw that Concord Station was trying to contact them. He also noted that the station appeared to be at red alert; its defense platforms were active, but he couldn't tell if the guns were aimed at the Invictus or the Sa'Nerra.

"We're receiving a message from the CIC on Concord," Kane said, before glancing across to Reeves. "We should probably let Lieutenant Curio know not to blow us to hell."

"Put him through on a secure channel," Reeves said,

realizing that his operations officer would have no idea he was on the Invictus, and likely considered the ship to be a threat.

"This is Lieutenant Curio to the unknown vessel approaching Concord Station," Curio began, speaking with calm authority. Reeves was actually impressed. "Halt your advance, transmit your ID and state your business immediately."

"Lieutenant, it's okay, it's me," said Reeves, pushing out of his seat and stepping in front of the holo projection of Curio so that his operations officer could see him.

"Commander Reeves?" Curio replied, clearly taken aback. "You are in command of the unidentified vessel?"

"That's right, Lieutenant, and I need you to clear us to dock in Fighter Bay One," Reeves replied, getting straight to the point. "I'll explain later, as much as I'm able to, anyway."

"Understood, sir, but I must warn you that your vessel and the Sa'Nerran ships are currently outside our perimeter of authority," the operations officer said, growing more agitated. "The Sa'Nerran ships arrived about an hour ago and have refused all attempts at communication. However, since they are beyond our perimeter and were not interfering with station business, I saw no reason to intervene."

"You did the right thing, Lieutenant," Reeves replied. He hadn't noticed that they were still outside of Concord's perimeter of authority, which meant that his hands – and Lieutenant Curio's hands – were tied. "Track the alien ships, but do not fire unless they breach Concord's perimeter without permission," he continued. "The last thing we need is to give the Imperator a legitimate excuse to blow the station to hell."

"Understood, sir, I will be standing by. Curio out." The holo image of the Eyrhu officer disappeared, leaving Reeves once again staring out at the Sa'Nerran Heavy Destroyer on the viewscreen.

"A conflict appears to be inevitable," said Ensign Three, with a calm stoicism that belied the seriousness of the statement.

"That seems to be our motto," Reeves muttered.

More alerts chimed out from Kane's console. At the same time, Reeves saw torpedoes snake out from the three Sa'Nerran Skirmishers.

"We have six incoming torpedoes," Kane called out. "The Skirmishers are accelerating toward us, though the Destroyer is holding position."

"They're using the Skirmishers to soften us up before the bigger gun comes in to make the kill," Reeves said, heading back to his seat. "Activate point defenses to take out those torps and prepare a spread of our own."

"Aye, sir, point defense cannons are tracking and engaging the targets," Kane replied. "We have torpedoes locked on to the lead Skirmisher."

"Fire!" Reeves called out.

Three plasma torpedoes shot out of their forward launcher like cannon shells and obliterated the lead Skirmisher. Plasma blasts then hammered into their shields as the remaining two alien warships returned fire.

"Shields holding at eighty-six percent," Kane said, as

the damage report readout updated. "These ships are hitting us with everything they have. That last volley alone nearly melted their guns."

"They know they won't last long, and are making every shot count," Reeves replied. More blasts hammered into their shields, then a second Skirmisher exploded as cannon fire from the Invictus raked along its hull.

"They're smarter than they look, I'll give them that," Kane said, as the Invictus maneuvered to get a shot at the final Skirmisher. "Cold-blooded too. It's like these skirmisher crews are just cannon fodder."

Suddenly, the bridge of the Invictus was rocked and Reeves could feel that they'd taken damage to more than just their shields.

"That blast came from the destroyer," Kane called out. "It hit us with its heavy cannon, aiming specifically at the weakened section of our shields."

Reeves cursed. Kane was right, and it was clear that the crew of the destroyer was a rung above the regular alien grunts.

"Moderate damage to hull armor, port side midships," Kane continued. "No critical systems are impacted."

"Rebalance the shields and take evasive action, Ensign, and try to sneak us inside Concord's defense perimeter if you can," Reeves called out to his android helmsman. "We'll need all the help we can get."

"Aye Commander, though the destroyer is making an effective gatekeeper," Ensign Three replied. "It is matching our maneuvers while maintaining its distance from the station, making it impossible to make a break for the perimeter without opening us up to a direct onslaught."

"If it won't move voluntarily then we'll make it move," Reeves said, gripping the side of his seat.

The Invictus' beam cannon fired, tracing a line through space and cutting directly across the path of the remaining Skirmisher. The alien vessel's starboard quarter was hit and the vessel spiraled out of control before exploding in a shower of sparks and flames.

"It's just us and the destroyer now," Kane said, fingers flashing across her console. "All weapons locked on."

"Start your attack run, Ensign," Reeves said. "Let's remind the Sa'Nerra what the Invictus can do."

"Aye, Commander, initiating attack run now," Ensign Three called back.

The Invictus turned hard and began powering toward the Sa'Nerran Heavy Destroyer. Flashes of plasma raced out from the larger vessel and the bridge was shook by the impacts.

"Firing..." Kane called out, sending a volley of plasma blasts back at the ship before launching a full spread of three torpedoes.

Reeves watched anxiously as their weapons slammed into the target, but the powerful destroyer's shields kept out the brunt of the impact.

"Moderate damage to the destroyer's shields," Kane confirmed. "And they intercepted our damned torpedoes too."

Reeves hammered a fist onto the arm of his seat, though

the curious alloy the ship was made from resisted the impact.

"Incoming torpedoes!" Kane's tone was urgent, and Reeves could sense her fear as keenly as he felt his own heart thumping in his chest.

"Point defenses to maximum!" Reeves replied. "Ensign, can we make a run inside the perimeter?"

"Attempting to move past the destroyer will allow it a clean shot at our weakened aft shields," the android replied. "I would suggest we destroy the vessel rather than attempt to run past it."

"Then bring us about for another attack," Reeves said.

A torpedo from the destroyer snuck through their point defenses and detonated. Reeves was almost thrown clear of his seat, and Kane was flung to the deck, but hauled herself up moments later, blood tricking from a cut to her head.

"Shields buckling," Kane called out. "We can't stand toe-to-toe with this thing for much longer."

"Ensign, tell whatever part of you is in engineering to boost power to the shields and give us everything the Invictus has left," Reeves replied.

"Aye, sir, shields stabilizing," Ensign Three replied. "I am preparing our attack run."

"Let's make this one count," Reeves said, nodding to his XO.

"Target locked, plasma and beam cannons ready," Kane replied, wiping the blood from her head and smearing it across her face like warpaint.

The destroyer's plasma cannons flashed again and the

Invictus was hit, but true to its word, the android had bolstered their shields. Reeves gritted his teeth and watched the range to target decrease until they reached the optimal firing range.

"Open fire, Major, give it everything," Reeves called out.

Pulses of plasma lashed the alien destroyer's forward shields, and Reeves saw the vessel make a desperate turn, in order to spread the damage across a wider section of the ship. The Invictus' beam cannon then raked across the destroyer's back, cutting a groove into its dense armor, but even that wasn't enough to put it down.

"Damn, this thing is unkillable!" Kane cried out, slamming her palms onto her console.

"I have a window," Ensign Three called out. "I believe I can make it inside Concord Station's perimeter of authority.

"Do it, Ensign, smartly," Reeves replied, feeling a swell of hope.

The Invictus turned and put on a burst of speed, and Reeves watched the destroyer closely, expecting it to withdraw. Instead, the enemy vessel turned and made a run for the station too.

"What the hell is it doing?" Kane said, thinking out loud.

"Get Lieutenant Curio on the line," Reeves said, feeling his heart-rate climb higher. He needed to warn his officer of a potential attack.

Suddenly, the destroyer opened fire with its beam

cannon, but this time it wasn't shooting at the Invictus. The powerful column of energy penetrated a small section of the station's shields, but the damage appeared to be minimal.

"That doesn't look like a critical area?" Reeves said, still trying to work out what the Sa'Nerran vessel was doing.

"I have Curio on the comm," Kane said.

Reeves pushed himself out of his seat and stood in front of the holo emitter. His operations officer appeared moments later, looking flustered.

"Sir, the Sa'Nerra have managed to penetrate our shields," Curio began, getting straight to the point. "The attack has damaged a bank of secondary command processors and severed our link to the starboard defense grid. We are unable to retaliate."

Reeves cursed. "Get your weapons back online as fast as you can, Lieutenant," he replied, realizing that it was now all up to them. "We'll take care of the destroyer."

"Aye sir, though standby, I have an idea," Curio replied.

Reeves was about to ask what the Eyrhu officer's idea was when the transmission was abruptly cut.

"What happened?" Reeves said, turning back to his XO.

"Unknown sir, but we're picking up a massive spatial anomaly," Kane replied, frowning down at the new data on her console. "It appears to be coming from the edge of Shadow Space."

"On screen..." Reeves said, raising his gaze to the panoramic viewer in front of him.

To his astonishment, the area of Shadow Space that

had appeared near Concord Station was growing. Out of the end of the central mass, a shadowy finger was extending toward the station like the root of a tree burrowing into the ground. Consoles and lights flickered on and off on the bridge and Reeves could see that every zone of Concord appeared to be affected too, as if all the electrical objects on the station had a loose power connection. He was about to order a report when a ship edged out of the darkness. It took him a moment to realize what it was, then his hopes sank.

"It's the Imperator's battlecruiser," Kane called out. "They must have travelled through Shadow Space to get here so fast." The tactical console chimed another alert and Kane scowled at the reading. "I'm picking up three other new contacts," his XO announced. Then she slammed her hand on the console and whooped. "They're coming from Concord Station, sir," Kane continued, meeting Reeves' eyes. "Three Jinx-class heavy fighters just came onto the board."

Reeves heard his station chime an incoming message and Kane put it through without delay. Captain Jesse Rush appeared in front of him, the man's steely eyes visible through the raised visor of a pilot's helmet.

"Abyss Squadron, reporting in, Commander," said Rush. "I hear you have some alien trouble you need help with?"

"Right on time, Captain Rush," Reeves said, feeling electricity tingle through his body. "Take your squadron and attack the heavy destroyer. We'll hold off the Imperator until Curio can get the station's weapons back online."

"Aye, Commander, you can count on us," Rush replied.

The holo image fizzled to nothing, and Reeves saw the trio of heavy fighters soar toward the wounded and scarred heavy destroyer. Reeves smiled as the elegant fighters moved to attack, then the viewscreen switched to show the Imperator's cruiser and the smile fell off his face.

"I have Lieutenant Curio again," said Kane.

Reeves nodded. "Put him through, Major. Let's hope he has some good news, because in our current condition, we can't hold off that cruiser alone."

The holo communicator turned on, and initially it only displayed Lieutenant Curio's empty station in the CIC, until the Eyrhu officer suddenly jumped into view.

"Apologies, Commander, I was momentarily indisposed," Curio began, eyes down to his console while he was talking. "Chief Raspe is working on a way to bypass the destroyed processors and reenable the defense platform."

"How long, Lieutenant?" Reeves replied, his eyes flicking from Curio to the cruiser that was powering toward them.

"The chief estimates several minutes," Curio replied, finally raising his eyes from his console. "He was unable to be more precise, and became quite agitated when I pressed him for a more exact figure."

Reeves blew out a heavy sigh. "Remind Chief Raspe that if he doesn't get the weapons back online in the next sixty seconds, there won't be anything left of Concord Station."

Reeves' sobering words appeared to have the desired

effect on Lieutenant Curio. "I will relay the message at once, and convey a suitable level of urgency."

"You do that, Lieutenant. Reeves out." The holo image of his officer disappeared and Reeves was left with the stark realization that they were on their own.

"Throw everything we have left into the weapons and shields," Reeves said, returning to his command chair. "If this ship has got any more surprises up its sleeve, now would be a good time to reveal them."

"I am afraid I am all out of tricks, Commander," the android replied, again with a stoicism that did not help breed confidence in their chances of survival.

"Then I guess we do this the old-fashioned way," said Reeves, locking onto the cruiser from the controls in his seat. "We slug it out and see who's left standing."

"Well, at least we won't have to wait long to find out," replied Kane, who now sounded as resigned to their fate as Reeves and Three were.

Like Reeves, Kane knew that two powerful ships fighting head-to-head would not take long. There would be no intricate ballet of moves; no parry-repost. They were like two old war galleons, running alongside each other and firing full broadsides at the same time.

"All weapons locked and ready," Kane said, hovering her hand over the controls to fire. "Power surge from the cruiser. It's getting ready to attack."

"Then respond in kind, Major," Reeves said, gripping the seat and bracing himself for a rough couple of minutes.

Plasma flashed from the guns of both ships, and torpedoes snaked out into space, crisscrossing each other within moments. The bridge was rocked hard and this time Reeves was thrown from his seat. Consoles blew out and other sections of the interior appeared to be melting, as if the ability of the Invictus to modulate and restructure its surfaces had been broken.

"Shields down," Kane called out, dragging herself back to her station. "Heavy damage to the plasma cannons. Several hull breaches detected, but none appear critical."

"What about the cruiser?" Reeves said, hoping that the Invictus had dealt as much damage as they'd received.

"The cruiser's shields have also buckled," Kane replied, brushing debris from her console. "It's also taken heavy damage, but its main plasma guns are still online."

"Hit it again, Major," Reeves said, eager to strike the killing blow before the Imperator got in first.

YOU LL

"Forward cannons not responding, I'm trying the beam cannon," Kane replied, before slamming her hands on the console again. "No response, it's still down."

Another explosion rocked the ship and Ensign Three was thrown from the helm control station to the deck.

"Ensign, are you okay?" Reeves called out, rushing to Three's side and helping the android up and back into its seat.

"I am damaged, but remained functional," Three said.

Despite its strange, almost featureless face, Reeves noticed that the android appeared to be in discomfort, and was hunched over the helm control as if winded. He wondered whether the damage to the ship caused the sentient AI to feel physical pain; it was a possibility he hadn't previously considered.

"I have an idea," Three added, maneuvering the Invictus to avoid another incoming volley from the cruiser. "There is not time to explain. You must trust me."

"Whatever it is, just do it," Reeves replied, heeding the android's advice and choosing to trust it.

"Major, prepare to fire aft torpedoes," Three said, glancing back at Kane. "Do not worry about the forward weapons. They are no longer needed."

Kane glanced across to Reeves and he nodded. "Aft torpedoes, standing by," his XO called out. Kane's expression then hardened like granite. "The cruiser is preparing to fire again. Whatever you're going to do, do it now!"

Ensign Three became entirely still, as if the android had merged with the vessel. Suddenly, the surge field generator came online, and the rising hum of the capacitor charging thrummed through the deck.

"They're firing!" Kane called out.

Reeves gritted his teeth and saw the cruiser's cannons glow hot. Then the Invictus surged, and for the briefest moment his consciousness was suspended and disembodied inside the surge dimension. A heartbeat later, and the Invictus was back in normal space. The suddenness of the surge left Reeves disoriented. Normally, surges lasted several seconds, but this one had been competed in the blink of an eye.

"Fire torpedoes, now!" Three called out.

"Torpedoes away!" Kane replied a split-second later.

Reeves watched as the weapons struck the alien cruiser, penetrating its shields and tearing into its hull. He felt a swell of hope rise inside him again, but the vessel was not destroyed. Then the cruiser began to turn toward them, and Reeves knew they'd played their final gambit.

"The cruiser is coming about," said Kane. "Torpedoes reloading, but I don't think they'll be ready in time."

Suddenly, a beam of energy lashed across the side of the alien battlecruiser, slicing an entire weapons pod off the massive vessel. Reeves adjusted the view on the screen and saw that the blast had come from Concord Station.

"Message from Lieutenant Curio," Kane called out. "Their defense platform is back online. He's asking if they should destroy the cruiser?"

Reeves had only seconds to make a decision. The consequences of destroying the alien flagship and its Imperator were momentous and unknowable. Would the death of the Sa'Nerran leader cause the warrior race to withdraw to Shadow Space to lick their wounds, or would it trigger an all-out war? Yet somehow, Reeves knew in his bones that war with the Sa'Nerra was inevitable, and he knew what he had to do.

"Order Lieutenant Curio to reduce that cruiser to ash," Reeves replied, standing tall.

"Aye sir, order relayed," Kane confirmed. Then she too stood back and watched.

Concord Station's turrets all turned toward the cruiser and their barrels began to glow hot. Reeves could see the emitter array for the beam cannon adjusting position, ready to fire again. He didn't care how tough the alien cruiser was – nothing could repel a full assault from Concord Station.

Bursts of plasma erupted from dozens of turrets all across the space station's twenty-kilometer-long body. Then there was a flash of light and the Sa'Nerran Heavy Battle-cruiser was gone. Reeves' head sank low. He'd taken his shot and missed. The Imperator had surged away.

CHAPTER 28
A BUNCH OF KNUCKLEHEADS

REEVES STEPPED off the rear ramp of the Invictus and circled around the Marauder-class Destroyer to survey the damage. That the ship was not already a smoldering pile of scrap metal was a miracle in itself, Reeves thought, as he moved further away to get a wider field of view. The pounding they had taken from the Sa'Nerra would have flattened any other ship Reeves had ever seen, from the mighty Bastion Navy Battlecruisers to the fearsome Quarr Interdictors. Yet somehow, the thousand-year-old ship had survived intact.

"Tough little ship," commented Kane, who had moved beside Reeves and was also peering up at the Invictus with her hands pressed to her hips.

"Tough is what you get when you overcook a steak, Major," Reeves replied, still surveying the craft. "This thing makes diamonds look as brittle as sugar cubes."

"I never overcook a steak," Kane replied, intentionally missing the point for the sake of being facetious.

"That's because you never cook," Reeves hit back.

"Does anyone cook anymore?" Kane replied, shooting Reeves a confused expression. "How the hell does food get made these days, anyway?"

"I don't care, so long as it tastes good," said Reeves. His eye had been turned by the arrival of the three Jinx-class fighters, which were being raised up from the fighter docking area on elevator platforms.

"Looks like you made a good pick there," said Kane, nodding toward the trio of fighters. "If it weren't for those pilots, the destroyer and the Imperator's cruiser would have double-teamed us and put us down for sure."

Reeves nodded, watching the pilots of the three craft race down the ramps and start celebrating and jostling each other.

"If Jesse Rush was unsure where he belonged before, then he shouldn't have any doubts now," Reeves answered.

"Who are the other two stick jockeys, though?" Kane asked, as the three pilots started walking toward them.

"I have no idea," admitted Reeves. "Our CAG has obviously been on a recruiting drive while we were away."

Captain Jesse Rush stopped in front of Reeves and Kane and threw up a stiff salute, which was closely mimicked by the two other pilots.

"Damn, it's good to back in the cockpit of a Jinx again," Rush said, lowering his hand to his hip once Reeves had returned the salute. "How did we do out there, sir?"

"Suffice to say, you saved our asses," Reeves said, smiling. Then he met the eyes of the other two pilots. Both were younger than Rush and had a hungry look in their eyes, which had become slightly tempered by the presence of their commanding officer. "Who are the other members of your squadron?" he continued. He remembered that his CAG had given the unit a designation, but his mind was too scrambled to recall it in that moment. "What was the squadron's name again?"

"Abyss Squadron, sir," Rush said, beaming from ear to ear. "I thought it was appropriate."

"I'd argue that it's actually pretty inappropriate, Captain, but I'll let it stand," said Reeves, slipping into 'commander mode', despite being amused by Rush's choice of name. Out of the corner of his eye, he could see that Kane was not attempting to hide her amusement.

"This is Ensign Kendra Fyre," Rush continued, gesturing to the pilot standing to his left.

"It's an honor to serve on the Abyss, sir," Ensign Fyre said. She had an almost unsettling intensity about her, like she was permanently on 'alert status'.

"Her callsign is 'Sparks' because she's hot stuff in the cockpit," Rush added, still beaming from ear-to-ear.

"Not just in the cockpit, from what I've heard," said the pilot standing next to 'Sparks'.

Ensign Fyre swiftly backhanded the man in the groin, and the pilot bent double, groaning and holding his crotch.

"And who is Ensign Punchbag?" Reeves asked, wincing slightly at the sight of the injured pilot.

"This Ensign Ray Sherman, sir," said Rush, shaking his head at the man. The pilot was a six-foot, solid-framed, square-jawed jock who Reeves guessed was probably as capable as he was cocky.

"Nice to meet you, Ensign Sherman," Reeves said, shaking the man's hand. From the look on the ensign's face, Sherman had obviously expected to have the more powerful grip out of the two of them, and was surprised when Reeves' arm was stronger. "What brings you to Concord Station?"

"It's simple, sir," Ensign Sherman replied, standing tall and pushing out his barrel chest. "I just want to kick some Sa'Nerran ass."

"Well, you'll get your chance, Ensign, I can promise you that," Reeves replied. The young pilot's answer had been predictably gung-ho, but he appreciated Sherman's enthusiasm.

"We call him 'Tank'," Captain Rush added, hooking a thumb toward Ensign Sherman.

Reeves laughed out loud. "Ray 'Tank' Sherman? You have got to be kidding me?" he said, raising an eyebrow at Rush.

"No, sir, he's a tank by name and tank by nature," Rush said, slapping Ensign Sherman on the shoulder. The pilot grinned at Ensign Fyre, who remained as intense as ever.

"So, nothing to do with Sherman tanks then?" asked Reeves, wondering if the quip had been entirely unintentional.

"Sherman tanks, sir?" Rush asked. "Are they a new addition to the Bastion ground forces?"

"Forget about it, Captain, it really doesn't matter," replied Reeves, accepting that few people had the penchant for ancient earth military history that he had.

"Yes, sir," said Rush, looking even more confused, as if

he'd put his foot in it, without knowing why, or even what 'it' was.

"And what about you, Captain, do you have a callsign too?" Reeves asked, quickly moving the subject on.

"Yes, sir, I'm 'Judge'," replied Rush, smiling again. "Because my word is the law."

The other two pilots snickered under their breaths as Rush said this, but the CAG shot them a look that quickly wiped the smirks off their faces.

"Technically, my word is law, Captain, but once again, I'll allow it," Reeves said. "Jesse 'Judge' Rush has a nice ring to it."

"Thank you, sir," said Rush, accepting the compliment.

"You and your squadron can hit the showers now, Captain, you've earned it," Reeves added. He knew his pilots would be eager to get back to their quarters, but he was also eager to get to the CIC.

"Yes, sir, though it's a shame that bastard got away," Reeves said, looking genuinely hacked off that the heavy destroyer had surged. "Along with the scar you gave it, we scuffed it up good, though. That's the sort of damage that doesn't just polish out."

"Scar is actually a good name for that Sa'Nerran brute. And, don't worry, you'll get it next time, Captain, of that I have no doubt," Reeves replied. He then nodded to 'Sparks' and 'Tank' in turn. "Good to have you all on the team, I know you'll do us proud."

There was a jarring chorus of "yes sir!" from the two ensigns, which surprised Reeves like a sharp slap across the face. All three pilots saluted stiffly before falling out and moving away, whooping and jostling each other again in celebration of their first mission.

"That was very inspiring, sir," said Kane, laying on the sarcasm even more thickly than usual.

"Stow it, Major, or you'll find out just how inspiring it feels to have my boot up your ass," Reeves hit back.

"They're a bunch of knuckleheads, but I like them," Kane added, shrugging. "Hopefully, our new CAG can rustle up a few more like them."

Reeves nodded while continuing to watch his pilots exit the hangar. "Based on the capabilities of the Sa'Nerran warships we've seen so far, I'd say we need a lot more of them."

Reeves became lost his in his own thoughts. Even with the Invictus, they were going to need a lot more firepower to take on the Sa'Nerra, and it seemed clear to him now that it was more firepower than any one realm alone could muster.

"Holy crap, have you seen this?" Kane called out.

Reeves felt his heart flutter, and turned to see Kane a few meters away, peering up at the hull of the Invictus. He ran over to her, expecting to see an exposed fuel cell or massive hull-breach that the landing inspection had missed. Instead, it looked like the ship had already spent several hours in a repair dock.

"How is that possible?" Reeves said, jogging around underneath the ship to re-inspect areas of damage that were no longer there. "I was sure this section was shot to hell."

"Dalton, look at this," Kane said, waving Reeves over to another part of the ship.

Reeves hurried to where his XO stood, beneath the starboard wing of the ship. Kane pointed up and Reeves couldn't believe what he was seeing.

"That's incredible," Reeves said, shaking his head. The damage to the section they were both looking at was repairing itself as they spoke. Broken structural beams were growing and knitting back together, like fresh bone fusing to old, while wiring and circuitry appeared to be fabricating themselves out of thin air. The whole section was glowing with an ethereal blue light, that was pulsing like a heartbeat.

"The Stembots are wondrous, are they not?"

Reeves and Kane both spun around to see Ambassador One behind them. She was wearing her exquisite ambassadorial suit, which made it look like she'd just stepped off the catwalk at a top fashion show.

"They are an evolution of the self-repairing armor plating that the original Invictus employed," the Ambassador continued. "The difference is that the Stembots can repair anything, and even regrow destroyed components, if fed with a sufficient amount of power."

"Damn it, Ambassador, don't sneak up on me like that, you nearly gave me a heart attack," Reeves said, pressing a hand to his chest.

Ambassador One frowned. "Your cardiac function is perfectly normal, Commander Reeves," the android said. "At least, it is for you, considering your genetically-enhanced physiology."

"She means that you're a mutant," Kane said, nudging Reeves with her elbow.

"Technically, you are now a cyborg, Major," Ambassador One added, smiling amiably at Kane. "Your body has adapted perfectly to the respirocytes, which is not always the case."

"How do you know about the respiro-thingys?" Kane asked, scowling at the android. "We've only been back a few minutes."

"I already know everything concerning your mission," Ambassador One replied, breezily.

Reeves then picked up on something the android had said, and wanted to return to it before the subject moved on.

"What did you mean when you said that bodies don't always adapt to the respirocytes?" Reeves asked.

"Organic bodies can often reject the purely synthetic blood, especially when in high concentrations," Ambassador One replied. "In the Major's case, the concentration is one hundred percent, so she is fortunate to be alive at all."

"Your counterpart in there never told me there would be risks like that?" Reeves said, feeling annoyed that he hadn't been consulted.

"I believe the phrase you used was, 'I don't care if you use black magic, just do whatever it takes to keep her alive'," Ambassador One replied, reciting Reeves' instruction word-for-word.

"Aw, that was sweet of you," said Kane, nudging Reeves again.

"Okay, I guess I did say that," Reeves admitted. "How do you know all this though?"

"Three and I have been in communication throughout your adventure, Commander," the android replied, while starting to walk toward the lowered rear ramp of the Invictus. "We can converse through the aperture relays."

Reeves and Kane followed the android then saw that Three was standing on the base of the ramp.

"Hello One, it has been a long time," said Three, nodding respectfully to the Ambassador.

"Too long, old friend," Ambassador One replied, returning the gesture. She then turned to Reeves and rested a hand gently on his shoulder. "How do you like your new commander?" she asked, smiling.

"They are remarkably alike, are they not?" Three said, mimicking One's smile precisely.

"Yes, they are, though not entirely alike," the ambassador conceded. "This one wears his heart on his sleeve, rather than beneath many layers of armor."

"That is a weakness the Sa'Nerra will exploit," Three replied, suddenly taking on a much darker tone.

"Perhaps," Ambassador One said, cocking her head slightly to one side. "But it was because of Lucas Sterling's humanity that Commander Reeves is here at all. The Sa'Nerra underestimated the power of the human need for companionship once before, and it cost them dearly." The ambassador then stepped onto the ramp of the Invictus and held Three's shimmering golden hand. "I underestimated it too."

"And I have also missed you, my friend," Three replied.

The two androids then turned to Reeves and Kane, each a shimmering reflection of the other.

"But now we have work to do," the two androids said, speaking in perfect unison. "War is coming, and we must be ready for it."

REEVES SWIVELED his command seat around in a circle, casually observing the stations on the CIC. It had been three days since he and Major Kane had returned from Thrace Colony with the Invictus, and in that time things had largely returned to normal. Night Sector still provided its extensive range of guilty pleasures, the traders of the Long Market were busy selling their wares, and the factories and industrial units in zones two and three were almost back to full capacity. The population of the station had even increased slightly over the last week, encouraged by the cooling off of military tensions along the new borders with Shadow Space. The fact that there was no longer a Sa'Nerran Battlecruiser looming outside Concord Station appeared to have helped too.

"My security report, sir."

Reeves spun around to see Sergeant Axia Calera standing between him and the holo viewscreen in the center of the CIC.

"Damn it, Sergeant, don't sneak up on me like that," Reeves said, taking the report from the Quarr security chief's hands.

"I wasn't aware that I approached in a covert manner, sir. I apologize if I did," Sergeant Calera replied, looking a little put out at being chastised so openly.

"What's the short version, Sergeant?" Reeves said, activating the paper and skim-reading its contents. Nothing was standing out to him as unusual.

"Instances of unrest have reduced by thirty-one percent in the last two weeks, sir," Calera said, proudly. "Most crime is concentrated around Night Sector and the Long Market, both of which have seen a much larger proportional decrease."

"I bet Sid Garrett isn't happy about that," snorted Reeves, smiling at the image of the gaunt-faced Lord of Night being inconvenienced by his new, stricter regulations.

"Mr. Garrett has largely abided by the new rules, sir," Calera confirmed, though rather than swell with pride at this success, the security chief appeared wary. "However, I believe he may have merely transferred some of his business dealings underground."

Reeves lowered the report and met Calera's eyes. "Explain, sergeant," he said, feeling a slight flutter in his gut.

"I have been receiving reports of increased activity inside the Slum, sir," the sergeant said. "As you know, it is almost impossible to patrol this sector, due to the inherent dangers to my enforcers. However, I am endeavoring to increase our security presence inside the Slum, and am working to build up a list of informants to assist us."

Reeves sighed. He'd experienced the dangers of the Slum first hand. The place was a rabbit-warren of damaged and half-finished sections of the station, which were not served by the regular transit terminals and conveyor systems. It was easy to get lost in the Slum, and consequently easy to hide there too. For someone such as Sid Garrett, it was the perfect place to transfer his more sordid operations to.

"Let me know what help you need, Sergeant," Reeves said, folding the report and pocketing it to read in more detail later. "We can't let Garrett gain a foothold down there. He's enough trouble as it is."

"Understood, sir, I will work up a list of recommendations, though I warn you that many will carry a significant additional cost," Calera replied.

"Give me the list and I'll see what I can do," Reeves said.

In truth, the station's finances were already at the brink of breaking point. The recent influx of visitors and residents, plus the ramp up of capacity from the industrial areas, had helped to bolster the station's balance sheet, but he was burning through credits like a starship burned fuel.

Suddenly, a young girl appeared beside Sergeant Calera. She was human, but dressed in traditional Quarr clothing; a dark colored top made from a heavy-duty looking material, black cargo-style pants and a long coat that almost reached the floor. The clothes were a stark contrast to the girl's striking red hair, which fell just above her shoulders.

"Aishi, you should not be here," Calera said to the girl.

Calera's tone was firm, but not harsh, and a million miles away from the security chief's usual precise and professional way of speaking. It was then Reeves remembered who the girl was. Aishi was the adolescent that Sergeant Calera and her life partner had adopted, after Reeves had shut down Garrett's obscene bordellos in Night Sector.

"I'm sorry, Custos, but These said to tell you that supper is ready," the girl said, brightly. She then noticed that Reeves was looking at her and waved at him. Not knowing what else to do, Reeves waved back and then felt a little silly for doing so.

"I will be along shortly, please wait for me outside," said Calera.

"Yes, Custos," Aishi said before running through the CIC and heading out of the main egress.

Reeves swiveled his seat around to watch her go and noticed that Major Kane was watching and smiling at her too, from her location at the main command console.

"I apologize, Commander, I know that Aishi should not be in the CIC," Sergeant Calera said, returning to her usual, professional way of speaking, though it was also clear she was embarrassed.

Reeves continued to swing his seat around until he was again facing his security chief. Ordinarily, he would have chastised Calera for allowing non-authorized personnel into the CIC, especially when it was a child, but in this case, he cut her some slack. He knew what the girl had been through, and what Calera had taken on, on top of her already very full plate.

"How's everything going with you three?" Reeves asked, including Calera's life partner in the number. He assumed that this was the person the girl had referred to as 'These'.

"Everything is fine, Commander, thank you for asking," Calera replied. The response was polite, but final. Reeves forgot how secretive the Quarr were, most especially about their private lives. However, he was still curious about one thing. "Aishi called you Custos; what does that mean?"

"The closest word in Bastion English would be guardian, sir," the security chief replied. She then quickly moved the subject on. "I will ensure that she does not enter the CIC again."

"It's fine, Sergeant, I'm happy to give Aishi access to the CIC if she needs to find you," Reeves said, spinning around in the seat again. "So long as she stays clear of the tactical console, anyway. We don't want her blowing up any incoming freighters."

"I would be happy to assist the girl by teaching her how to fire the beam cannon, sir," said Lieutenant Stas Rosca from the tactical station.

Not only did the Skemm's ethereal, wispy way of talking make the statement sound oddly menacing, but it was difficult to tell whether his officer was being serious or not.

"That will not be necessary," Sergeant Calera replied, stating her intentions very clearly.

"It's okay, Sergeant, the Lieutenant was just kidding," Reeves said. He then frowned and spun his seat around to face the tactical station. "You were joking, right Rosca?"

"Of course, sir," Rosca replied, airily. "If you say, so."

Reeve's scowl deepened. As usual, his Skemm officer's eyes were cast into shadow beneath his pronounced, furrowed brow, which made it hard to ever know when Rosca was being serious. Reeves glanced at Kane to gauge her reaction, since his XO was the station's resident expert in sarcasm. If she was smiling then Rosca had being joking, and if his XO appeared perturbed then the Skemm was not. However, Kane looked just as bemused as Reeves did, and shrugged at him before returning to work on the command console.

"You have a council meeting in thirty standard minutes, sir."

Reeves jerked around and saw Lieutenant Harpax Curio standing beside Sergeant Calera, who had remained where she was because Reeves had forgotten to dismiss her.

"Will everyone stop sneaking up on me?" Reeves snapped at Curio, making the Eyrhu officer's thin lips purse into a pout.

Reeves then turned to Calera. "You're dismissed, Sergeant, thank you," he said, allowing his security chief to return to her ward, and to her supper. As usual, Calera had continued her shift for far longer than her allotted hours.

Lieutenant Curio held out another piece of paper and waited for Reeves to take it.

"This is the agenda for the meeting, sir," Curio said. "I

thought you might like to see it ahead of time. Major Kane asked me to prepare some notes too."

"Thank you, Lieutenant," Reeves said, taking the paper. He briefly skimmed it, finding the agenda to contain the usual mix of tiresome administrative matters that the quarrelsome group of diplomats wished to address. He noted that Fang Gruba, the Bukkan Ambassador, had specifically raised the question of Reeves' and Kane's whereabouts. He sighed heavily in anticipation of the raucous ear-bashing he was going to receive from the disagreeable Bukkan diplomat.

The main command console and tactical console then chimed an alert. Lieutenant Curio hurried back to his station, while Reeves glanced over his shoulder to receive the report from Major Kane.

"A surge field is forming, but it's not from one of the established apertures," Kane said, the concern evident in her voice.

"On screen," Reeves said, scowling and turning back to the holo viewer at the front of the CIC. The image flicked on and Reeves watched an aperture began to form in space.

"A ship is emerging, sir," said Lieutenant Rosca, making the statement sound both intriguing and ominous.

Reeves kept his eyes focused on the newly-forming aperture, hands gripped around the arms of his seat. Then there was a bright flash of light, and the alert alarms wailed.

"It's a Sa'Nerran Battlecruiser," Rosca continued, speaking with more urgency. "The configuration matches the Imperator's flagship."

"Red alert!" Reeves called out, throwing himself out of

his seat. "Shields to maximum and bring the defense platform online."

"Aye sir, engaging defense platform," replied Rosca.

Reeves turned to his XO. Her eyes had sharpened and
she had already adopted the posture of Kane the soldier.

"Get Rush and his knuckleheads in their launch tubes,
but tell him to standby," Reeves ordered.

"Aye, sir they're already on their way," Kane said,
looking beyond Reeves to the image of the cruiser on the
holo.

"The Sa'Nerran cruiser is holding position, sir," Lieutenant Rosca said, sounding calmer, but no less enigmatic.
"It is outside Concord's perimeter of authority." The
tactical station then chimed another alert and the Skemm
officer was quick to provide an update. "The battlecruiser
has launched a shuttle, sir. It is heading toward the station."

"Keep a turret locked onto the shuttle, but focus our
main guns on that cruiser," Reeves said, scowling at the
new arrival. It wasn't one of the Sa'Nerran Hornet fighters
that they'd seen before. To Reeves' eye, it just looked like a
regular transport shuttle.

"I am receiving a text message from the shuttle,
Commander," said Lieutenant Curio from the operations
console. "It is a request to dock. The message contains full
ambassadorial clearance, sir."

"It's the damned Imperator," said Kane, shaking her
head. "It thinks it can just waltz back in here after what it
did?"

Reeves checked his own consoles, but the message and
the clearances were valid.

"Is the shuttle armed, Lieutenant Rosca?" Reeves said.

"Negative, sir, the shuttle contains no weapon systems," Rosca replied, as Reeves circled around to stand beside Kane at the main command station.

"We could just blow it up, and be done with it," Kane said. There was a mischievousness to the suggestion, though Reeves knew that she wasn't entirely joking either.

"That would be nice, but I don't want to start a war just yet," Reeves said. "And having the Imperator back here at least lets us keep an eye on it."

"It'll certainly make the council meeting more fun than it was going to be," replied Kane, smirking.

"Lieutenant Rosca, stand down to yellow alert, but monitor that cruiser closely," Reeves called out. "If it so much as drifts inside our perimeter of authority by a millimeter, I want to know about it."

"Aye, sir," replied Rosca. The alert immediately stopped and the lights in the CIC returned to normal.

"Lieutenant Curio," Reeves then called out, locking eyes with his Eyrhu operations officer.

"Yes, sir?" Curio replied, clearly intrigued as to what his commander's next order was going to be.

Reeves blew out a heavy sigh, then gave the command. "Grant the Sa'Nerran shuttle clearance to land, and prepare for its arrival."

CHAPTER 30
IT HAS BEGUN

COMMANDER REEVES RESTED on the central podium of the council chamber with his head in his hands. Ambassador Gruba had been addressing the assembled diplomats for five minutes straight, barely pausing to take a breath. Reeves had already forgotten what he was talking about, and was past caring. He considered that he should probably chastise himself for his apathy, since it was part of his role to facilitate good relations between the realms. However, it all seemed so insignificant and pointless to him. War was just over the horizon, and when it arrived, all of Gruba's petty nonsense would be thrown into sharp relief.

Massaging his tired face, Reeves straightened up and met the glowing eyes of Ambassador One. As usual, she had attended the meeting, but said virtually nothing, beyond succinctly addressing any urgent matters relating to the human population. To her side was an empty podium belonging to the ambassador of the Sa'Nerran empire.

Reeves had half expected the Imperator to have attended the council meeting, and it was his primary motivation for attending himself. However, the Imperator's shuttle had docked in zone four and the alien leader had been swiftly escorted to the embassy district by his honor guard. Nothing had been seen or heard from the Sa'Nerra since, yet the Battlecruiser still loomed in the distance, just beyond Reeves' reach.

"Are you listening to anything I'm saying, Commander?" Gruba barked. It was the word 'commander' that had suddenly roused Reeves from his catatonia.

"I don't think it's possible for anyone within a light year of this room not to hear you, Ambassador," Reeves hit back. "Now do you have any final matters to bring to this council's attention, or are you going to yield to another representative?"

"As I have just requested, though it is clear you were *not* listening, I demand to know where you and Major Kane went just over three weeks ago," Ambassador Gruba bellowed. "It is unprecedented for the commander and executive officer to be absent for such a protracted period of time."

"I took a vacation," Reeves said, giving an intentionally pithy response.

"With your subordinate?" Gruba barked. "For three standard weeks!"

"What can I say, she's a great traveling companion," Reeves replied.

The Bukkan's face was becoming increasingly flushed,

and Reeves realized he should probably give a serious answer, before the ambassador keeled over and died.

"It was essential station business, Ambassador, and therefore not a matter for this council," Reeves added, more firmly. "As I understand it, Lieutenant Curio dealt with all matters that required my attention while I was away, so I really don't see the problem."

"The problem is that the senior staff of this station abandoned their posts during a period of great uncertainly and danger," Gruba retorted, slamming his huge fist onto his podium.

"Did you get attacked by the Sa'Nerra while we were gone?" Reeves asked.

"Well, no..." Gruba admitted.

"Then there's no problem," Reeves said, shrugging.

"In fact the Sa'Nerra chose the precise moment of your return to engage in hostile action," whispered the Skemm ambassador, Thessala Topal. "I find that curious, don't you Commander Reeves?"

"A coincidence, that's all," Reeves replied, with his best poker face.

"What I also find curious is how Skemm ships have been seen rendezvousing with Sa'Nerran vessels close to Shadow Space," said Titus Vedrix, the Quarr ambassador.

"We are merely ensuring that the Sa'Nerra agree to the terms of our accord," Ambassador Topal replied. "You Quarr always jump to the wrong conclusions."

The Skemm ambassador had a way of making everything sound like a warning or a threat. Reeves found her deeply unsettling, like a wicked witch from an ancient fairytale.

"I agree with Ambassador Topal," said the Eyrhu Ambassador, Hostillian Zeno. "There is nothing sinister about maintaining diplomatic relations with the Sa'Nerra."

"You would say that, Ambassador Zeno, since we have monitored your vessels conducting the same clandestine liaisons," Titus Vedrix hit back.

"Apparently, they were not clandestine at all, Ambassador Vedrix," the Eyrhu diplomat replied. "Unless you are spying on the great Eyrhu Theocracy?"

Reeves held up his hands and got the room's attention, fearing the meeting was about to descend into a brawl.

"None of this is helpful," Reeves called out, speaking loudly enough to drown out even the boisterous Ambassador Gruba. "Now, if there is no further business for this council, I suggest we adjourn."

The doors to the council chamber then swung open, revealing the Imperator, flanked by two of its honor guard. Behind them was Major Kane, along with Sergeant Calera and six armed Security Enforcers. The Imperator marched inside the chamber, while its honor guard warriors remained outside, watched closely by four of the enforcers. The remaining two enforcers followed Kane and Calera inside, stalking behind the Imperator with anxious looks on their faces.

"You're late, Imperator," Reeves called out to the leader of the Sa'Nerran Empire. "We were just about to adjourn."

"Have you already adjourned?" the Imperator replied, pausing en route to its podium.

"No, but we..."

"Then I still have the right to address this council," the Imperator interrupted, continuing to its position beside Ambassador One and the Quarr diplomat.

Ambassador One didn't even look at the seven-foot warrior, while Ambassador Vedrix glowered at the Sa'N-erran, making no attempt to conceal his displeasure at being situated so close to it. Major Kane joined Reeves on the central podium, while Sergeant Calera and the two enforcers stood off to the side, hands resting on the grips of their pistols.

"Weapons are not permitted inside this chamber!" Gruba bellowed.

"New rules, Ambassador Gruba," Reeves replied, calmly. "While an aggressive force remains on this station, my Enforcers will be permitted greater discretion in order to keep the peace. That includes in here, and it also includes Paradise."

Gruba looked like he was about to burst a half dozen blood vessels. "That is an outrage!" the Bukkan bellowed. "That goes against the founding agreements of this station."

"Like I said, things have changed," Reeves replied, standing firm. He then pointed to the Imperator. "If you have a problem with that, then take it up with the thing responsible for the extra security measures."

Gruba's eye flicked across to the Imperator, who slowly turned its head and fixed its gaze onto the Bukkan ambassador.

"No, I do not believe that will be necessary," Gruba said, stuttering through the words. Reeves had never seen the Bukkan climb down so quickly, or in such cowardly fashion.

"Good," said Reeves, smiling at Gruba, before again turning to the Imperator. "Now, say what you came here to say, Imperator, and make it quick."

"I would have brought this information to the attention of the council sooner, had its chairman been present," the Imperator said, glowering at Reeves.

"I'm not sure how that can be true, considering you were on Thrace Colony with your friends, the New Earth Movement," Reeves hit back.

The looks on the faces of the other ambassadors were as expected; a mix of shock and disgust. Reeves had wanted to expose the Sa'Nerra's dealings with Shepard publicly at the council, so that Ambassador One could officially take the information back to the Bastion Federal Government.

"Lies," the Imperator hissed.

Reeves shrugged. "I guess that will be for the Bastion Federal Government to decide."

"How do you know this information, Commander Reeves?" said the Skemm diplomat, Thessala Topal. Her small eyes were just about visible beneath her permanently-furrowed brow.

"That's not important," Reeves said, again refusing to entertain any questions about his own whereabouts.

"He knows nothing, because it is lies," the Imperator snapped, turning to the Skemm ambassador and causing her to visibly shrink inside her long, hooded cloak. "But if the humans of Bastion wish to challenge the Sa'Nerra, there will be consequences."

"That sounded like a threat, Imperator," said Ambassador One, smiling genially at the alien leader. "Was that a threat?"

"It was a warning," the Imperator replied, not bothering to look at One as it spoke. Then the Imperator turn to Ambassador Titus Vedrix. "A warning that the Quarr repeatedly ignored."

Ambassador Vedrix shifted uncomfortably, but retained his Quarr-like imperiousness in the face of the accusation from the Sa'Nerran leader. Reeves felt a chill run down his spine; he could sense something dark was coming.

"The Quarr has continued to disrespect the terms of the ceasefire," the Imperator went on, still staring at Vedrix, who was matching the warrior's gaze seemingly without fear. "Despite the Sa'Nerra agreeing to allow its inhabitants off the colony world we have claimed, the Quarr have armed and enflamed an insurrection." Reeves met Kane's eyes; it was clear she could sense it too, as could the other ambassadors. "Sa'Nerran ships have also been attacked and destroyed..."

"This is the work of rebel forces within our society," Ambassador Vedrix cut in, standing tall and speaking with confidence. "These rebel elements do not represent the Quarr Empire, and we are not responsible for their actions. We need to investigate these allegations and..."

The Imperator suddenly reached across to Vedrix and grabbed the man by the throat. "Your time is up, Quarr," the Imperator hissed, slowly lifting Vedrix off his feet.

Sergeant Calera and the armed enforcers quickly moved in.

"Release him, right now," Calera barked, aiming a pistol at the Imperator's head.

"You are unwise to threaten me, Quarr," The Imperator snarled.

The doors to the council chamber flung open and two Sa'Nerran honor guard warriors stormed inside, armed with Concord Station plasma pistols. Reeves saw the four other enforcers lying motionless on the ground, just outside the chamber.

"Your orders, sir!" one of the Enforcers, called out, still aiming his weapon at the Imperator.

"Everyone, stand down," Reeves bellowed. He aimed a finger at the alien leader. "That includes you, Imperator. We do our fighting outside of this chamber."

The Imperator's eyes locked onto Reeves and the alien bore its jagged teeth. Reeves could still see the burned flesh on its face from their previous encounter.

"As you wish, descendant," the Imperator hissed, throwing Titus Vedrix to the deck.

The leader of the Sa'Nerra then hissed to its honor guard warriors in its native language, and the guards in their distinctive crimson armor backed down. Sergeant Calera also lowered her weapon then commanded her enforcers to do the same.

The Imperator pushed past Calera and the enforcers and approached Reeves, before halting in front of his podium and turning to face the assembled diplomats.

"As of this moment, the Sa'Nerra and the Quarr Empire are at war," the Imperator announced.

The statement caused a stillness to descent over the chambers, as if the alien leader had just announced someone important had died.

"I advise the other realms to take notice of this day," the Imperator continued. "Abide by the terms of our agreements, or there will be consequences." Raising its hand, the alien leader aimed a long, leathery finger at Ambassador One. "The Bastion Federation should take note. There will be no further warnings."

The Imperator then turned to face Reeves, standing almost eye-to-eye with him, despite the fact Reeves was on a raised platform.

"Now you can adjourn the meeting," the alien warrior hissed, before turning and marching toward the door. Its honor guard warriors followed, tossing down the weapons they had taken from the enforcers as they did so. Then as abruptly as the Imperator had arrived, it was gone.

"Session adjourned," Reeves called out.

The ambassadors quickly departed the chamber without another word spoken between them. Reeves saw Titus Vedrix climb to his feet, looking more embarrassed than he was injured. More than that, the proud Quarr diplomat looked shaken, even afraid. The man had good cause to be afraid, Reeves realized. The stubbornness of the Quarr Empire had provoked the Sa'Nerra into war.

Reeves waited for the others to leave, until only himself, Major Kane and Ambassador One remained. The android approached the podium, an unusually somber expression on her face.

"It has begun," Ambassador One said, breaking the silence. "But be under no illusion, the Quarr are only the beginning. Whether provoked or not, the Sa'Nerra will bear arms against all six realms. It is only a matter of time."

"Then we need to get to the bottom of the Progenitors' role in all this fast," said Reeves. There was no need to lower his voice or speak in abstract terms; the council chamber was protected against electronic means of snooping. "And we need a way into Shadow Space, so we can find out what we're dealing with."

"Three has been calculating the position of the closest Progenitor world," the android continued. "The planets move periodically; we believe so that the Sa'Nerra can harness the energy of new stars in order to feed the expanse of Shadow Space."

Kane recoiled. "They move entire planets?" she asked, sounding extremely dubious about what the ambassador had said.

"Yes, much in the same way that you move ships through apertures, except on a slightly larger scale," Ambassador One replied, cheerfully.

"*Slightly?*" Kane looked at the android like she was a lunatic.

"It doesn't matter how they do it, only that they do," Reeves said, keen to move their discussion along. He'd been on Concord Station too long already since returning from Thrace Colony, and was itching to get back on mission.

"Let us know when Three and the Invictus are ready. In the meantime, the Major and I will continue to monitor the Imperator and keep this place from falling apart."

"I will be in contact soon, Commander Reeves," Ambassador One said. She then nodded to Reeves and Kane and departed the council chamber.

Reeves leaned up against his podium and let out a long, slow breath. From the high of the successful mission, he had quickly fallen to a low ebb. He'd hoped that the war he knew was coming was still some months away – weeks at worst – yet it had already arrived. And it had arrived without fanfare or any warning. The Quarr were a strong, capable warrior race in their own right, but Reeves knew the Sa'Nerra as well as any being alive, Ambassador One excluded, and he knew they didn't stand a chance. Not on their own.

"This galaxy is going to hell a lot sooner than I expected," Kane said, also resting against the podium alongside Reeves. "Even with the Invictus and those two sentient androids, I can't see what the hell we can do to make this better."

"We have to bring the realms together," said Reeves. When he thought about it, the answer was obvious. Yet the simplicity of the seven words he'd just spoken belied the enormity of the task they described. "We have to show them who is pulling the Imperator's strings, and what that means for all of us if we don't come together."

"We can't even get six members of each realm to be in a room together without bickering and trying to tear each

other's eyes out," Kane replied, stating the harsh, but unde-
niable truth. "How the hell are they going to fight together
if they can't even stand to be in the same place for more
than an hour at a time?"

Reeves blew out another heavy sigh. "I don't know
Katee, but for some reason, I think we're the only ones who
can make it happen." He then turned to Kane and smiled.
"It's actually all your fault, you know?"

Kane looked aghast. "How the hell is this my fault?"

"Because you convinced me to take this damned job,"
Reeves hit back. "I could be doing a cushy private security
gig on a safe planet, escorting some rich asshole to a gala
dinner from his penthouse suite. Instead, I'm in the middle
of a galactic war, and have two different asshole factions
that both badly want me dead."

"That second part is most definitely not my fault,"
Kane said, still sounding indignant. She then smiled and
nudged Reeves with her shoulder. "Admit it, though, you
wouldn't have it any other way."

As usual, Reeves found Kane's glibness to be endearing.
However, she was also right. Whether it was facing demons
from his family's distant past, or confronting a resurgent
warrior race that was also inexorably linked with his
history, he was right where he needed to be.

"Come on, let's go and grab something to eat, before we
get back to saving the universe," Reeves said, wrapping his
knuckles on Kane's shoulder then jumping down off the
podium.

"Ow, that actually hurt," Kane complained, rubbing the
spot where Reeves had punched her.

"Don't be a baby, I only lightly tapped you," Reeves hit back, raising an eyebrow at Kane.

"Just for that, you're buying dinner, and I get to choose where," Kane said jogging to catch up with Reeves.

"I dread to think what class of eatery you'd choose," Reeves hit back, imagining some dingy diner in Mid Town or, worse, a fusion restaurant in the Karaoke district of Night Sector.

"Actually, I quite fancy trying Starlight," said Kane, breezily.

Reeves scowled at his XO. She had a look about her; a look that he knew meant mischief.

"You do know that Starlight is the most expensive and exclusive restaurant on the station, right?" said Reeves, eyeing his XO suspiciously. "You're nuts if you think I'm paying for us to go there."

"You owe me twenty credits, remember?" said Kane, still smiling. "That should cover us for a little light supper."

"That'll barely cover the drinks at that place," Reeves hit back, though he was exaggerating. "And how come I owe you twenty?"

"You lost both of our wagers on Thrace Colony," Kane replied. She had taken the lead and was already directing them toward the Cultural Quarter, where Concord's best eateries were located.

"You'll have to remind me, Major," Reeves said, still suspicious of his XO.

"You bet that I wouldn't talk my way into the workers bar, and that we'd get off that rock without blowing something up," Kane said, her smile widening. "Well, I did, and we very much didn't, which means I'm up twenty."

Reeves cursed. As usual, his XO was right. He considered continuing to plead his case that spending ridiculously over the odds at a restaurant which was popular mainly because it had a panoramic view of stars and a nearby nebula was a waste of money. Then he realized how many times he'd almost died on Thrace Colony and changed his mind.

"What the hell, let's push the boat out," Reeves said, causing his XO to whoop and slap him enthusiastically on the back. "But no shots."

"Maybe just a couple?" Kane said, shrugging and flashing her eyes at him.

Reeves laughed and shook his head. There was no point arguing with Kane when she had her mind set, and he realized he didn't really want to, anyway. War had broken out in Quarr space, and in a week or two, he'd be heading into the unknown in order to learn why. He figured he was owed a decent meal and a drink or two.

Commander Dalton Reeves and Major Katee Kane turned down a side-street and headed toward the restaurant with a starlight view. The ordeals and challenges they'd already survived would have been enough to fill a lifetime for most people, but he was strangely hungry for more. And he was also keen to get to know his new ship, and its unique personality. It was a ship that had ferried his ancestors across the galaxy and carried them through a war. Now, it would need to do the same again for him. And despite having no reason to believe it, Reeves knew the

Invictus wouldn't fail him. And he knew he wouldn't let it down either.

The second great Sa'Nerran conflict had begun. And Dalton Reeves, descendant of war, was ready for it.

The end (to be continued).

CONTINUE THE JOURNEY

Continue the journey with book three: **Ancestor of War**. Click the cover to learn more.

More by G J Ogden. Click the series titles below to learn more about each of them.

Omega Taskforce series (6-books)

Dark and gritty - BSG meets Star Trek's Section 31.

Star Scavenger series (5-books)

Firefly meets Indiana Jones. Amazon Best Seller.

The Contingency War series (4-books)

A best-selling sci-fi adventure with a unique twist...

Darkspace Renegade series (6-books)

A fast-moving military sci-fi series with epic villains.

The Planetsider Trilogy (3-books)

A unique post-apocalyptic sci-fi action-adventure.

Audible Audiobooks

Star Scavenger series - click here

The Contingency War series - click here

Omega Taskforce series - click here

The Planetsider Trilogy - click here

Subscribe to G J Ogden's newsletter

Click here to sign-up

ABOUT THE AUTHOR

At school, I was asked to write down the jobs I wanted to do as a "grown up". Number one was astronaut and number two was a PC games journalist. I only managed to achieve one of those goals (I'll let you guess which), but these two very different career options still neatly sum up my lifelong interests in science, space, and the unknown.

School also steered me in the direction of a science-focused education over literature and writing, which influenced my decision to study physics at Manchester University. What this degree taught me is that I didn't like studying physics and instead enjoyed writing, which is why you're reading this book! The lesson? School can't tell you who you are.

When not writing, I enjoy spending time with my family, walking in the British countryside, and indulging in as much Sci-Fi as possible.

Subscribe to my newsletter:
http://subscribe.ogdenmedia.net

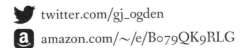 twitter.com/gj_ogden
amazon.com/~/e/B079QK9RLG

Made in the USA
Middletown, DE
03 September 2022